Urchin and
the Heartstone

M. I. McAllister
The Mistmantle Chronicles

Urchin of the Riding Stars
Urchin and the Heartstone

THE MISTMANTLE CHRONICLES

Urchin and the Heartstone

M.I. McAllister

BLOOMSBURY

First published in Great Britain in 2006 by Bloomsbury Publishing Plc
36 Soho Square, London, W1D 3QY

A CIP catalogue record of this book is available from the British Library

Hbk ISBN 0 7475 7512 6
9780747575122
Export pbk ISBN 0 7475 8281 5
9780747582816

All papers used by Bloomsbury Publishing are natural, recyclable
products made from wood grown in well-managed forests. The
manufacturing processes conform to the environmental regulations
of the country of origin.

Typeset by Dorchester Typesetting Group Ltd
Printed in Great Britain by Clays Ltd, St Ives Plc

1 3 5 7 9 10 8 6 4 2

www.mistmantle.co.uk
www.bloomsbury.com

For Marilyn Watts and Alison Sage

Great Heart of my own heart, whatever befall
Still be my vision, thou ruler of all

Prologue

On the Isle of Whitewings, three animals met in an underground chamber by night. One was Brother Flame, a tall, thin squirrel in a priest's tunic. The second was Larch, a small female hedgehog with a serious, pointed face. And the third was Cedar, a squirrel the colour of firelight, darting urgently into the chamber.

'It's too late,' she said. 'They've gone.'

'Then they're sure to find the squirrel and bring him here,' said Flame gravely. 'They won't dare come back without him.'

'He'll be in great danger,' said Larch. 'Did you find out his name?'

'Urchin,' said Cedar. 'Urchin of Mistmantle.'

She spoke the island's name carefully, as if it were

something precious. Cedar had never been to Mistmantle, but she had dreamed of it all her life.

Chapter 1

Wild seas and storming rain had battered the coast of Mistmantle all night, making squirrels scurry down from lurching tree-tops and hide in the roots. But by morning the gale had passed and the island lay washed and sparkling, with the wet stones of Mistmantle Tower gleaming pale pink and gold in the summer light. Squirrels darting from the windows on errands scrabbled to keep their grip as they ran down the walls. On the rocks around the tower columns of moles saluted and stood to attention as Captain Lugg the Mole trained them, and in the tower itself there was breathless bustle. The island was preparing for the coronation of Crispin the Squirrel.

Delicious wafts of spice and heat came from the kitchens where moles, squirrels and hedgehogs chopped nuts, lifted sticky golden cakes from ovens, and hung bunches of mint in the windows to keep the flies away. Otters piled up casks of wine in the cellars. Dancers and choirs ran up and down stairs looking for somewhere to practise, acrobats rehearsed on turrets and hung up tightropes which Mother Huggen the Hedgehog used as washing lines for the choir robes, and young animals hurried from the Spring Gate with splashing buckets of cold water for thirsty animals. Hedgehogs struggled to carry robes and Threadings down the stairs to the vast Gathering Chamber, where carpenters sawed and hammered to finish a new gallery.

The Gathering Chamber was the most impressive room on the island, but today it was crammed with stacked-up benches, robes, busy animals preparing for the coronation and more animals trying to look busy so they'd be allowed to stay and help. Threadings, the stitched, woven and painted pictures showing the stories of the island, lay draped across chairs until somebody could hang them up. In the middle of all this, Urchin, a young squirrel with unusually pale fur, was trying to find a way out.

Captain Padra the Otter had given him a very simple order – 'just nip down to the shore, Urchin, and ask Arran to come up' – but it was easier said than done. Urchin may have been Captain Padra's page and a Companion to the King, but at this moment he didn't feel at all significant. He was just a very young squirrel trying to get out of the door while a dozen large hedgehogs carrying stepladders were coming the other way, and somebody had just left a stack of cushions in the doorway because there was nowhere else to put them. It was easiest to jump out of a window and run down the tower wall.

The fresh, warm air was wonderful, and sunshine soaked into his fur. He delivered his message to Padra's wife, Captain Arran, who jammed her captain's circlet on to her rough, tufty fur and made her way round the tower to the Gathering Chamber.

Urchin paused for a moment, absorbing the sun and the fresh sea breeze. A few leisurely otters rowed, fished and taught their little ones to swim in the shallows as if they didn't know a thing about a coronation or the flurry in the tower. It was late summer, too beautiful a day to spend it all in the tower. He looked out to sea, and looked again.

Enchanted mists surrounded Mistmantle. No animal who truly belonged to the island could leave by water and return by water. The mists prevented it, and few ships found their way through them to the island. But something was moving in the mists now. Shading his eyes with his paw, Urchin watched. First he saw something, then he didn't, then he did. He should let Padra know.

He ran round the tower again and skimmed up to the window of the Gathering Chamber. As his best friend, Needle the Hedgehog, was spreading red-velvet cushions on the window seat he was very nearly knocked back down again. He managed to keep his balance and scramble over, but Needle's spines were exceptionally sharp and he couldn't avoid being prickled. He wriggled his way through the crowd to Padra and caught the smile on his face, but Padra always looked as if he were about to laugh.

'Captain Arran is on her way, sir,' he said, 'and I think there's a ship coming. Something's moving in the mists.'

'Strange,' commented Padra. 'Visitors for the coronation?' Needle glanced round the Gathering Chamber as if trying to work out where to put them.

'You two, go and have a good look,' said Padra. 'Send word if you need me, but I'll be down present-ly. Get a bit of fresh sea air and sunshine. And, Urchin, look out for a squirrel called Juniper.'

'Juniper?' repeated Urchin.

'Young squirrel, bit younger than you two, dark fur,' said Padra. 'He has a crippled hind paw so he was brought up in hiding, but he's free now. He needs to get to know other animals. He's had a lonely sort of life and lived among otters more than squirrels –

which hasn't done him any harm, of course, but he needs to meet other young squirrels. I mentioned you, and it turned out that his foster-mother had already told him about how you brought Crispin back to Mistmantle. He really wants to meet you.'

'Captain Padra, sir!' called someone, and Padra was hurried away by a hedgehog carrying a robe. Urchin ran down the tower wall again and waited on the shore until Needle, trundling over the rocks, caught up. There was no sign of anything in the mists now – maybe it had just been a trick of the sunlight.

'That must be Juniper,' said Needle. At the water's edge stood a squirrel who looked a little younger than Urchin, thinner and darker than most squirrels. One hind paw was small and curled. Not long before Captain Husk had tried to have all weak or injured young animals put to death, and many of them had been brought up in hiding.

Juniper must have heard his own name, because he had turned so that Urchin could see a pointy face. He was watching them shyly as if waiting to see whether they would be friends or not and hoping they would, and Urchin knew what that was like. He himself had always been 'that very pale squirrel', the orphan squirrel, the odd one out. He scampered down the sand, followed by Needle, and Juniper twitched a nervous smile. His eyes were dark and bright as berries.

'Are you Juniper?' asked Urchin. 'I'm Urchin.'

'A Companion to the King!' said Juniper with admiration.

Urchin tried to make the sort of easy, laughing reply that Captain Padra would have come up with, but unfortunately he couldn't think of one. 'Um . . . suppose so,' he said, and nodded at Needle. 'Needle's a Companion to the King, too. Where are you from?'

Juniper turned and pointed towards the forest stretching out to the west and rising into the hills. 'Do you see, sir, between the trees, just beyond the dark row of firs?' he said, and his voice was soft with shyness. 'Past there, sir, there's a waterfall.'

'I'm not a sir,' said Urchin. 'You lived at the top of the waterfall?'

'No, s— no,' said Juniper. 'Behind it, in the caves halfway down. Damson the squirrel found me when I was a baby, and looked after me. I never went anywhere else much because she had to keep me hidden, but now I'd like to live in the wood.' His ears twitched. 'So long as I can still see Damson, that is. She brought me up, and she's old now. She shouldn't be alone.' He looked down shyly at his paws, then up at the tower. 'Who are all those hedgehogs?'

Urchin and Needle turned to look. A group of tall

male hedgehogs stood in a huddle on the rocks.

'They're some of the Hedgehog Host,' said Needle. 'It was one of Husk's ideas. When Husk was in power the strongest of the male hedgehogs were sent away to do mining and quarrying right over on the North Corner, in the Rough Rocks. Even married hedgehogs with families, like Docken – he's Thripple's husband, Hope's daddy – they all had to go. They've been set free now, but they still sort of stay together and call themselves the Hedgehog Host. Some of them might be promoted to the Circle, like Docken and . . . um . . . that tall one that all the hedgehog maids fancy. Gorsen. Gorsen the Gorgeous, or at least he thinks he is. Gorsen and Docken work at the tower.'

'That must be good,' said Juniper with a wistful look that Urchin understood. Juniper was a bit like himself a year ago, when he had longed to be a tower squirrel but hadn't liked to say so. A very wet otter was loping up the shore towards them, smiling brightly. When he reached them he screwed up his face and shook himself dry with a flurry of spray.

'Fingal!' said Needle. 'You did that on purpose!'

'Just the thing for a hot day,' said Fingal, who was Padra's younger brother and had the same pleasant look about him.

'Have you seen any sign of a ship, Fingal?' asked

Urchin. He'd lost sight of it now – perhaps it was steering round the island, trying to find a way through the mists.

'No,' said Fingal, and glanced over his shoulder. 'Still no. Should I? Oh, hello, Juniper. Don't often see you here.'

'So you two know each other?' said Needle.

'The otters sort of brought me up, too,' explained Juniper.

'Don't know about bringing him up, but you know how it is,' said Fingal. 'Where there's water, there's always an otter or two. Nobody has a clue who Juniper's parents are. Damson found him all by himself and kept him secret in the days when they killed anything with half a whisker out of place, so we all taught him the really useful things, like swimming and sliding down waterfalls.'

'I don't know who my parents are, either,' said Urchin to Juniper. 'Apple the Squirrel looked after me.'

'Oh, I know about *you*,' said Juniper with admiration. 'Only, living where I did, I didn't get to hear about everything that happened on the island. I've heard bits of the story, about Captain Husk and everything, but –'

'Oh, it's simple,' interrupted Fingal. 'King Brushen was the king, but it was Husk who really made all the rules. Husk was so clever nobody realised just how bad he was, him and his Lady Aspen. Husk had Crispin sent into exile, my brother Padra took Urchin as his page and taught him to do all those pagey things, and Urchin went off to find Crispin and now Crispin's the king. He hasn't been crowned yet, but he's still the king. That's all. Anyone want to skim stones?'

Urchin understood more and more why Captain Padra had kept his talkative, carefree young brother out of the way while Husk was in power. Fingal chose two round, flat pebbles and loped down to the shore with them. Needle edged closer to Urchin, who turned to face her so he wouldn't be prickled.

'No ship,' she said. 'If there was one, I expect it had to turn back. They usually do. Do you think Juniper can manage to skim stones? I mean, with his bad hind paw. His balance must be affected.'

'I won't show him up,' Urchin whispered back. Fingal flicked a pebble across the water and watched it skip twice before it sank. Needle's throw wasn't good, and as Juniper seemed to be holding back, Urchin went next. He couldn't quite bring himself to make a hopeless throw, but it wasn't a good one either. The stone bounced once, and sank.

'Your turn, Juniper,' he said.

The pebble flew from Juniper's paw. Once, twice,

three, four, five times it skimmed over the water. Urchin gave a gasp of admiration.

'Well done!' called Needle and Urchin. Juniper turned and smiled shyly as if he thought he should apologise.

'The otters taught me that,' he said.

'Can you teach me?' asked Urchin. For a moment he was afraid he'd said the wrong thing – it was as if he was asking to know Juniper's secret – but he soon realised it was exactly the right thing. He had put Juniper in charge.

'It's – it's all in the wrist,' said Juniper, clearly astonished to find himself teaching anything to Urchin. 'You do it like this.'

They went on skimming stones, as Urchin improved his aim and Juniper grew more confident. By the time they were running out of suitable stones, Urchin felt as if he'd known Juniper for years. They were friends, and he knew they always would be. It was as simple as that.

'There's a whole heap of stones by the jetty,' said Fingal. 'The ships use them for ballast, but you can always find a few for skimming.'

'What's ballast?' asked Juniper.

'Rubbishy stuff for putting in ships to make the right weight,' said Fingal. 'But nobody minds if we skim them.' He turned to look for a flat stone, then suddenly straightened up and seemed to be watching something. 'Look! Look, can you see that?'

All of them looked out to sea as Fingal pointed. Slowly, still misted and unclear, a ship was emerging. They watched her, minute by minute, the mists still hanging thinly about her like smoke. The stones were left untouched. Urchin called to two young mole sisters nearby, Jig and Fig, and sent them to tell Padra and the king.

He had expected billowing sails and flags, maybe, hung from the masts, coming to celebrate Crispin's coronation. But the ship that now appeared looked as if the previous night's storm had battered her into defeat. The mast tip hung crooked, the sails were in tatters, and she limped to the island like a dying animal.

Chapter 2

The Gathering Chamber of Mistmantle Tower had been cleared at last, and only a few animals remained. It looked more enormous than ever, with every window thrown open against the summer heat. Three squirrels – Longpaw the messenger and Russet and Heath, who were both members of the group of senior animals called the Circle – waited at the door in case they were needed.

In front of the great curving windows was the dais, with a single throne at the centre, and before it, on a cushion of deep green satin, lay a circlet of gold. This was no plain captain's circlet. It was beautifully wreathed with golden oak and beech leaves and acorns, and gleamed like fire when the sunlight caught it. But Crispin the king was not seated on the throne, and not even touching the crown. He was perched on the edge of the dais with the squirrel priest, Brother Fir, beside him. In the middle of the hall Padra and Arran stood very still while hedgehogs draped their ceremonial robes of turquoise and silver round their shoulders, whispered to each other, tugged the robes into place, and occasionally put in a pin. Thripple, a senior tower seamstress hedgehog with a hunched back and a crooked look about her, knelt on the floor by Padra, spreading the hem of his robe and shuffling back to inspect the look of it.

'It's just on the floor, Captain Padra, but not trailing,' she said.

'That's how I want it, thank you, Thripple,' said Padra. 'Crispin, I know how you feel about wearing the crown, but you should try it on for size.'

'No I shouldn't,' said Crispin. 'It's something I feel strongly about. I don't even want to be called "the king", and all this "Your Majesty" business. Yes, I know we've been over all this before, and that they have to call me something other than Captain or whatshiswhiskers.'

'They need to know they have a real king,' insisted Padra. 'They need the feeling of having a leader. And it helps the Companions to the King if they know who they're companions to, Your Whatshiswhiskers.'

'Yes, I know,' said Crispin. 'But I won't wear the

crown until Fir puts it on my head at the coronation. It's a solemn moment, and it won't be if I've already worn it.'

'It won't be if it falls over your eyes,' said Padra.

'It's been measured,' said Crispin. 'I don't even want to touch it until I'm crowned. It wouldn't be right. It would be like holding the Heartstone.'

'The Heartstone is completely different,' said Padra. 'Ouch!'

'Sorry, Captain Padra,' said Thripple, and sat back on her heels to inspect the robe. 'Now, sir, are you absolutely sure you don't want it longer?'

'If it's any longer it'll get sat on by a mole,' said Padra. 'And when you see your husband, tell him the gallery's finished and there's room for all the Hedgehog Host in there.'

'Oh, Docken and me and all of us are most grateful for it, Captain,' she said, and twisted awkwardly to follow his gaze up to the newly finished gallery. 'There's such an awful lot of them, sir, to fit in.'

'And you can't pack hedgehogs in closely,' observed Arran. 'Not without serious consequences. But Gorsen and Lumberen had a look at it themselves, and they were pleased with it.'

Thripple had opened her mouth to say that Gorsen was a most particular hedgehog and if the gallery was good enough for him, it was good enough for everyone. But she said nothing, because at that point Gorsen the hedgehog himself marched into the Gathering Chamber, bowed smartly to Crispin and saluted.

'There's a deputation of young'uns to see Your Majesty and Captain Padra,' he announced. Gorsen was a tall hedgehog with a bronze tip to his spines, large black eyes and a purposeful stride, and his striking good looks had won the attention of most of the single female hedgehogs on the island.

'I told them Your Majesty's busy,' went on Gorsen, 'but they're all mightily excited about something and they say it's important, and Urchin sent them. Your young Hope's among them, Mistress Thripple.'

'Tell them all to come in, please, Gorsen,' said Crispin as Thripple's eyes brightened. 'And send a squirrel down to the kitchen for some strawberries.'

They heard stifled giggling before Jig and Fig, the mole sisters, appeared with Hope the hedgehog between them. There was a cry of 'ooh, Mummy!' from Hope, who scurried as fast as he could to Thripple before he remembered where he was and turned to bow to the king.

'Please, Your Majesty –' he began.

'That's Brother Fir,' said Thripple gently. Hope was very short-sighted.

'Please, Your Majesty,' repeated Hope as Padra

picked him up and pointed him in the right direction, 'King Crispin, sir, Captain Padra, sir, there's a ship arriving and Master Urchin said you should know, urgent says it's Urchin, no, Urchin says it's urgent, Your Majesty, Captain Padra, sir, sir.'

'Urchin mentioned it before,' said Padra. 'I'll go, shall I, Crispin?'

'And if Your Majesty can spare me, I shall have a little look for this ship from my turret,' said Brother Fir, slowly standing up and rubbing at his lame leg. 'Hope, would you like to come with me? But your legs may be too tired to manage the stairs. I believe we should wait for a minute or two and eat strawberries. They renew one's energy, you know.'

On the shore, animals had gathered to watch the approaching ship with her tattered sails and slow, halting progress. Otters swam in the shallows and ran up and down the beach, wanting to help with mooring her. Squirrels and hedgehogs stood in little clusters on the rocks, shielding their eyes against the sun. It was unusual, a ship arriving, especially one as battered as this. It was well worth watching, especially for small animals bored with gathering the berry harvest. Now and again a mole or two would emerge from a tunnel, peer about, sniff, and, not caring much for boats, disappear again. Urchin, Needle and Juniper stood close enough to the water's edge to let the waves lap over their paws as Apple, Urchin's foster-mother, bounded across the sand towards them. Apple was very round for a squirrel, and left large pawprints. She was telling them what she thought about the ship long before she reached them.

'Ooh, look at that, or I should say look at her, shouldn't I,' she said, and stopped to take a deep breath. 'She don't look too big, nor too healthy, neither. She must have been in the storm, I wonder who's on there, poor souls?'

'I can see someone moving on deck,' said Needle. She scrambled on to a rock and stretched on to her claw tips. 'Wait a minute – yes, there's a hedgehog.'

Urchin hopped up beside her and stretched up on his claw tips to see. 'And there's a squirrel turning the wheel,' he said. 'I can see its ear tufts.' A gentle splash nearby made him turn from the ship to the water and Fingal bobbed up in front of him, his eyes bright, his whiskers dripping. He was enjoying this enormously.

'Should we swim out and offer to tow her in?' he asked.

Urchin looked round to see who Fingal was talking to, then realised it was himself. It wasn't as if he were a captain or a member of the Circle. He was still a page, but he was also a Companion to the King, and other young animals seemed to think he'd know what to do. At moments like this, he asked himself what Padra would do.

'Yes, go on, then,' he said. Fingal rounded up a few more otters by splashing them, and with twists, turns and somersaults they swam out to the boat.

'Show-offs,' said Needle. Urchin turned to grin at Juniper and stopped grinning when he saw Juniper's face. There was a tight, anxious frown.

'Are you all right?' he asked. His eyes on the ship, Juniper nodded. A squirrel and a hedgehog were leaning over the rail, stretching out to see the island, and something flashed so fiercely in the sunlight that Urchin had to squint. One of the hedgehogs must be wearing some sort of silver jewellery. Or was it a sword hilt? It flashed again as a hedgehog wearing a deep purple cap leant over the side of the ship and cupped his paws to his mouth, and Urchin saw the broad silver chain he wore about his neck. He was still too far away for his voice to carry well, but Urchin caught a few words.

'What's he saying, can't hear a word. Is he talking funny?' demanded Apple.

'Something about "wings" and "birch",' said Urchin. 'I didn't get the rest.'

'Well, what's that supposed to mean?' said Needle, leaning from side to side to get the best view she could. 'They all look a bit battered, don't they?

Those hedgehog spines need grooming and the squirrel looks all sort of – sort of washed out.'

'Her's had a wetting, bless her,' said Apple.

'Yes, that's what a soaked squirrel looks like,' said Urchin, who had been in a storm at sea himself and remembered it vividly. The otters had caught the ship's ropes and, grinning hugely, were hauling her in. The hedgehog in the velvet hat and silver chain leant forwards, cupping his paws again, and Urchin waded into the sea to hear him.

'We come from King Silverbirch, King of the Island of Whitewings,' shouted the hedgehog. 'We are in great need, and beg to be taken with all speed to King Crispin.'

Urchin supposed he was the one who should say something, but he wasn't sure what. 'King Silverbirch's ship is most welcome,' he called back, because it was polite and harmless and gave him time to think. Something swished swiftly in the water to his left, and to his great relief he saw the gleam of a gold circlet.

'Captain Padra, sir!' he said. 'They've just greeted us. They're from an island called Whitewings, from King Silverbirch.'

'And well and truly wrecked on the way,' remarked Padra, raising his head and shaking the water from his ears. 'I've heard of Whitewings, we've

29

traded with them in the past. Is that Fingal with the ropes?' He loped from the water to stand beside Urchin. 'Fingal, bring her in in a straight line!'

'She looks even more battered now she's close,' said Needle.

'Bad enough without Fingal ramming her into the jetty,' said Padra. 'He never looks where he's going. Shall we go to meet them, Urchin? Oh, you've met Juniper.' He turned to Juniper with a broad smile that turned to concern. 'Are you all right, Juniper?'

In spite of the summer morning, Juniper was shivering. He blinked, swallowed hard, and took a deep breath as if breathing had suddenly become a struggle.

'Yes, Captain Padra, sir,' he said, but his voice was low and shaky. 'I think it's just the sun, sir. I'm sorry, sir.'

'Find a bit of shade, or a pool,' said Padra kindly. 'Any sensible animal stays in the wood or the water in weather like this. I wouldn't be on land if not for the coronation. Urchin, come with me and we'll welcome them. And do something about your tail tip.'

Urchin twisted round to look over his shoulder, found a few burrs and wild raspberries that seemed to have stuck to his tail, and pulled them out with his teeth. Then he followed Padra on to the jetty and stood a pace behind him.

'Won't the ship have to be searched, sir?' he whispered.

'I've given orders for it,' Padra whispered back, and raised his voice to greet the lordly hedgehog in the bow.

'Captain Padra the otter greets King Silverbirch's envoys in the name of Crispin, King of Mistmantle,' he called. 'Come in peace, and be welcome.'

With a bit of creaking and bumping, the gangplank was lowered. Down marched the hedgehog, his head held high and his silver chain flashing in the sun. Side by side behind him came another male hedgehog, rather short and thick-set with short spines, and a stern-looking female squirrel. They both looked a little older than Urchin. And lastly followed a small squirrel, about Urchin's age, who looked as if she wasn't enjoying this at all. Urchin thought she must be seasick. They all carried silver-grey satchels and wore pale yellow cloaks badly stained with sea water, and their faces were strained and worn. Advancing along the jetty, the leading hedgehog looked Padra in the eyes – but there was a swift glance towards himself that made Urchin feel uncomfortable. As for the other Whitewings animals, he felt that they were trying very hard *not* to look at him.

'You wish to be taken to King Crispin?' said Padra.

'With all haste,' said the hedgehog. He had a deep voice and an air of grave authority. 'Our need is very great.'

'Then I'll escort you to the tower myself,' said Padra, and turned to the younger animals, who had gathered on the shore. 'Crackle, Sepia, off to the tower before you draw another breath. Give word to the king, then to the kitchens. Our visitors have taken hard weather, and need hospitality. Chambers should be prepared for them.'

The squirrels dashed away. Padra turned back to the envoys.

'Pardon me, but your ship must be searched. Captain Lugg will be in charge of it. I regret this, but not long ago ships arrived in Mistmantle carrying unwelcome visitors, and now we inspect all vessels. Needle will carry your satchels, and may we help you with your wet cloaks?'

Urchin discovered what was meant by 'helping with cloaks' when Padra took the four damp, salt-smelling garments from the animals and passed them to him to carry as they escorted the visitors across the sand. They were long, heavy cloaks, so it was a struggle to hold them high enough to keep them from trailing in the sand and still see over the top. Lugg's moles and hedgehogs were pattering down to the ship to search it, but there was no sign of Juniper until Apple's loud and unmistakeable voice carried across the sand.

'Never mind, son, you'll feel better for it,' she was saying. Urchin looked over his shoulder to see her bending over Juniper, who was being sick into a rock pool. 'There, now, son. Better out than in, probably you've just had too much sun and excitement and that, that's all it is.'

Urchin hoped the visitors hadn't noticed that.

Chapter 3

Hope had peered short-sightedly down from every window in turn, and was now sniffing his way happily around Fir's round turret. The airy little room smelt of berry cordial, fresh raspberries, pine cones, herbs and candles, all of which he managed to find. It was a simple room with an air of soft breeze, sea and prayer about it and had very little for him to bump into. With some difficulty he climbed on to a stool beneath a window and smelt lavender and rock roses as they tickled his face from the window box.

'I have some pebbles by the hearth,' said Fir. 'You may like to play with them.'

He bent stiffly and picked up a basket that glowed with smooth stones, sea-washed, some white and flecked with silver, some green marble, some the palest pink, some the colours of peaches and apricots. Hope sniffed, pressed his face against the cool pebbles, and dug his paws into the basket, turning the stones over and rubbing them against his cheek. He laid them out in patterns and attempted, not very successfully, to build with them.

'We are to have visitors,' said Fir, glancing out of the window. 'Hm. They had no easy passage, and the mists may have held them off. They must have been most determined to get here, and somehow the mists let them through. There's Urchin carrying their cloaks. And dear Apple, and a young squirrel being terribly ill. Hm.' He pulled a few straggling stems of thyme from the window box, wrapped them round newly cut flowers for Hope's mother, and watched very keenly as Hope pushed the pebbles about. Hope seemed content to play all morning, and Fir made no attempt to hurry him.

'Please, sir,' said Hope after saying nothing at all for a while, 'I heard somebody talking about the Halfstone of Mistmantle. I don't know what it is, and the pebbles made me think of it again.'

Fir chuckled softly. 'The *Heartstone*, Hope,' he said. 'The Heartstone of Mistmantle. It looks like any old pebble, just like one of these, but it has a most special quality. It is a gift of the Heart to the island. The Heartstone can only be held in the paw of a rightful ruler or priest of Mistmantle. Nobody else can hold on to it, unless they carry it in a bag or a box, of course. That makes it a vital part of the coronation. At King Crispin's coronation I will place it in his paw, and the whole island will know he is their true king.'

There was a knock at the door. 'That's Urchin's knock,' said Fir. 'Come in, Urchin.'

He turned to Urchin with a twinkling smile of welcome, but Urchin thought he looked old and tired. Fir had seemed older and slower ever since the struggle with Husk, as if it had drained the strength from him.

'The king requests you to come to the Throne Room, Brother Fir,' said Urchin with a bow.

'Then tidy up the pebbles, the two of you,' said Fir. 'Pop them in the basket. Urchin, tip some water into that bowl so that Hope can wash his face. There's nothing like a young hedgehog among the berries for making a mess. And I notice, Urchin,' he glanced at Urchin with a lift of the eyebrows, 'that King Crispin keeps his visitors indoors on such a bright and beautiful day.'

'Yes, Brother Fir,' said Urchin. Fir might be looking old, but he still didn't miss anything. He knew that if Crispin kept his visitors indoors, it was because he wanted secrecy.

'Hm. I see,' said Brother Fir. 'All tidy now, Hope?'

Gorsen of the Hedgehog Host stood on duty outside the Throne Room door, his fur gleaming, bowing deeply to Brother Fir before opening the door. The Throne Room was a simpler, airier place than it had been in the last days of King Brushen. Sunshine brightened it. Crispin stood by the window, his deep red fur gleaming in the light, Padra beside him. The sun was so strong that Urchin found he had to squint, and could hardly see Crispin's face. It was much easier to look at the animals from Whitewings, who were now well groomed. Food and wine had been set out for them on a table, but they still looked so solemn that Urchin felt he must have done something wrong as soon as he hopped in.

Needle stood dutifully by the empty fireplace, her paws folded and the satchels neatly stacked behind her. Urchin bowed to the king and, as usual when he wasn't sure what to do, glanced at Padra for a prompt.

'Brother Fir, Urchin,' said Padra, holding out a paw to them, 'come and meet our visitors. This is Lord Treeth of Whitewings.'

The lordly hedgehog with the silver chain bowed stiffly to Fir and inclined his head towards Urchin.

'Urchin, Companion to the King?' he enquired gravely.

Urchin bowed. 'Yes, sir,' he said.

'Lord Treeth is a distinguished Lord of Whitewings, and the Ambassador of King Silverbirch,' went on Padra. 'And attending him on his embassy are his highly trusted attendants. Bronze . . .'

The stocky, short-spined hedgehog nodded briefly at Urchin with something that was half a grin and half a grimace. He looked to Urchin like an animal who could hold his own in a fight.

'. . . and Trail,' said Padra. The older female squirrel gave a very straight-backed curtsey with her chin up. Urchin felt as if she were inspecting him to see if his claws were clean.

'. . . and Scatter,' finished Padra. The smallest squirrel managed a wobbly curtsey and a brave attempt at a smile, and Urchin smiled back with sympathy. She still looked seasick.

'Lord Treeth,' said Crispin. 'Your story concerns us all, but in particular it concerns Urchin. May I ask you to repeat it? Be seated, all of you.'

The visitors settled themselves on stools, Urchin and Needle on the floor. Glancing up Urchin saw that now Crispin was seated, with the back of the throne behind him, his face could be seen very clearly. He looked sharper and more attentive than ever. With great dignity Lord Treeth straightened his back, placed his empty cup on the table, and began.

'Whitewings has always been a peaceful island, and a fair one. The brightness of silver sparkles in its waterfalls and gleams in its rivers, and mines of silver lie hidden in its depths. Swans dwell on our lakes and shores. On the rare occasions when our ships have breached the Mistmantle mists, we have been glad to trade with you. In the past, Mistmantle animals have married into Whitewings.

'Suddenly this year, in the spring, we found ourselves with a wave of newcomers from Mistmantle, seeking to live in Whitewings. They told us of a war on Mistmantle which had caused them to flee for their lives, and we took them in. I am forced to admit that we have regretted it. We welcomed them and made them at home in our island, expecting them to be like all the Mistmantle animals we had ever met – pleasant, helpful, good-natured. But these animals were not at all like anyone else from your island. They were loud and boastful, swaggering about the island, showing off, unwilling to work except for their own benefit. They were unfriendly, huddling together, keeping their own company, avoiding the rest of us.'

Urchin could feel Trail's eyes on him as if he were

to blame for all this. He wanted to squirm.

'This was bad enough,' said Lord Treeth. 'When some of them were caught stealing from our stores we put them in prison cells for a time, to teach them that we would not tolerate thieving. When they were released, they stirred up their companions to wreak mayhem on our island. They live as outlaws, waging war upon us.' He turned to look gravely at Urchin. In fact, in the pause that followed, they all seemed to be looking at him.

'I'm very sorry to hear it, sir,' he said, wondering what it had to do with him.

'By this time,' said Lord Treeth, 'we had realised that these animals were exiles from Mistmantle, following the downfall of Captain Husk. The exiles had brought us violence and unrest, but they also brought something most precious. They brought hope. They brought us the most important news there is.'

He paused again. In the power of the moment, Urchin stayed silent.

'We have a prophecy on our island,' said Lord Treeth, 'so old that nobody knows how long ago it was spoken, but it has been passed on through generations. Far, far away in the past, it was said that a time would come when the creatures of Whitewings would be in great need. A squirrel would come to our help, and be the island's deliverer. This deliverer would be . . .'

He paused again, as if he wanted to be sure of everybody's perfect attention. Urchin's fur bristled. He felt he knew what was coming.

'. . . a Marked Squirrel,' said Lord Treeth. 'By that, we mean a very rare type of squirrel, hardly ever seen on these islands.'

Urchin already knew what Lord Treeth would say. Heat burned in his face.

'A squirrel pale as honey,' went on Lord Treeth. 'A squirrel, Urchin, like yourself. When the Mistmantle animals told us of such a squirrel on their island – a Marked Squirrel who had already crossed the sea to bring King Crispin home – we saw hope. The Mistmantle exiles had brought us chaos, but they had also shown us where we could find deliverance.'

He was no longer looking at Urchin. He was looking past him towards Crispin, as if this must be settled between king and ambassador.

'And so,' finished Lord Treeth, and his deep voice resonated through the throne room, 'King Silverbirch beseeches the help of King Crispin. We know you are an honourable king. We have heard of your courage and nobility. We implore you to send a small band, only a small band, of warriors to our aid. But also, because our need is so great, and only one creature can help us, we ask that the Marked Squirrel may come with them. King Silverbirch has sent you tokens of his great esteem.'

He waved a paw to Trail and Bronze, who opened the grey satchels. The boxes they took out were painted in purple and silver, and as they lifted the lids something sparkled. Urchin almost gasped at the beauty of the gifts. There were silver and gold nets filled with hazelnuts and tiny apples, a green sword belt embroidered with crimson, and bracelets woven of the finest strands of twisted silver. Finally, from a nest of crimson velvet folds, he lifted a shining sword and held it high across both paws.

Urchin's eyes widened. The hilt of the sword was so intricately worked that it could have been made from threads or grasses, but every twist and every fibre was a strand of pale silver. Lord Treeth turned to him and, to Urchin's wide-eyed astonishment, held out the sword.

'A gift for the Marked Squirrel,' he said. 'May you use it in the service of your own king and ours.'

It was so beautiful that Urchin could hardly look away from it, but though he wanted it with all his heart he couldn't extend even a claw towards it. *It can't be for me. I'm not meant to accept.* Padra's paw was on his arm.

'Captain Padra, please take Urchin's sword for

him,' said Crispin. 'Lord Treeth, I am confident that Urchin will never use a sword dishonourably.'

'Thank you, Lord Treeth,' said Urchin, and with an effort he looked away from the sword. Something in Crispin's face warned him to say no more.

'The moles will escort you to your chambers,' said Crispin, making it clear that the discussion was over. 'You will want to rest after your journey, and you will eat with me here this evening. Needle, my Companion, call Gorsen in, please.'

Gorsen marched in so smartly that Needle had to dodge out of his way. He bowed impressively.

'Gorsen, make sure our guests have all they need,' said Crispin. 'And send me Docken.'

With great courtesy, Gorsen ushered the visitors from the room. The small squirrel, Scatter, still didn't look well, and Urchin felt sorry for her.

Presently, Docken arrived. He was a bit dishevelled, but he always looked like that. Mistress Thripple could do wonderful things with every sort of thread and fabric, but not even she could make her husband look well groomed.

'Take over guard duty, please, Docken,' said Padra. 'Absolutely nobody is to be admitted.'

'Understood, sir,' said Docken, and took his place outside the door. Padra closed the door after him and leant against it, looking across the room into

Crispin's eyes.

'Yes, that's what I thought,' said Crispin. 'But let's hear from all of you. Brother Fir?'

Chapter 4

At the shore the younger animals still hung about the ship, waiting to see if the moles would find anything exciting and passing the time by playing with pebbles, skimming stones, jumping off the jetty or playing coronations and taking turns to be Crispin. Occasionally there would be chants of 'Find the king, find the queen, find the Heir of Mistmantle', which was an old Mistmantle game in which three animals were sent away to hide while the others covered their faces and repeated the chant ten times before running off to look for them. As the animals being hunted had great fun distracting attention from each other and the squirrels would climb up anything that didn't run away, there was a lot of chasing and shrieking. Needle was holding the paw of her small brother Scufflen as he paddled in the waves with little squeals of excitement. Sepia the squirrel, whose beautiful singing voice had captivated the whole island at the Spring Festival, hung back a little, sometimes watching them, sometimes gazing past them.

In these past months, life had astonished Sepia. She had grown up in a birchwood near a waterfall, the youngest member of a family who were always very busy and very organised, always gathering nuts and storing them neatly, making cordials and medicines, running messages – her brother Longpaw was one of the fastest messengers on the island, and carried messages for the king. Sepia had always felt she was the smallest and least important member of her own family and the colony. She wasn't all that good at any of the things that mattered, like gathering and storing, and she could never quite keep up with the other squirrels. Everyone else had such a lot to talk about that Sepia, who had a quiet spirit to begin with, became used to the fact that nobody listened to her very much. So she had made a world of her own, making up songs in her head, dancing when nobody was looking, and, when she could be alone, running down to the caves behind the waterfall. She had a favourite place there where the damp walls gleamed and her voice echoed and sang back to her, and there was nobody there to tell her to stop singing and do something useful.

Then, on a spring day, she had been visited by Arran the Otter. Sepia was used to otters – there were always a few of them near the waterfall – but she had never before met Arran, who was a member of the Circle and a very important otter. Arran had brought her a message from an even more important otter, Captain Padra. The captain had heard her singing, and would like her to sing for King Brushen at the Spring Festival.

At the Spring Festival, she had been so nervous that by the time she had to sing her mouth was dry and if her legs hadn't trembled so much she might have run away. But when it was time for her to step forwards, Arran had whispered to her, 'It's all right. Just sing the way you sing in your cave,' and Captain Padra himself had given her such a kind smile of re-assurance that she had fixed her eyes on him and sung just for him, because he gave her confidence. Then she had become caught up in the battle for Mistmantle, and had helped to save Padra, Arran and the whole island. Suddenly, she mattered.

Suddenly, too, she had new friends. Fingal, Crackle the Squirrel, and Needle the Hedgehog were all her friends. Urchin, too, though she was a little in awe of Urchin who had crossed the sea and brought Crispin home. But the animals who had shared in that vital day stayed together. Never mind that Fingal never took anything seriously, that Crackle was so afraid of being unpopular she'd be friends with anyone, that Needle could be bossy. They were her friends. If she wanted to escape into a dream world, or be very quiet by herself for a while, none of them minded. But now that she was at the tower every day learning to be a real musician, she didn't need to dream quite so much.

Fingal swam in and out of the staithes, popping up now and again and playing hide and seek with a little she-otter called Skye who was just learning to swim. When Captain Lugg finally marched from the ship with a troop of moles and hedgehogs behind him, the animals instantly stopped playing and rushed to press round him. Apple jumped on to the jetty, which creaked. Skye darted back to her mother.

'Found anything, Captain Lugg?' asked Apple.

'Spies and swords?' asked Fingal hopefully, and the little ones clamoured to know if there was any exciting cargo, and what was it like in there, and could they go on board and have a go at the wheel.

'Certainly not!' said Lugg. 'It's a king's state vessel. No weapons. No warriors hiding. Crew unarmed, and not many. I'm reporting to the tower. But she has a ship's boat,' he went on, winking at Needle. 'A little lifeboat. Surprised they haven't needed it. The crew have permission to lower it, just in case any littl'uns might like to play in it.'

There were cheers and shrieks of delight, and presently the ship's boat was lowered jerkily over the side. As the smaller animals swarmed into it, Apple sat down heavily.

'It's a big disappointment,' she pronounced, and sighed. 'I couldn't help wondering if they'd brought a nice young princess along. Or a few to choose from. Mind you, she wouldn't have to be a princess, it's more important that she's a nice –'

Fingal, who had been admiring the boat, bobbed up from the water.

'You're not trying to marry Crispin off, are you?' he said.

'Well, and why not, and it's *King* Crispin to you,' said Apple defensively. 'It's a hard lonely business being king, he needs somebody beside him, a better squirrel than Crispin never set paw to a branch, and besides it's a waste, a nice squirrel like him not having a wife. There must be somebody on the island, though I don't know that he's got his eye on anyone.' She shook her head and sighed again. 'If I were younger or he were older, I'd have a go myself.'

Fingal disappeared underwater. A giggle of bubbles rose to the surface.

'But, Mistress Apple,' said Sepia gently, 'it's not

long since Whisper died. He must still be grieving for her.'

'Who's Whisper?' asked a small hedgehog.

Sepia lifted the hedgehog carefully on to her lap. 'Was, not is,' she said. 'When Crispin had to go away, he lived on an island with swans and squirrels. He married a squirrel called Whisper. Urchin met her and he said she was kind and lovely, and Crispin adored her. But she died, and Crispin can't want to marry anyone else yet.'

'All the same, there should be a family,' said Apple firmly. 'And the sooner the better. A proper family in the tower, little squirrels all running and climbing about, that's what we want.'

Fingal surfaced and tried to answer, but he was still laughing too much. He rolled over and slapped his tail against the staithes.

'I see what you mean,' said Sepia thoughtfully. 'Otters are water creatures, and I'm sure Padra won't want to be king.'

'Our Padra?' said Fingal and abruptly stopped laughing. 'Hail and plague, he'd have to be, wouldn't he?'

'Haven't you never worked that out?' demanded Apple. 'If there's no family, it's the next senior captain gets kinged, or queened, or whatever. And I'm sure your Padra would be a very good king, but otters don't like being away from water just like moles would rather keep away underground.'

'I can't see Arran in a crown, either,' said Fingal. 'She can't even keep her circlet on.'

'There you are, then, it's like I told you,' said Apple. 'We have to get the king married, and in the meantime, take good care of him and make sure he doesn't get ill nor hurt nor nothing. Have you got any big sisters, Sepia?'

In the Throne Room Urchin watched the solemn faces of Padra, Crispin and Fir. His paws tingled. It was exciting to know that, sooner or later, Crispin would ask for his opinion. He just hoped he wouldn't say anything silly. Padra and Fir had spoken already.

'So,' said Crispin, 'three of us are agreed that we must help Whitewings, as it's the animals we sent into exile who are causing their troubles. But putting Urchin at risk is another matter. Now, Urchin.'

Urchin's ears twitched nervously. Crispin smiled and leant forwards casually on the throne, folding his paws as if he and Urchin were chatting in Anemone Wood, not having a solemn meeting in the Throne Room.

'I haven't let you say a word up to now,' he said, 'because I was pretty certain that you'd say, "Yes,

Your Majesty, send me. I'll go." You might not want to go, you'd rather be here with the rest of us, you might be terrified, but you'd do it.'

'I was going to ask if it could wait until after the coronation,' admitted Urchin.

'*Everything* can wait until after the coronation,' said Crispin firmly. 'You may be the Marked Squirrel who's going to deliver the island. It's just as likely that you're not – or at least, not yet.'

Urchin looked down at his claws. There should be something exciting about the idea of being the Marked Squirrel of a prophecy. But he didn't know anything about Whitewings, or how he was supposed to deliver it, or even where it was, or whether they'd let him keep the sword if he didn't.

'How can I tell if the prophecy means me?' he asked.

Crispin turned to Fir. 'How can he tell?'

'He can't,' said Fir simply. 'Prophecies are all very useful in their way, but they must be handled with care. They can cause all sorts of wrong guesses.'

'Is there such a prophecy, Brother Fir?' asked Padra.

'Oh, yes. Hm. Yes,' said Fir. 'A Marked Squirrel will deliver Whitewings in its time of need. Squirrels of your colour are most rare, but I believe Whitewings is one of the places where they are, occasionally, seen. Or so they say.'

'Are they?' said Urchin. 'Are they?' And a shiver ran through him with a hope and excitement he had never known. Fir's words had stirred something so deeply hidden inside him that he hadn't recognised it before.

'Please, Brother Fir,' he said, and found he was stammering, 'please, if there are squirrels like me on Whitewings, might that be where I come from?'

'*Occasionally*, Urchin,' said Fir, and Urchin's hopes darkened, 'very occasionally, there is a squirrel like yourself on Whitewings. But they are very rare. I think your mother must have belonged somewhere further away. You're very special, you know, Urchin, wherever you come from.'

'Thank you, Brother Fir,' said Urchin quickly, and bent his head to hide his disappointment. Sometimes, when he caught sight of his reflection, he would wonder what it would be like if the other squirrel in the water or the window could be real, a squirrel like himself, so he wouldn't be the only one with pale fur. Mostly, nobody noticed the difference any more. He himself forgot that he stood out in a crowd. But it had been so good, for a moment, to think that he might find out where he came from and know who he was. When he had thought he came from Whitewings, his heart had urged him to go there. He swallowed hard, and curled his claws.

'You don't have to go,' said Crispin firmly. 'They offered you a sword, and Padra intervened. If you'd accepted it, it would have been as good as agreeing to fight their battles for them.'

'Oh!' said Urchin. 'I didn't know that.'

'Exactly,' said Padra drily. 'I hope they weren't trying to trick you, offering something so hard to refuse. You must bear that in mind, Urchin. They really shouldn't have offered it.'

Urchin gave a little nod to show he understood. He'd been right about that sword. It really was too good to be true.

'But, please,' he said, looking from Crispin to Padra and back, 'just for a moment, just now, when I thought it might be the place I come from, I really wanted to go there. I wanted it for my own sake. So I suppose I should be ready to go for theirs. I don't know if I'm the squirrel in the prophecy, or what I'm supposed to do when I get there, but if I don't go, Your Majesty, I'll always wonder what would have happened if I did. So I'm willing to go, if you want me to – or as willing as I can be, when I don't know what I'm letting myself in for.'

'Well done, Urchin,' said Padra, and knowing that he was impressed made Urchin feel better about everything.

Crispin nodded. 'Wait outside, please, Urchin, while we talk further,' he said. 'And you, too, Needle – unless there's anything you want to say?'

Needle had stayed silently by the fireplace all this time. Urchin saw the way her sharp spines bristled, and the tight scowl on her face.

'It's nothing to do with me,' she said brusquely. 'But since you've asked, Your Majesty, I think Lord Treeth's looking down his nose at us, the same goes for that Trail squirrel, and Bronze looks like a claw thug. If I were Urchin I wouldn't want to go with them, but if he must, I'll go too.'

'That's very noble of you, Needle,' said Crispin, 'but if Urchin goes he'll have guards and warriors to protect him. He mustn't be in danger from Mistmantle exiles, or from the mercenaries who fought for Husk.'

'Yes, Your Majesty, but I think I should be there all the same,' she said. She bowed with a tight little pursing of her mouth, and left the chamber side by side with Urchin. They found Docken still on duty outside, his spines sticking out in various directions. The empty stone corridor was pleasantly cooler than the Throne Room, and they scurried straight to the open window. Three hedgehogs were struggling up the beach carrying a dark wooden sea chest between them.

'That must be Lord Treeth's belongings,' remarked Docken, looking over their shoulders. 'He must be planning a long stay. Expect it's full of robes.'

'He looks like the sort of animal who likes dressing up,' said Needle, and leant out further to watch. 'I keep getting the Hedgehog Host mixed up. That big one's Lumberen, I know that.'

'Yes, that's Lumberen. Not bright, but a good worker,' said Docken. As he spoke, the very large hedgehog at the front stepped in a rock pool so that the chest tilted dangerously. Urchin couldn't hear what the other hedgehogs said, but he knew it wasn't polite.

'And the two at the back with the cross faces are Sluggen and Crammen,' said Docken, pointing out two hedgehogs who appeared to be scowling with effort. 'They always look like that. These days they've got nothing to scowl about, but I suppose they've got into the habit of it. And,' he said, turning to meet someone in the corridor, 'here's Gorsen. You've got all those visitors sorted out, then, have you?'

Gorsen, who was rubbing something into his paws, looked even more perfectly groomed than before. Urchin supposed he was trying to impress the envoys.

'Far better work than slaving underground day

and night for Captain Husk,' said Gorsen. 'King Brushen would never have allowed it if he'd known the half of what was happening. I've put Lord Treeth in Lady Aspen's old sitting room. It was far too good for her.' He marched smartly away with a scented waft of resin oil.

'He even puts sniffy stuff on his paws,' observed Needle.

'Gorsen thinks of everything,' said Docken. 'He'll be a member of the Circle one of these days. He's the kind who gets places.'

Urchin's mind was still on the other side of the Throne Room door. He supposed it would be all right, going to Whitewings, only – well, only he was still learning how to be a court squirrel, and he was making new friends, like Juniper. Juniper might be like a younger brother, and he'd often wanted a brother. Then again, if Juniper was going to be sick every time he saw a boat he might be the sort of younger brother who wore out your patience. When the Throne Room door opened, he straightened up.

'Come in, Urchin,' called Padra, and he walked into the Throne Room and bowed with his fur prickling. Padra was smiling reassuringly, but then, Padra would.

'Urchin, we've come to a decision,' said Crispin. 'The envoys and crew can stay until after the coronation. Lord Treeth won't be pleased – he can't wait to get you off the island – but he'll just have to put up with it. When the coronation is over I'll send an advance party of our moles by tunnel to make their own judgement of the situation and report back. *If* they agree with what Lord Treeth told us, we'll send a small fighting force to sort out a few Mistmantle animals who need to learn better manners, and *if* they advise it, you will go with them, but only if I know that there's a bird or a tunnel to get you safely home.'

'Are there really mole tunnels under the sea?' asked Urchin. He'd always doubted it.

'Oh yes,' said Crispin. 'The moles don't like telling the rest of us about them, except to swear that they exist. But apparently they were made thousands of years ago when the sea bed wasn't the sea bed at all, and the islands weren't islands. I suppose they could get a small squirrel through one if they had to.'

Urchin didn't like tunnels, but if he had to go through one to get home, that was that. And he might not have to go there at all, and certainly not yet. He could forget it until after the coronation.

'And now,' said Crispin, 'we have guests to entertain. Lord Treeth will eat here with the captains, Fir and myself, and I'll have a table set up in the chamber next to this, for you and Needle and the young

Whitewings attendants. And, Urchin, all we have said here is of the highest secrecy. Not a word to anyone. Even Needle. All she needs to know is that she has to be pleasant to the Whitewings envoys.'

'Yes, sir,' said Urchin, catching the laughter in Padra's eyes. All he had to do now was persuade Needle to be nice to animals she didn't like. Delivering an island would have been easier.

Chapter 5

The small chamber was decorated very beautifully for the young Whitewings attendants. Colourful arrangements of summer flowers, deep purple irises, creamy roses and deep red peonies spilled from window sills and crowned the tables. Cushions had been spread on benches and on the floor. In the late evening sunshine all the windows were open, and the sea glittered beyond them. The curtains, creamy-white and patterned with leaves, lifted softly in the sea breeze.

The evening was turning out better than Urchin had expected as they shared supper and stories. Bronze, Trail and Scatter were much friendlier now than they had been in the Throne Room. Scatter looked better than she had before, though she still seemed frail and shy. She wore a little ring of hawthorn berries on her wrist and stayed close to Trail, who constantly asked her what she'd like to eat and whether she felt well.

Needle was on her best behaviour, whether or not she was enjoying herself. Chilled cordials had been brought from the cellar with berries and flower heads floating on the top, and there were hazelnut cakes, cheese, tiny vegetable pastries and sweet frothy things made from fruit, cream and honey. Urchin stopped worrying about whether he'd be going to Whitewings and how to get back.

Bronze had looked like the kind of hedgehog nobody argued with, but he was turning out to be good company. When Needle asked him, with cold politeness, what sort of journey they'd had, he launched into a tale of how as soon as the storm began Lord Treeth retired to his cabin with a pillow on his head and stayed there ('He kept a whole cabin to himself, too!' said Scatter) and when he came back on deck he'd forgotten about the pillow, which had impaled itself on his spines and was still on top of his head, and when they managed to pull it off you couldn't see His Lordship for feathers.

Scatter giggled. She asked Urchin and Needle about their part in the battle for Mistmantle, and listened with fascination. She sucked stickiness from her claw tips, Bronze told another funny story, he and Needle got hiccups, and Trail told them how Lord Treeth had tried to be heroic and help to furl the sails and ended up hanging on with all four paws to the mast and waiting to be rescued.

Urchin laughed politely, but unease was slowly creeping into him. This didn't feel right. He wouldn't tell stories about Padra the way these animals told them about Lord Treeth. But then, Padra wouldn't do silly things like that in the first place.

Needle moved away to the window. Urchin could tell she was tired of Scatter giggling and Bronze telling his tales, but unfortunately Bronze followed her.

'The nights are drawing in earlier now,' he said. 'Sunset's beginning.' Trickles of gold were spreading across the blue evening light.

'Ooh, do you think we'll see that riding stars thing?' said Scatter in excitement. 'When the stars all dance around the sky and everything? That happens in Mistmantle, doesn't it? I'd love to see that.'

'It won't be tonight,' said Needle, and explained patiently as if she were speaking to a small child. 'Brother Fir would have told us. Riding stars don't happen often, and when it does it always means something, for good or for harm. We've had enough harm on Mistmantle.'

'But it'll be a lovely sunset,' said Trail. 'We'd see it

better from the other side of the tower. Shall we go and see *King's Arrow* by sunset?'

'*What* by sunset?' said Needle.

'It's the name of our ship,' said Trail. '*King's Arrow*. She looks wonderful in this sort of light. Shall we go and see?'

'Shouldn't somebody know where we are?' said Scatter nervously, and looked to Needle for help. 'We should tell Lord Treeth, but we can't interrupt them while they're in the Throne Room. He'd get cross.'

'I'll tell them,' said Needle, and couldn't resist adding, 'Our king won't get cross. I'll catch up with you later.' Urchin was pretty sure she wouldn't hurry. She'd probably had enough of the company by now, and he'd better get them out of her way before she forgot to be polite. He gathered up the visitors' cloaks and they pattered down the stairs and out of the tower. The fresh air was still pleasantly warm, the summer evening was scented with thyme and chamomile, and the ship lay calm after her wild crossing, with the fire-bright sky beyond her. Her small boat nestled half-screened behind her like a shy child with its mother.

'That boat should have been raised back to the deck,' said Bronze.

'She's a beauty, though!' said Urchin, looking with admiration at the little lifeboat. Her lines were sleek, her sail was furled, and she even had a canopy folded back against the starboard side.

'She's small, but she's built to be a boat we could survive in after shipwreck, even on a long crossing,' said Trail. 'She has that canopy for shelter, and there are storage boxes under the rowing benches and the seats in the stern, to make room for cloaks and provisions. Shall we show you?'

'I'll go first!' called Scatter and ran along the jetty, wobbling a bit on the wooden slats. 'Somebody give me a paw?'

Bronze sighed. 'I don't know why we had to bring her,' he said. 'Clueless. Can't get in and out of a boat without falling in. Give her a paw, would you, Urchin?'

Juniper dashed along the path that wound from Falls Cliffs and darted up the first tall tree he found. The quickest way to the bay was through the pine treetops to Anemone Wood and beyond, and so he leapt from tree to tree, the tips springing back beneath him, faster and faster. He must reach the bay, though it had been the scene of one of the worst moments in his life.

He didn't understand what had happened to him as the Whitewings ship had drawn near. He only knew that as she came in something grey and tight had seemed to press him, as if smoke had filtered into his eyes and throat. A sense of horror had made his stomach turn with nausea, his heart had raced, he had turned hot and cold – then, with the lurch that followed, it had been all he could do to find a rock pool and be sick.

Juniper had known moments like that before. They had been rare and terrible, but never as bad as this. He could remember feeling this anxiety, this fear and horror, once when he had been very small, and once just before a baby was taken away to be culled. It was as if he knew beforehand that something terrible would happen.

It had been such a wonderful morning until the bedraggled ship had come in and horror had enfolded him. Being wretchedly sick was bad enough, but he had done it in front of all his new friends. In front of Urchin of the Riding Stars, his hero! Today his hero had become his friend, and he had immediately ruined it all by vomiting in a pool while Urchin escorted distinguished guests to the tower. He couldn't help being sick. The horror had overwhelmed him. But that same sense of fear about the ship was the very thing that now sent him rushing back to the bay, his ears flattened back, his paws outstretched, his tail spread like a banner behind him. Urchin needed help. It was as if the darkness had been lifted from him and wrapped around Urchin, and he would do anything, anything, to save him.

In the Throne Room, the remnants of a meal lay on the table and wine shone in glasses. Needle stood politely with her back straight, her spines smoothed down and her paws folded, patiently answering yet more of Lord Treeth's questions. She had meant to deliver her message and leave – she wanted to see her family, and there might be leftovers from the table to take to little Scufflen – but Lord Treeth insisted on taking an interest in her. He asked her so many questions about her family and about the other hedgehogs on Mistmantle that she cast pleading looks at Crispin to rescue her. He stood up.

'Needle, do you go back to your family tonight?' he asked.

'I was hoping to, sir,' she said. He swept a few cakes into a basket.

'Take these,' he said, 'with my greetings to your parents. Captain Lugg, will you escort Needle home?'

'There's no need, sir,' she said, feeling happier already and curtseying as she took the basket. 'Shall I –'

She stopped. There were scufflings outside, a high, tearful voice and a loud, urgent rapping on the door.

'What on the island's this?' said Lugg, his paw on his sword hilt.

'Enter!' called Crispin. As the door swung open, the sound of a squirrel sobbing grew louder.

Gorsen marched in, his face grim. Scatter was holding his paw and rubbing tears from her eyes.

'You won't be in any trouble, Miss Scatter,' said Gorsen gravely. 'Tell the king what you told me.'

Scatter struggled through her tears, and couldn't speak. Crispin knelt in front of her. 'Take a deep breath,' he said gently. 'Don't be afraid of me.'

Scatter's lips trembled.

'He's gone, Your Majesty,' she stammered.

'Who's gone, Scatter?' asked Crispin.

Needle found her skin was clammy. Her limbs felt weak, and she clenched her paws.

'Urchin,' whispered Scatter, and her voice rose into a wail. 'He went in the little boat . . .' and, hiding her face against Gorsen, she sobbed wretchedly.

Sweating and breathless in the fading light, Juniper reached the shore, sniffed the evening air and looked about him. Nobody was in sight.

The ship lay at her moorings, and Juniper forced himself to look hard at her. She would have no power to frighten him if he faced her. With her tattered sail, she looked helpless and harmless. Then he saw a small boat moving far off on the water, drawing steadily nearer to the mists.

'Padra, fetch guards and go after him,' ordered Crispin, 'but not beyond the mists.' Padra ran from the room. Needle would have followed, but a glance from Crispin told her to stay. 'Now, Scatter,' he went on, 'tell me exactly what happened.'

Scatter still gulped and gasped as she tried to speak. From the flowers on the table Crispin gave her a pawful of soft petals to dry her eyes, and at last she spoke.

'The ship's boat was still down,' she sniffed. 'It shouldn't have been, and if only it hadn't he would never have gone. But as soon as he saw it he said he'd just go to Whitewings. He said it was his own risk and he wouldn't put anybody else in danger if he went alone, and Y . . . Y . . . Your Majesty wouldn't have to order him. Please, *please*, Your Majesty, we all tried to talk him out of it, but he was so determined, he – he kissed the ground, and held up his paw and made a vow about it – he would have gone all by himself, and got lost, so Trail and Bronze went with him, and he . . . he . . . he said . . .'

She burst into fresh weeping, and Gorsen hugged her tightly.

'He said Your Majesty would understand,' she

sobbed. 'He said, if he was the Marked Squirrel – *that* Marked Squirrel – it was the only honourable thing to do.' She buried her face against Gorsen.

'Oh, Your Majesty,' said Lord Treeth heavily. 'What can I say? We would never have knowingly put your Companion in danger.'

Needle's spines bristled as she watched Lord Treeth's face. He wore a look of concern and sorrow, but it seemed to her that it could have been painted on. She slipped her paw into Arran's, not for comfort, but to keep herself from flying at Lord Treeth with her claws out.

He's lying, Your Majesty. She thought the words hard at Crispin, wishing he could read her mind. *They're both lying.* It was all too convenient, Urchin going when Whitewings wanted him so much.

'They'll look after him,' sniffed Scatter.

'Oh, Trail and Bronze will look after him,' said Lord Treeth. 'They are the best of our young. Brave, skilled, and expert sailors. He's safe with them.'

Silence followed, a tight, chilly silence. Needle had never been afraid of Crispin, but she felt afraid even to look at him now. *King Crispin knows*, she thought. *He knows they're lying.*

'Fetch a guard squad, Gorsen,' ordered Crispin tersely. 'Arran, get every available otter to join Padra in searching the waters as far as the mists, but no further.'

Arran slipped from the room, and Gorsen rapped out orders from the doorway. Paws scurried along the corridor, and, as a squad of moles and hedgehogs lined up before him, Crispin turned without smiling to Lord Treeth.

'These animals will conduct you and Scatter to your chambers,' he said. 'Captain Lugg, go with them. We will discuss matters further in the morning. Brother Fir, Needle, come with me, please.'

Outside, the air had turned cool. Crispin, Fir and Needle felt the breeze tug at their fur as they stood on the cold, wet sand. No light showed on the water. It seemed a long time before Padra's sleek wet head appeared in the shallows and he scrambled to the shore.

'Not a sign,' he said. His voice was grey with defeat and anger burned in his eyes. 'Nothing. Sorry, Crispin.'

Needle stared wretchedly out at the empty sea. She knew Padra was angry at himself for not catching up with Urchin and bringing him back. She knew what that felt like.

If only I'd gone with them to the shore. If only I'd delivered my message to the king and then gone straight down to join them. I'd had enough of the Whitewings lot and I was glad to get out of it. I should have stayed with him. If only I could go back to suppertime and change what happened. If only I could start again.

'Padra, you've done all you could,' said Crispin. 'Come to the Throne Room and I'll tell you everything that Scatter said.'

Miserably, Needle edged closer to Crispin.

'Please, Your Majesty,' she said, 'Urchin's Padra's page and your Companion. He wouldn't have gone away without your permission.' Speaking quickly to get it over with, she added, 'Please, King Crispin, I'm sorry. It's my fault, if I'd stayed with him he'd still be here.'

Crispin took her paws in his. 'Of course it's not your fault, Needle,' he said, but she didn't feel comforted. She looked to see where Brother Fir was and what he was doing and saw him alone at the end of the jetty, the breeze ruffling his pale tunic, one paw raised towards the empty darkness under the stars.

Chapter 6

'Don't believe a word they said,' grumbled Lugg. 'He didn't go of his own will. He was took.'

The captains had gathered in the Throne Room. Needle had followed them and nobody told her to go, so she stayed.

'Needle, did the other Whitewings animals try to persuade him to go?' asked Crispin.

'Not when I was there,' she said. 'We just chatted and had fun, and somebody suggested we should go back to the jetty to see the sunset. I can't remember whose idea it was, but Scatter said somebody should tell you where we were. I was tired of Bronze showing off and Scatter giggling, and Urchin was happy to look after them, so I thought I may as well . . . may as well . . . leave him to it. I'm sorry. Lugg's right. He wouldn't have gone without your permission.'

'Needle,' said Crispin, and knelt beside her, 'none of this is your fault. Can you tell me why you stayed so long with us in the Throne Room? It was because Lord Treeth kept you talking.'

'That was a trick,' said Lugg. 'Gave them time to get our Urchin away. Our Urchin's been took. If you'd stayed with him, Needle, they would have took you, too.'

Crispin walked away and leant against a window sill, facing them.

'We may hope for the best, but we have to act for the worst,' he said firmly. 'We can't trust Lord Treeth and Scatter, but they may be innocent and are still our visitors. They are to be kept in their chambers and guarded until we have Urchin home. Keep the ship's crew under guard, too.'

'Strange, that,' said Padra. 'Lord Treeth is a very important animal. If this was a plot to take Urchin away, why was he left behind?'

'To make trouble,' said Lugg.

'He won't get the chance,' said Crispin. 'We'll have Gorsen in charge of his guard. Because we can't leave by water and return by water, following by boat isn't possible. Lugg, what can you tell me of the tunnels?'

'We can reach Whitewings that way, Your Majesty,' said Lugg. 'Been in 'em myself. Not all the way to Whitewings, but my father took me down there and taught me the ways of 'em. Long journey, though.'

'How long?' asked Crispin.

'Six days and nights. Maybe seven, even eight. Depends on the moles and the route, Your Majesty. There's two of 'em.'

'I believe it's only three or four days by boat,' said Padra, 'so Urchin and his captors will be there before them.'

'Then, Lugg, send moles at once,' said Crispin. 'True and trusted moles, six to each route.'

'Can't attack Whitewings with a dozen moles, with respect, Your Majesty,' said Lugg.

'You're not to attack it,' said Crispin. 'I need a small, discreet force to see what's really happening, and report back. And if Urchin needs rescuing, as I'm sure he will, be fast and sure and rescue him. Take whatever you need from the armoury, but without weighing yourselves down. And tell them, Lugg, that I won't be crowned before they come back, so they won't miss anything.'

'We're assuming that Urchin can get back through mole tunnels,' said Padra.

'Might be a tight squeeze some places, but he's not full grown yet,' said Lugg. 'And we can dig 'em out a bit wider if necessary. Slow us down a bit, but we'll get him out. Permission to go, Your Majesty? Get him out before he grows any more?'

'Go, Lugg,' said Crispin. Lugg bowed smartly and trotted away.

'Before anybody else leaves,' said Crispin, drawing himself up, 'I have a solemn promise to make in front of witnesses.'

There was a cold swish of metal as he drew his sword and laid it on the floor before him. Arran stood up and folded her paws. Needle copied her.

'I swear before you all,' said Crispin, 'on all that I love and on my honour as your king, that I will not be crowned until Urchin of the Riding Stars is returned to us alive. If he is not, I will be uncrowned until my death.'

There was a moment of solemn silence, broken by Fir. 'As to that, I think he'll return alive,' he said. 'But you couldn't be crowned yet anyway, Crispin, not quite thoroughly and properly. The most extraordinary thing has just come to light. The Heartstone is not the Heartstone. It is a fake.'

Darkness pounded in Urchin's head. Inside and around him, everything churned and rocked. His eyes wouldn't open. His mouth was dry with a sour, fusty taste.

Wherever he was, he was in the wrong place.

Damp and chilled, he was lying on something hard. He should be in a dry nest in his chamber at the Spring Gate – he tried to call for help, but couldn't. Even the effort to open his eyes was too great.

'You gave him too much,' said a female voice. 'You might have done permanent damage.'

'He'll be more damaged when King Silverbirch gets him,' growled someone else.

The rocking went on. Urchin forced his eyes open, and was still in darkness. Flexing chilled, stiff claws, he reached for his sword.

He hadn't been wearing a sword. There was nothing there.

'He's moving,' said the female. Her voice brought a fuzzy picture into Urchin's swimming head. He remembered Trail and Bronze – those were the voices he had heard. Where was Needle? And the small squirrel – he remembered helping her into the boat, and then Bronze holding him and forcing a drink between his teeth . . .

A hinge creaked, and the sound hurt his head.

'What are you doing?' growled Bronze.

'Finding him a blanket,' said Trail. 'He mustn't take ill. We have to get him back alive.'

'Get one for me too,' said Bronze. 'It's freezing in these mists.'

The mists! Urchin heaved himself up, struggling

against the arms that seized him. He tried to balance, and couldn't. There was a tightness about his paws as he fought to move, his tail wasn't balancing him, and as his eyes focused and his dizziness cleared he knew exactly, wretchedly, how things were. His hind paws and tail were tied, his forepaws were tethered to rings on each side of the boat, and they were deep in the mists.

If he could get out now, he might be able to swim for it. There was some slack in the ropes holding his front paws. Gathering all his strength he heaved, struggled and kicked out with his bound feet at Trail.

'Vicious little freak!' she snapped. 'Bronze, help me!'

Growling and cursing, Bronze came from the rowing bench to help. Urchin could make out the shape of a sword at his side.

'Get down, you,' snarled Bronze, with a push that sent Urchin sprawling backwards – but the fall brought the sword within reach. Urchin darted a paw at it, but his limbs had grown stiff, and before he could reach the hilt Trail had whipped the sword from its sheath. She slapped the flat blade on to his wrist with a sting that ran all the way to his shoulder. Gasping with pain, he felt the cold sword point at his throat.

'It's a long way to Whitewings, and there's nobody

here to help you,' she said. 'You may as well cooperate.' She dropped the sword in front of Bronze. 'You
should have seen that coming. Good thing I did.'

Urchin kept very still. Trail was right. He was at
their mercy. He put up with her draping a blanket
across him as if he were a baby. Bronze had settled
down to row again, and each creak and dip of the
oars took him further from Mistmantle.

'It's like this,' said Bronze. 'You're a court squirrel,
you're under orders from the king and that otter, you
obey orders, right? Well, we're court animals, too,
under orders from King Silverbirch and Lord Treeth,
and if they tell us to snatch the Freak and get him to
Whitewings that's what we have to do. Fair enough?'

Urchin's mouth felt dry and swollen as he spoke.
'My captain and my king,' he croaked, 'wouldn't
order me to trick another animal and kidnap him.'

'Oh, shut up, Freak,' said Bronze. 'You fell for it,
didn't you?'

I fell for it. It didn't help to know that. He wondered if they'd missed him yet, and a little brightness
entered his misery.

'They'll be looking for me,' he said. 'They'll know
I've gone.'

'No they won't,' said Trail smugly. 'Why do you
think Scatter isn't here? She stayed to tell them you
came of your own choice, and she'd act it up for all

she's worth. Only thing she's good for. So they're not going to send anyone looking for you, are they, not past the mists? They wouldn't risk never getting back.'

Urchin didn't answer. Trail didn't know what she was talking about. She didn't know Crispin. The idea of Crispin *not* doing something was too appalling to think of. If Crispin didn't do anything, and if he couldn't escape – and the chances of escape were so small they were ridiculous – he might never get home again.

Perhaps King Silverbirch would just tell him what they wanted him to do and he could do it and go home. Unfortunately, that seemed unlikely. All this talk about a Marked Squirrel seemed hollow. They weren't treating him at all like an honoured guest and saviour of the island – and Bronze's words about the king made him so uneasy he hoped he'd only dreamed them.

He reminded himself that he had left the island by water before and returned, and that time he had been storm-tossed and nearly wrecked, and hadn't known where he was going. The Heart that cared for Mistmantle had cared for him, too. He found a quiet place in his own heart, and from that still point inside himself, he called silently for help.

Great Heart of Mistmantle, keep me, as you kept

me before, even beyond the mists. Bring me home.
Bring me back to Mistmantle.

He twisted to look out at the grey water behind
him. Was that an animal, gliding behind the boat?
But it couldn't be. Just a shadow on the waves. When
he looked again, it had gone.

In the grave silence of the Gathering Chamber of
Mismantle Tower, Needle stood with an oval box in
her paws. It was a beautiful thing, made of softly
glowing pale pink stone with flecks of silver and gold
wavering through it. She had been sent to Fir's turret
to collect it, and it was so important that Heath and
Russet, squirrels of the Circle, had been sent with her
as an escort.

'Thank you, Needle,' said Brother Fir, and took off
the lid.

The stone lay in a nest of straw and muslin. It was
no bigger than a pebble, smooth, almost heart-
shaped, the same colour as the box it lay in, with a
gleam of gold at its heart. Needle watched Fir lift it
from the box.

It had to be the Heartstone. It had to be. Brother
Fir must be wrong to say the Heartstone was a fake.
It was too sacred a thing to be tampered with.

'It looks like the Heartstone to me,' said
Crispin. 'But I've only seen it once, when King

Brushen was crowned.'

'Hm!' said Fir, and tossed it into Padra's paws. 'Catch!'

Padra caught it by instinct. It lay in his paw, not moving as he looked from the stone to Fir.

'Give it to Needle,' said Fir.

Needle wanted to say no – she wouldn't dare touch the Heartstone – but Padra was already passing it to her with such a grave expression that she didn't like to argue. She took the stone very carefully in both paws, feeling the eyes of Fir, Arran, Padra and the king resting on it as she held it. It made her nervous so that her paws shook a little, but it stayed still.

'That is *not* the Heartstone,' said Fir. 'It is convincingly like the real thing. For a time it even convinced me, and I am the only animal left alive who ever held the real one. But it didn't *feel* right in my paw. The weight, the balance, and there is something of a . . . a . . . what can I call it? something that calls to me from the Heartstone, as if it were a living thing. Just to make absolutely sure, I put this one in with a basket of pebbles for that delightful little hedgehog to play with today. He carried it about in his paws and in his mouth, he built with it, he made patterns with it. Never dropped it once. The real Heartstone would have been halfway across the floor as soon as he touched it.'

'So what's happened to the real one?' asked Arran.

'You can be sure Husk was responsible, whatever it was,' said Padra.

'Certainly, certainly,' said Fir, scratching his ear. 'Husk intended to be crowned, but he knew he wouldn't really be the true king and so wouldn't be able to hold on to the Heartstone at his coronation. Wouldn't do, would it? All those animals packed into the Gathering Chamber, all stretching up on their hind paws to watch, and the Heartstone leaps out of his paw like a frog. Hm? So he had a copy made, and disposed of the real one.'

'How?' said Crispin. 'How can we find it?'

'I wish I knew,' replied Fir simply. 'I know of no power that could destroy the Heartstone, so it must still be somewhere. I only hope it will help us to find it, for there's no knowing where it is. You're the king anyway, Crispin. By the laws of the island you have been king since the death of King Brushen, and you were acknowledged as king that very day. That's what you are, whether or not you're crowned using the Heartstone.'

'But I should be,' said Crispin. 'It's the right way. It must be found.'

'Does that mean we should all go looking for a small stone that could be anywhere?' asked Arran.

Crispin's whiskers twitched. 'And for whoever made this one,' he said. Fir's eyes brightened.

'I hoped you'd think of that,' he said. 'It must have taken great skill to make such an excellent copy.'

In spite of the seriousness of the situation, Needle suddenly felt better than she had since Urchin disappeared. Now she had something to do, something worth doing that would take her mind from worrying about Urchin. In her heart, she made a vow.

I promise that I will search for the Heartstone, and will never stop searching until I find it.

She'd need a plan. And she'd need other animals to join in. It was time to do some organising.

Chapter 7

In a little turret room in the tower, Scatter the squirrel stretched up on her hind claws to look down from the window. Nobody had ever told her how beautiful Mistmantle was. How could she ever have imagined this, the changing green woodland, the blue of harebells, the clusters of berries like jewels on the currant bushes, the pale gold shore? What a shame she'd never be able to enjoy it.

If this was a prison cell, it was a surprisingly nice one. She had expected to be thrown into a dark hole in the ground, but they had locked her into a sunny little room with a bed, a chair, and water and biscuits on a table. When she looked down she could see animals gossiping as they gathered baskets of summer fruit or carried water from the springs. Lord Treeth was in the chamber next door. She had heard him complaining to the guards about it. He had talked about her, too.

'Scatter is expendable,' he had said. *Expendable*. She didn't know what that meant, but she supposed it must be something good. King Crispin had seen through her lies – she had known that might happen, but she had carried out her part anyway. If he had her put to death, she would be dying for Whitewings. So 'expendable' must be a nice thing to say about anybody. It was like 'expert' and 'dependable'. It wouldn't be so bad being killed, if she was being expert and dependable for her island. She didn't like the king of Whitewings, but he was still the king.

Someone knocked sharply at the door. She sprang up, cold and bristling with fear. Oh, they had come for her already! Would she be shot by archers? Or stabbed? She hoped it would be quick. A stern female voice came from outside the door.

'Scatter of Whitewings,' said the voice, 'I am Mistress Tay the Otter, historian and lawyer of Mistmantle.'

A mole voice interrupted. 'You can't speak to the prisoner, Mistress Tay,' said the mole.

'I can, I may and I will,' replied Tay. 'You may refuse to let me into her cell, but as the authority on our laws I must inform her of her rights.'

'Not without the king's permission, you don't,' said the mole. 'You'll have to speak to him.'

'I fully intend to,' said the otter firmly. 'Scatter of Whitewings, you are charged . . .'

Scatter pressed her paws hard against the door. 'Oh, please,' she called, 'please just tell me when they're going to kill me, and how?'

To Scatter, the silence seemed to last for ever. Then the otter answered, sounding faintly surprised.

'Kill? This is Mistmantle. We do not have a death sentence. You are charged with deceiving the king and aiding in the abduction of Urchin, Companion to the King. The king orders that you should be given food, water and shelter, but kept under guard awaiting His Majesty's decision regarding your case as under the fourteenth rule of the Circle and Court of King Brooken and the third and fourth orders of the Tower Guard. But we most certainly do not put our prisoners to death. I will now go to the king and seek permission to enter this chamber.'

No death sentence! Life was wonderful! And so was Mistmantle!

As darkness gathered, Scatter fell asleep. In the deepest hour of night, in the next chamber, Lord Treeth silently opened the lid of his sea chest.

'Out you come, Creeper,' he whispered. 'We will

soon have someone to assist us.'

Urchin grew utterly sick of the dull, lifting sea. Even when he shut his eyes, he could still see it. He gazed at the horizon for any sign of land or, much better, a ship that might rescue him.

He didn't even know why he was wanted on Whitewings and whether they really wanted him to save the island. At least he'd have more idea what was going on when he got there, so when the first faint line of land came into sight, he didn't know whether to be relieved or terrified.

He sat up straighter, scanning the horizon, twitching his ears. Once he got there, he could plan his escape. If he were really lucky the court would be full of hedgehogs, and he could outrun and outclimb any hedgehog easily. But where would he run to on an unknown island?

'Heart keep me,' he prayed. There was nobody else to help him.

Bronze was tipping pawfuls of shrivelled berries into broad leaves. 'That's his,' he said, nodding at Urchin who had just enough freedom of movement to feed himself. 'Who's been at the fresh water, then?'

Trail, who had bent to give Urchin his food, drew herself up. 'Exactly what are you suggesting?' she asked icily.

'I'm not suggesting anything,' said Bronze. 'I'm saying. There's less fresh water than there should be. I've been rationing it, I should know.'

'Then you're not rationing it very well, are you?' said Trail.

'Well, if I took it, I wouldn't be saying anything about it, would I?' growled Bronze. 'There's only you, me and him, and he can't reach anything much. And there's an apple missing, and some of that bread from Mistmantle, and I haven't been eating it.'

Urchin watched with intense interest, saying nothing. If they squabbled, they'd forget to watch him. He wriggled, flexed his paws, and stopped abruptly when Trail turned on him with a glare.

'It's you, stealing, isn't it!' she snapped.

'How can he, idiot?' growled Bronze.

'I don't know how he's done it, but it was him,' she insisted. 'You don't watch him properly when it's your turn. I have to do everything myself.'

'And I suppose you do all the rowing yourself, too?' snarled Bronze. As Trail spun round to face him, she screened Urchin from his eyes.

Urchin could get his paw close enough to his mouth to eat. Could he bite through his bonds? Trail had moved now, and Bronze was looking over his shoulder to continue the argument. Stretching and twisting, Urchin gnawed the rope on his wrist.

'Are you saying I don't watch him?' demanded Bronze.

Trail straightened up. 'You're not watching him now!' she said in triumph, and turned on Urchin. He whipped his wrist away from his mouth, but it was too late.

'What are you up to!' she demanded as she climbed over the rowing bench. 'What's happened here? You verminous freak, you've been chewing this!'

'Nice try,' said Bronze, and crouched forwards over the oars to talk to him. 'Listen, you half-coloured freak from an island of idiots, just behave and you won't be harmed. You're supposed to be the deliverer, though you don't look like delivering much at the moment. Not even yourself. Leave him alone, Trail.'

Urchin gazed out at the land that seemed to come no nearer and told himself he should never have tried that. Escape was impossible. He should have talked to Trail and Bronze, tried to get at least one of them to be friendly and urged them to tell him all about Whitewings and about themselves. He might have persuaded them that they'd all live much more happily if they took him back to Mistmantle and stayed there – it was the sort of thing Crispin would have done. He would have made his enemies his friends.

What would Crispin have said if he'd seen that pathetic attempt to free himself?

He knew exactly what Crispin would say, and Padra, too. *Never mind, Urchin. Put it down to experience.*

He made a promise in his heart. *I will come back. I will come back to Mistmantle, to my friends and my king.* The coast of Whitewings was becoming clearer. He could see cliffs, and a few sparse trees. Looking down to keep the glare from his eyes, he saw a squirrel's paw on the side of the boat.

He shut his eyes and looked again. Definitely a paw.

'What are you looking at?' demanded Trail.

'A fish or something,' said Urchin. Instinct told him that they should not know about the paw. When he looked again, it had disappeared.

In the tunnels under Whitewings, moles ran whispering, one to the next, and the next, and the next. A message was being hurried underground as far as the round chamber where Brother Flame was finishing his morning prayers.

'Pardon me, Brother Flame,' said a mole in a low, urgent voice. 'Boat sighted. Small one. Here soon. Must be them.'

Chapter 8

L ongpaw and the fastest of the squirrels flew through treetops, bending the tips of firs, shaking the cones, carrying in one paw or in their teeth the leaves bearing King Crispin's claw mark. Otters twirled through the water, whispers ran through tunnels and burrows, through dreys and into tree roots. From the windows of the tower trumpets flashed in the sunlight with a sharp, shrill call. Animals heard the message and ran to tell one another until the whole island knew that Urchin had been taken away, the real Heartstone was missing, and Crispin would not be crowned until they were both returned.

Animals wept, raged, ran to the tower to learn more of what had happened, cried out their prayers to the Heart. Ripples of rage and indignation spread through the woods, hills and shores. Squirrels scrambled up the highest trees to gaze out to the mists. *He's OUR Urchin, how dare they? Heart keep him, where are they taking him? And who had the nerve to meddle with the Heartstone? Whatever happened to it, you can be sure it was to do with Husk.* But even more than they cared for the sacred stone, they cared and fretted for Urchin. And everyone asked where was Apple, and who was going to tell her?

On Crispin's orders, Apple had been one of the first to know. Longpaw had dashed through the woods to search for her and found her watching a group of squirrels practising their dances for the coronation party. Apple, fanning herself with a fern, had just chosen a pleasant young squirrel to bring to Crispin's attention when Longpaw gave her the message. Attended by Longpaw she stood up, paws on hips, to march to the tower and hear everything about it.

The day lengthened. Late golden light fell on the water where little boats bobbed near the mists, and now and again a sleek round head would rise to the surface. On Crispin's orders the otters were keeping watch from the sea, as members of the Circle watched from the turrets of Mistmantle Tower. Needle, with little Scufflen falling asleep in her arms, sat miserably on the jetty, kicking her paws. Sepia sat beside her, keeping quiet because there was nothing worth saying. Fingal swam listlessly round the staithes. Every time Needle kicked the jetty Scufflen opened his eyes and squeaked until Sepia, who had always wanted a younger brother or sister to look after, lifted him from her paws and cradled him herself, singing lullabies.

'I'm still thinking about the Heartstone,' said Needle. Scufflen's eyes opened and shut again, and Fingal bobbed up beside them to see if anything interesting was happening. 'I know what it looks like, I've seen the copy. I can describe it so we all know what we're looking for. The thing is, it could be anywhere on the island.'

'Who's "we"?' asked Fingal.

'Won't it be wrapped up in a box or something?' said Sepia.

'It might not,' said Needle, still kicking her heels at the jetty. 'If anyone found a stone in a box, they'd know it was something special. Husk would need a box or a bag or something to carry it in, but he could tip it out. If he never wanted it to be found, he'd have to have thrown it on the beach, maybe, where nobody would notice it in all the other pebbles. Or drop it down somewhere nobody could ever find it.'

'Difficult, on this island,' said Fingal. 'I should

think he threw it out to sea, so it would get washed away.' He turned a somersault in the water. 'But it would get washed back again.'

'Couldn't it sink to the bottom?' said Sepia quietly, not wanting to disturb Scufflen.

'Or be swallowed by a watersnake?' said Fingal cheerfully. 'Shall I kill one for you and see if it's eaten the Heartstone? Oh, but if it swallowed it, it couldn't hold on to it, could it, so I suppose the poor old watersnake would –'

'Oh, please, Fingal!' said Sepia.

'We should start by beachcombing,' said Needle, as they didn't seem to be taking this seriously enough. 'We'll divide up the shore between us and whoever else will help. Crackle will. And all your musicky friends, Sepia, you can get them to help. Fingal, you'll need to get some otters.'

'What, to kill watersnakes?' he asked.

'No, for beachcombing,' said Needle with irritation, and stretched up to watch a young squirrel running from the tower. 'There goes Gleaner!'

'Oh, get her to help, then,' said Fingal, splashing on his back in the water.

'Certainly not!' said Needle. 'She can't be trusted. She used to be Lady Aspen's maid.'

'So?' said Fingal.

'She was devoted to Aspen, and Aspen was as bad

as Husk,' said Needle. 'And before that, she was always a mean little squirmyfur.'

'She's not so bad now,' said Sepia. 'She's very grateful to Crispin because he didn't send her into exile or shut her in a dungeon for years. We could invite her to help.'

'No, we couldn't,' said Needle. 'But I wish I knew where she's off to. You can't trust her. I'll organise beach patrols and talk to Fir.'

'You do like organising, don't you?' said Fingal.

'I'll look in my song cave,' said Sepia thoughtfully. 'There are always pebbles there. Some are very pretty ones. It might be among them.'

'How would it get there?' asked Needle.

'Spat out by a watersnake?' said Fingal.

'I wouldn't need to know how it got there,' said Sepia gently. 'I'd just have to find it.' She spoke dreamily as if to herself, rocking and patting the sleeping baby hedgehog in her arms. 'It's a good place for singing. You run down Falls Cliffs to get in round the side, where it's driest, and there's a small entrance to squeeze through, and you come out into a cave behind the waterfall. The waterfall makes a noise, but when you go further it opens into the loveliest high chamber with a place that lets light in, and it's – oh, it's like nowhere else. The walls glow and there's a little rock pool thing and a spring and then . . .'

'Yes?' said Fingal.

'. . . and then you sing,' she finished simply.

'You mean, *you* sing,' said Needle.

'And it sounds so strong, because the echo brings it all back to you,' said Sepia earnestly. 'It's like – like somewhere holy, and the music is all around . . .'

She stopped. It was too precious, too special, to tell them that she felt as if she rode in the night sky when she sang in her cave. It was just the sort of place where something as magical and wonderful as the Heartstone might turn up. The thought of her song chamber made her yearn to go there.

'Find some squirrels,' said Needle, bringing her back down to earth. 'Fingal, you can –'

'Find a watersnake and do it in?' he asked hopefully.

'Organise the otters,' she said. 'I'm going to tell Fir what we're doing.' She took Scufflen from Sepia's paws and hurried away as he blinked sleepily over her shoulder. Fingal shook his head.

'Hasn't anyone told her?' he said. 'You can't organise an otter.'

'Sh!' said Sepia. 'Somebody's calling.'

'Fingal! Fingal!' It was a cry from an old voice, a cry strained with anxiety and distress. Sepia sprang up and ran to meet the elderly squirrel hobbling towards them.

'Mistress Damson!' she called. 'What's the matter?'

'Have you seen Juniper?' demanded Damson quickly. 'Fingal, have you seen Juniper? You two being friendly, I thought you might know where he is. Only he never came back last night, and I haven't seen him all day, and neither has anyone! Have you seen him, Fingal? Have you seen him?' She clutched Sepia's paw tightly, and turned to her with a look of desperation. 'Sepia, have you seen Juniper?'

Chapter 9

With a growl of gravel, the boat ran aground on the shores of Whitewings. Guards had already seen them, and armed hedgehogs and squirrels stood in rows on the shore, though it was still barely light. Nobody else was about except two swans bobbing on the water, watching their reflections. They wore something that looked like silver collars, but at such a distance Urchin couldn't be sure.

Trail and Bronze heaved him to his hind paws. He stretched and rubbed at his wrists as Trail sliced through the bonds, but Bronze held him fast.

'Don't even think about it,' snarled Bronze, but Urchin had already looked for chances of escape and seen none. There were archers among the guards, so he wouldn't get far. Dragged through the shallows to the shore, he craned his neck to see further. *Know your territory*, Padra would have said. And as Trail and Bronze left him in the care of three guards, two holding his arms and another holding a sword to his throat, he thought he may as well take a good look at the island.

The sands were dull grey, almost white. Ahead of him rose grey and white cliffs so steep that he had to tip back his head and narrow his eyes to look at them. Here and there a straggly bush clung to the cliff side. Some long, shiny twists ran down the cliffs – Urchin thought and hoped they were freshwater streams until he saw that they were gleaming veins of silver. Here and there was a gaping rocky place that looked like the entrance to a cave – that might be worth remembering. He was trying to see a pathway through the cliffs when he heard a rhythmic clanking of metal that somehow reminded him of Lugg's guards practising their drill on Mistmantle, but this was no rehearsal. Soldiers were marching, louder and closer, and their tread was menacing with purpose. He could tell now where the cliff path must be from the sound, and the sunlight flashing from weapons.

'Shackle the prisoner's paws,' ordered Trail. 'The Lord Marshall is coming to escort him to the king.'

'But I've only just been untied!' protested Urchin, but nobody was listening to him. Iron shackles were clamped round his forepaws and fastened to the guards' own wrists, and he was marched across the sands towards the foot of the cliffs. He was trying to keep a count of how many animals carried weapons – too many, in his opinion – but as yet another column appeared from another direction, he gave up trying. How many did it take to arrest one young squirrel? Who did they think he was?

Chained, unarmed and surrounded by hostile animals, it astonished Urchin how little afraid he was. Everything was so strange that it seemed to be happening to somebody else, and besides, there wasn't time to be afraid. The animals marching towards him wore metal breastplates, and several had helmets, some rounded, some oblong, some plain and some decorated. But the puzzling thing was that everything about these animals – fur, armour, weapons – looked dusty. A thin layer of something like ashes lay over them.

Urchin lifted his chin and marched across the sand with his paws tethered and his head up, determined that if Crispin and Padra could see him, they'd be proud of him. At the foot of the cliff path he was jerked so fiercely to a halt that he just managed to stay on his paws as the guards saluted.

'Stand to attention for the Lord Marshall!' barked a hedgehog.

Down the path marched a broad-shouldered, short-furred squirrel, his face hidden by an enormous metal helmet that made him look far taller than any squirrel should be. *It's only a helmet*, thought Urchin, but with its grim slit of a mouthpiece and the jagged, claw-like spikes around its crown it was meant to be terrifying. The large paw resting on the sword hilt looked hard and powerful. One hind paw, Urchin noticed, looked as if it had been damaged, but it was the only sign of weakness about him.

'Lord Marshall,' began Bronze, 'I bring you the –'

'I can see who he is,' growled the Lord Marshall, and with a rough heave he pulled off the helmet.

Urchin's stomach tightened. Against the sudden weakness in his legs, he forced himself to stand firm. He must not show the fear that gripped him as he looked up into a grinning face he had hoped never to see again. This was the squirrel who had been at Husk's right paw, a grim, surly bully with claws that gripped like iron.

'Good morning, Granite,' said Urchin. *Heart help me*, he thought.

In the early light over Mistmantle, Needle picked her way through wet shells and fronds of brown seaweed to the water's edge. It was too much to hope that

Urchin would be coming back, but she couldn't help going to look, just in case, before speaking to Crispin about the planned visit to Sepia's song cave. The boats on watch had not moved, and their lights still glowed. They had been given pennants to fly at any sign of Urchin's return, but every single one remained furled.

Something at the tower caught her eye. A light glowed in a window, then vanished and presently appeared at the next, as if somebody were carrying a lamp along the corridor. It could be anybody's light – but Tay's chamber was on that landing, and the scholarly otter was not often about so early. Tay had supported Husk in the past, and Needle had never trusted her since.

A firm step squelched the wet seaweed behind her. Before she turned round she knew that it must be Gorsen, who always marched like that. Lumberen followed, slipped on a patch of wet weed and landed heavily on his back.

'You're out early, Needle!' said Gorsen. 'Looking for Urchin?'

'He's not here,' grunted Lumberen as he picked himself up. Lumberen never said anything clever, but Gorsen said he was very loyal, and certainly he was big and strong enough to be useful in a crisis. Her father said Lumberen had fought heroically in the fight against Husk's forces.

'Lumberen and I are guarding the Whitewings prisoners next,' said Gorsen. 'Sluggen and Crammen are doing the night watch. Of course, Needle, they're not really prisoners, they're under house arrest in very comfortable tower rooms. It makes you wonder what King Brushen would have made of it.' He tilted back his head and took a deep breath of the cool, salt air. 'D'you know, Needle – the other animals don't understand this, but you're a hedgehog, like me – the Throne Room is a place for quills, not red curly tails. Don't misunderstand me – King Crispin's an excellent king and I'm proud to serve him. We never had a better captain than Crispin. But a king? There's aspects of kingship that only a hedgehog appreciates. He's doing his best, but it takes spines to be a king.'

'He's a good king, and I'm his Companion,' she reminded him sternly. A gleaming pebble caught her eye and she snatched it up, but it lay motionless in her paw and she threw it away in disappointment. 'I have to go now. I need to report to the king.'

As Gorsen and Lumberen marched off to the tower and two pretty young hedgehogs pointed to Gorsen and giggled shyly, Needle hurried up to the Throne Room to find Docken on watch at the door. He didn't look like at all an animal on guard duty. His spines were as untidy as ever and he was bending to listen to Hope, who was standing on his hind legs and jigging with excitement.

'So can I go, Dad, please, please, *please*?' Hope was saying. 'Mummy says I can if you say yes.'

'You want to go to the waterfall?' said Docken uncertainly. 'You don't know about waterfalls.'

'I will when I've been there,' pleaded Hope. 'Please, Fingal's coming and he's sort of almost grown-up and he's Captain Padra's brother and Fingal knows all about waterfalls, he used to be one, I mean, he used to live in one, he told me about it and there's a boat there and he can row it and we're all going to look for the Heartstone, *please*?'

'I didn't know you were coming, Hope,' said Needle, feeling a little put out. This was a serious attempt to find the Heartstone and she had thought that only she and Sepia were going. Fingal must have invited himself and Hope. Typical. Hope was sweet, but he was an infant and needed looking after, and Fingal would only mess about in the water and forget what they were there for.

'Are you going, Needle?' asked Docken.

'Oh, yes. Me and Sepia,' she said. 'But we might be away for more than one day, and we'll be in caves most of the time. It could get cold, and he's very young.'

'Oh, but if you're going, Needle, it's all right,' said

Docken. 'You're a safe pair of paws.'

'I'll tell Mummy!' cried Hope in delight and scuttled away in the wrong direction, dangerously near the top of a steep stair. Needle rushed after him in time to see a curled-up ball of hedgehog spin to the bottom of the stairs, land and lie still.

'I'm coming!' she yelled, but before she could move the spines uncurled. Hope's nose appeared first, twitching.

'Oops,' he said.

'Are you all right?' gasped Needle.

'Oh, yes,' said Hope, and began the laboured climb back up the stairs. 'I forgot which way round I was.'

'He usually gets it right,' said Docken, and Needle hoped it was true. Having satisfied herself that Hope had survived unharmed as usual, Needle asked to see the king and curtsied her way into the Throne Room.

As she straightened up, she knew that important matters were being discussed. Padra, Arran and Fir were with the king, and something about the grave atmosphere in the room made her feel she'd better hurry.

'Sorry if I'm interrupting, I'll be quick,' she gabbled. Breathlessly she rattled out her plans to Crispin, who stood up and held out both paws to her. Fir, Arran and Padra stood, too, as it wasn't polite to sit when the king was standing.

'Don't stay longer than one night,' said Crispin, taking her paws. 'If you do, I'll send search parties. I don't want to lose anyone else. Take warm cloaks, and provisions from the kitchen.' He took a beech leaf from a heap at his right paw and marked it with his claw. 'There's my token.'

'Thank you, Your Majesty, and by the way Tay was about very early this morning,' said Needle quickly. 'At least, I think it was Tay. There was a light moving in her gallery.'

'Thank you, Needle,' said Crispin. 'I know all about that. You may go.'

They waited until the door had closed behind her. The solemnity had lifted while she was there, but it settled again now.

'Brother Fir,' said Crispin, 'please go on with what you were saying.'

'It's all very simple and easy to understand,' said Fir, folding his paws. 'Priests generally do keep pretty well, but we don't last for ever. All that cleansing of the dungeon, you know, it had to be done thoroughly and it rather wore me out. It really is time I began to train a new priest. I would have done it before, you know, but . . .' his shoulders lifted and fell in a heartfelt sigh, 'all the young animals I had in mind for priests have gone on to do other things –

becoming captains and kings, that sort of nonsense. So, though we shall need a new priest, I'm afraid I haven't the faintest clue who it will be. We need a new lawyer and historian, too, for when poor old Tay finally wears out, but I've found one of those, if Your Majesty approves.'

'Who is it?' asked Crispin.

'Squirrel called Whittle,' said Fir. 'Already knows all the stories inside out, and has a head for law.'

'*Whittle?*' said Arran. 'He's as scatty as a sandfly. He'd leave his tail up a tree if it wasn't attached to him.'

'Oh, undoubtedly,' said Fir. 'But I'll help him organise his thinking. He does think, that's the main thing.' He rubbed his right ear tuft. 'What's next?'

Crispin reported on the Whitewings prisoners. Tay was determined to visit them and he usually went with her, and had been to their apartments earlier that morning. Lord Treeth refused to speak to anyone except to scream insults and complain about the food, and much of the furniture had been removed to save him the trouble of hurling it at the door.

'He's made a terrible mess of Aspen's old room,' said Crispin, 'but Scatter really looks forward to our visits. I think she's lonely.'

'I think she's a designing little schemer,' said Arran.

'She may be both,' said Padra.

Appointments to the Circle were discussed next. One or both of Gorsen and Docken could be promoted soon, perhaps with a view to becoming a captain one day. The search for Juniper was not encouraging. Russet and Heath, the squirrel brothers from the Circle, were in charge, but there was no sign of him from one end of the island to the other.

'Apple could help,' said Crispin. 'Then she might stop trying to marry me off.'

'Not a chance,' said Padra.

'Why doesn't she just round up all the eligible females and parade them past you?' said Arran.

'That's exactly what she is doing,' said Crispin. 'Padra, Arran, find something useful to do and stop laughing. And think of this.' His face brightened into warmth and excitement. 'The moles that we sent to Whitewings to rescue Urchin must be halfway there by now! I wish he knew about them.'

'He soon will,' said Padra.

Granite looked Urchin slowly up and down from the tufts of his ears to his hind claws. The cool breeze from the sea ran through Urchin's damp fur, but he tensed his limbs and forced himself not to shiver, not while Granite was inspecting him as if he wanted to cut him into little pieces and was choosing where to start. He may as well stand up to him.

'Why do they call you Lord Marshall, Granite?' he asked.

'Why are you still only a page, you scrawny little freak?' growled Granite. 'We're marching to the Fortress. It's a long way, Freak, so we keep a smart pace. It'll do you good. As a great favour, I advise you to mind how you speak to King Silverbirch when we get there.' He jerked the shackles so that Urchin staggered. 'And,' he added as they marched off, 'look out for Smokewreath. There's a squirrel to be afraid of. But if you meet Smokewreath you won't have anything to fear! Not for long!' With a harsh laugh and another jerk at the shackles, he marched them up the steep steps in the rock.

The sudden exercise after his days and nights in the boat made Urchin's legs and paws ache, and Granite forced a fast pace. At least when they reached the top of the cliff, he'd be able to take a good look at the island. *Know your territory.* Looking for anything that could help him escape would distract his attention from armed animals, chains and aching paws. Finally, reaching the top with sweat clinging to his fur, he took his first good look at Whitewings.

For miles ahead it seemed almost completely flat – there were mountains in the far distance, but nowhere else to make a change in the landscape or offer a hiding place. The woods seemed to be made up of thin, delicate trees with small leaves – birches, mostly, with pines and larches, but they didn't look healthy. They were starved, with thin, papery leaves and sparse needles, and there seemed to be a fine pale film of grey dust over everything. He wasn't sure what it was, but the dust and the spindly trees made the landscape more like winter than late summer. He could see scrawny purple heather, dark creeping bilberry, and broom, which would have to do if he needed a place to hide. Far off, grim columns of smoke lifted lazily into the sky.

For this bleak place, he had been dragged away from Mistmantle.

Inland the landscape had a touch more greenness, but it was still flatter and greyer than anything he could have imagined. Nobody was harvesting anything – but there wasn't much to harvest. The guards were surly and spoke little, even to each other, so there wasn't much to be learned by listening to them. Nervous-looking animals scurrying past stopped now and again to look, point at him and whisper, but at a glare from Granite they tucked their heads down and scurried away.

'We don't have any of that Mistmantle nonsense here,' said Granite. 'Keep 'em busy, keep 'em scared.

Shall I tell you what we do if they don't behave themselves?'

Urchin didn't answer. Granite went on, 'We have good archers here. The best.' Urchin could hear the grim smile in his voice. 'Dead shots.' He turned sharply on a hedgehog in the guard, and Urchin noticed for the first time that the animal seemed close to tears. 'That's right, isn't it?' Granite was growling now. His lips were almost touching the hedgehog's ear. 'Dead shots, aren't they?'

'Yes, Lord Marshall,' trembled the hedgehog.

Granite straightened up with a snort of satisfaction. 'Shot his brother yesterday, didn't I?' he said. 'Cheeky little runt told me he wasn't well enough to work, isn't that right?'

'Yes, sir,' whispered the hedgehog wretchedly.

'Yes, and I happened to agree with him,' said Granite. 'So I shot him myself. Gave what was left to Smokewreath. That's what we do here, isn't it?'

'Yes, sir,' said the hedgehog, biting his lip against tears. Rage seethed in Urchin.

I wish I really could be the deliverer of this island. It needs delivering.

'Move, Freak,' said Granite with a rough push.

When they had marched so long that Urchin was almost asleep on his paws they stopped and passed round flasks of water which tasted stale and metallic.

111

More marching, more dust, more aching limbs. Occasionally animals passed, some pushing barrows, glancing at him with curiosity and darting away when they saw Granite. The mountains seemed further than ever, and he was hungry. Far away and to the left on high ground was a larch wood which might be a useful place to hide, but he soon found that they were marching towards it. The Fortress must be in there somewhere. Although he was almost too tired to care, he tried to think of what he'd say to King Silverbirch.

A squirrel plodded past, dragging something on a rough hurdle of woven sticks. Urchin craned his neck to see what was on it.

'Keep going, Freak!' barked Granite, but Urchin had seen what lay on the hurdle. It was a dead sparrow, its beak open in death and its wings half spread as if it had been struggling to fly. Dark, dry blood stained the feathers.

'Curious?' said Granite. 'It'll be for Smokewreath. He needs dead things for his craft. It's wonderful what he can do with a dead body, just ask that hedgehog. We don't hold with your priests here – we don't have any doddery old squirrel hobbling about and saying prayers. We have a sorcerer. His magic keeps the king powerful and the island safe, and helps us to find silver. The more magic he does in that little chamber of his, the stronger we are. Now, there's the Fortress.'

Urchin looked ahead through the slender tree trunks. Beyond them were dark walls, battlements and something that flashed in the sun.

'There it is,' said Bronze proudly. 'The Fortress. Better than that fancy tower on Mistmantle. This is a real stronghold.'

They marched upwards through circle after circle of trees and, as the clash of guards presenting arms grew louder, the Fortress came into view. Urchin craned his neck. A high, square building squatted on the hill, built from the pale timbers of birch trunks and layers of dark grey stone veined with white and silver. Thin silver wires snaked round tree trunks and twisted into patterns in the slate-grey roof. Silver crisscrossed the windows and twined up the lintels of the doors that hedgehogs heaved open for them. They looked thick and solid, those doors. The hedgehogs stood back, saluted Granite and stared at Urchin.

'Say goodbye to the sunlight, Freak,' muttered Granite, and led Urchin down a corridor so grey and dark after the daylight that Urchin felt he was being swallowed into blackness. When his eyes had adjusted he was astonished at how crowded the corridor looked, until he realised that he was looking at reflections. Mirrors lined the corridor so that in the grim light there were more guards, more Granites, more Trails and Bronzes, everywhere he looked.

Urchin wished he had a sword, if only as something to hold on to. He must be brave, or at least look brave, for as long as he possibly could. In the mirrors he could see Bronze, standing with his shoulders squared and an infuriating sneer on his face as if he were copying Granite. Come to think of it, he'd been shadowing Granite all the way.

'Better than Mistmantle,' growled Granite. 'If you're a lucky little freak, the king will be having one of his good days. If he's in a rage, you'd better duck. Of course, I don't want the king to be angry with you.' He put on a soft, purring voice that made the hedgehogs chuckle. 'I don't want the nasty big king to be angry with the poor little freaky-weaky, do I? Well?' he went on, as Urchin didn't answer. 'Do I, Freak?'

'I don't know,' said Urchin. 'Do you?'

'Oh, no, Freak,' he said, and tweaked the fur on the back of Urchin's neck. 'I want him to give you to *Smokewreath*!'

They had arrived at a wooden door so polished that it gleamed. Blue stones studded it. Patterns curved and twisted across its surface, and the silver handles gleamed. Squirrels in tunics and helmets guarded it, and Granite nodded at them as he rapped at the door with his sword hilt. The doors creaked open a little from the inside, and Urchin caught a glimpse of a shining floor.

'Urchin the Freak for His Splendour King Silverbirch,' announced Granite, and gave Urchin a push in the back that sent him stumbling into the High Chamber of King Silverbirch.

Chapter 10

When the shore was deserted and Urchin had been marched away, a half-drowned squirrel crawled from the water.

The world swirled about him and waves pounded in his aching head, but he could see a cave. Pained with cold, Juniper crawled across the shore.

Had it been three days? He wasn't sure how long he'd been in the water. He'd tried so hard to save his hero, his friend. He'd meant to get into the boat, to seize Bronze's sword or gnaw through Urchin's bonds, but by the time he'd caught up with them he was too chilled and exhausted to do anything except cling to the stern and try to hold on. Time after time he had tried to climb up, but every effort had left him falling back into the water, and swimming to catch up. So much for saving Urchin. It had been all he could do to save himself, scrabbling with a free paw for a mouthful of bread or the water bottle when they weren't looking.

It hardly mattered now. He had no idea where he was any more, or why. He knew that his name was Juniper. He had a vague memory of Damson, and knew she was too far away to help him. His breathing hurt, everything hurt. He was too cold to shiver. Paw by paw he crept into the darkness of the cave, and sank down. Paws came towards him so softly that he barely heard them until somebody was beside him.

It was no good. Too late to run away, even if he could.

A gentle paw was on his head. A low voice, a female hedgehog voice, was whispering urgently.

'Who's this? He's soaked and frozen! Flame! We need a fire!' Someone was helping him to his paws, asking his name. Through half-closed eyes he saw a tall thin squirrel in a priest's tunic running towards him – then the priest was pulling off the tunic, wrapping him in it, and at a run they were carrying him away. Or was he dreaming? It was as strange as a dream, and as confusing.

He caught little of what they said to each other as they ran deeper and further into tunnels, but he heard 'dangerous' and 'quickest way'. Suddenly, they had stopped. The priest carrying him was huddling back against a wall, inching his way along in absolute silence. The hedgehog had become so quiet that Juniper wasn't even sure she was still there. Juniper looked round, trying to see what was so dangerous that they needed to creep past like this. Then he clenched his teeth.

The same dark and terrible horror he had felt as the ship arrived at Mistmantle washed through him again. Some evil thing must be close. He must look it in the face and know what it was.

From the tunnel, a short passageway opposite them ended in a dark orange firelit glow from a half-open door. In absolute silence they slipped past, but the hot glow of firelight showed Juniper the things that hung on the walls beyond that door.

Dead things. A squirrel, a hedgehog. Knives. Nets of things that looked like claws, teeth, and ears, but they couldn't be, surely . . . then there was a sound of tuneless chanting in a dry, rasping voice, and a laugh like the grating of steel and stone. A different kind of cold prickled through Juniper and made his fur bristle. He wanted to shut his eyes, but he couldn't. He swallowed hard. They edged further and further away from the evil glow and its appalling chanting until he could see and hear it no more, and the nausea left him – then they were running again, in and out of passageways and tunnels until suddenly they were in a round chamber with a feeling of peace and safety about it, and somebody was kindling a fire in the hearth, and the hedgehog was giving him a drink that warmed him all the way through, and wrapping him in a blanket.

'I'm Larch,' she said, rubbing his shoulders with the blanket. Her eyes were kind and concerned. 'Do you feel any better now?'

He nodded. Now that he was no longer so numb, he might manage to speak soon, but he was still bewildered that all this warmth and gentleness could exist so close to that terrible dungeon, or whatever it was. Larch turned to speak to the priest.

'Pity we had to come past Smokewreath's lair, but there wasn't time to waste,' she said. 'Where's Cedar?' She turned back to Juniper. 'Were you with the Marked Squirrel?'

'M . . . m . . . marked . . .' stammered Juniper.

'Urchin,' she said urgently. 'Were you with Urchin?'

He wasn't sure how far he could trust these animals, but he had to. 'He shouldn't be here,' he mumbled through chilled lips.

'I know,' said Larch. 'We'll do what we can for him, and we'll take care of you, too.'

A squirrel with flame-red fur appeared in the doorway.

'Here's Cedar,' said Larch.

Urchin had been trying out various defiant speeches in his head, but the effort to recover his balance made him forget them, and the sight of the chamber made him forget everything else. Beneath his paws the floor gleamed so brightly that he couldn't understand why it wasn't slippery, and his astonished reflection gazed back up at him. On three sides there were windows with mirrors between them, and everything was decorated with silver – coils and twists of silver, silver engraved with patterns, silver shining from goblets and trays. The attendant squirrels and hedgehogs wore silver helmets and polished swords. And on the dais, proud and straight-backed on the high silver throne, was King Silverbirch.

He was a tall, lean hedgehog, and his face was stern under the silver crown of birch leaves. On the arms of the throne his claws were long and sharp as talons, and painted silver. A high-collared cloak of silver cloth was fastened at his throat with a twisted clasp. His gaze was piercing and his voice, when he spoke to Urchin, was like a note on a tight string.

'Closer,' he ordered.

Urchin stepped forwards, the chains on his wrists clanking as his guards moved with him. He would try to behave as if Padra were watching – but a flash of sunlight from a mirror so dazzled him that he had to shade his eyes with a paw.

The king's face brightened with a wild delight that was terrifying. Then he gave a peal of laughter.

'I dazzle him!' he laughed, and leapt from the dais with his paws outstretched. 'Welcome, Marked Squirrel from Mistmantle! Lord Marshall, why did you chain him? What sort of welcome is this?' He laughed wildly, and took Urchin's paws in his. 'Take these chains off! Has he eaten? Has he had anything to drink?' He waved a young squirrel towards him. 'Let him drink from my own cup! Bring him bread, bring him almonds, bring him berries and apples! Make his chamber ready!'

Urchin was too amazed to speak, but there was no need to. The king stepped back, holding him by the shoulders at arm's length and looking him up and down as attendants hurried about with keys and, to his enormous relief, released his chains.

'A Marked Squirrel!' he cried in delight, and turned Urchin round as if he wanted to show him off. 'Well! Just look at him, all of you! Look at that colour! Welcome, Urchin of Mistmantle!'

Urchin had expected rage or hatred, and this welcome didn't reassure him. The king's wild excitement was disturbing.

'Granite, what have you done?' demanded the

king, and Urchin saw the smirk on Bronze's face. 'He's our honoured guest! Dearest Urchin, I am so sorry! Bring him a chair! Not *that* one! Bring him cushions!'

Urchin rubbed at his wrists. The king was either mad or playing games, or perhaps he himself had gone mad and none of this was really happening. A basket chair filled with cushions was brought for him, and the king put a cup into his paws. Thirsty as he was, he was uneasy about eating or drinking anything they gave him – he'd already been drugged once – but he didn't have much choice. He sipped cautiously at the wine, found it very strong, and tried not to pull a face.

'Did you have a good journey?' asked the king anxiously, and seated himself on the throne again. 'You must be tired.'

As if Padra were watching, thought Urchin. 'Your Majesty,' he said, 'your envoys told King Crispin that animals from Mistmantle were terrorising this island and that you needed his support. In particular, you asked for me. I was brought here against my will and marched across Whitewings in chains. If there is any service you need from me, tell me what it is, and if I can do it without harm to Mistmantle or to innocent animals, I will. Then send me back.'

The king stared as if astounded, then gave such a

shriek of laughter that Urchin winced.

'Oh, I know,' he said. 'Yes, lots of your old friends from Mistmantle are here, but most of them are terribly, terribly helpful to us. I don't know what we'd do without them. There's our excellent Lord Marshall, to begin with. And some of them have come in so useful to dear Smokewreath.' He frowned, and wriggled his paws. 'He should be here to meet you, but they gave him a little kill today, a hedgehog, and he can't be torn away from it. The thing is, dear Urchin, you're so precious to us, we had to get you here, whatever the cost. All they told you about rescuing us from naughty Mistmantle animals, it was terribly good, wasn't it? Lord Treeth had to tell you that. It isn't true, but we thought Crispin would fall for it. Those two animals who brought you here, they've done so well, I'm promoting them to the Inner Watch! Isn't that wonderful!'

'Thank you, Your Majesty!' said Trail and Bronze.

The idea that he was being paraded as a trophy was too much for Urchin. 'You mean,' he exclaimed, 'your ambassadors lied to King Crispin to get me here, whether I wanted it or not? What is it that you really want me for?'

The silver cloak billowed. The king swept down on Urchin, seized his throat and forced his head back. For a terrifying moment Urchin felt the strong, sharp talons, looked up into the wild eyes and heard the snarl deep in the king's throat. Then the king laughed again.

'Poor little thing!' he said, and let go so suddenly that Urchin swayed. 'You don't understand. You will.' He turned to Granite.

'He understands more than you think, O Splendour of Silver,' said Granite. 'He's not as stupid as he looks.'

'Explain to him, Lord Marshall Granite,' said the king.

'It'll be a pleasure,' said Granite. He stamped forwards, carrying his damaged paw badly. The long march must have put a strain on it. 'Listen, Freak.'

'Freak!' exclaimed the king with delight, but Granite went on.

'His Majesty King Silverbirch is the Shining Majesty of the Splendour of Silver,' growled Granite. 'He's not one of the petty lordlings you're used to on Mistmantle. This is a real king, and if you had any manners you'd bow.'

At the thought of bowing to this king Urchin squirmed inside, but he knew it might be dangerous not to. Slightly and stiffly, hating himself, he bowed.

'He's a splendid king, the kind of king Captain Husk would have been,' said Granite. 'And a great king gets whatever he wants. So if he knows that a

Marked Squirrel is to be the island's deliverer and he thinks the island needs delivering, and there's a Marked Squirrel on Mistmantle, then we get it for him, right? Your Majesty, shall I put the Freak in its cell for you?'

'I should show him off,' said the king thoughtfully. 'The question is, how to make the best use of him to get what we want? I shall take advice about it. I should like to know what the dear Commander thinks, she knows such a lot about so many things. Yes, take him to his room.'

'Delighted to, Your Majesty,' grunted Granite. Trail, Bronze, Granite and two hedgehogs marched forwards and escorted Urchin back through the hall of mirrors, up a winding stair.

'You'll have all you need,' said Trail. 'Don't try to escape. There are archers everywhere.'

'Enjoy your home comforts,' said Granite. 'I'll give it three days. Four, if your luck holds.'

Urchin was pushed into the turret and heard the clang of bolts and locks behind him, then was a shuffle of paws. At least two guards would be at the door.

He took a good look at the room, closed his eyes, and opened them again in case he was dreaming. With its deep soft rug, draped curtains, a table set generously with food and drink and plump, colourful cushions, his prison cell was furnished more luxuriously than the king's chambers at Mistmantle.

They still hadn't told him what he was supposed to do, but he didn't want to wait to find out. There had to be a way out. Deep-blue curtains, tasselled and brocaded, hung at the only window, but when Urchin examined it he found it locked fast and protected with iron bars set into the stone. A bed had been made up with blankets, and he dived underneath it to scratch at the floor. It was made up of small wooden floorboards. He might be able to lift one and escape, if he could first find out what was underneath – dropping into a guard room wouldn't help. There was a fireplace, too, but no fire laid in it, so with the energy of hope he jumped into the grate and darted up the chimney.

It soon became a tight squeeze, then even tighter, and though Urchin drew in his shoulders and made himself as small as he could, the chimney was too narrow for him. Furious with frustration, he wriggled down again, brushed soot roughly from his fur, and threw himself into inspecting every inch of the cell. He searched the fireplace, looked under the rug, ran up the walls and scrabbled with his claws at the ceiling, and finally dropped back to the ground and kicked the cushions. He was far from home, trapped and furious at the injustice of it.

'I'll get out,' he said out loud. 'Heart help me. I

promise you, King Crispin. I promise you, Captain Padra.' He kicked the cushions again, and looked enviously down from the windows at the squirrels outside enjoying their freedom.

But were they free? Like the animals he had seen on the march, they were outside but they didn't look free at all. They had a timid, scared air about them, hardly ever stopping to talk to each other, glancing anxiously over their hunched shoulders. At this time of year they should have been harvesting food, but wood and stone were heaped in the barrows they wheeled about, and he understood now about the grey film over everything. It was a layer of dust from the mines. As night darkened, he said a prayer for his friends on Mistmantle, settled down among the cushions, and didn't even try to sleep.

He did sleep, though, lightly and at last, and woke in the dark. Someone was in his room. He felt their presence. He heard them breathing. Beneath his fur, a shiver crept through his skin. There was a sour, fusty smell, like singed fur and vinegar. It drew closer.

Urchin stayed still, his eyes shut, listening. It would be safer not to provoke them. *Stay still. They'll go sooner that way.* Somebody whispered, and he recognised King Silverbirch's voice.

'Isn't he a little treasure? And we've got him safe

and sound. We need to make the most of him.'

The squirrel voice that replied was slow and so hoarse that it rasped like a sword on stone. Urchin's fur bristled and his claws curled.

'If he's *that* squirrel,' it whispered, 'we should kill him at once.'

'Now, now, Smokewreath,' said the king, 'you can't have him yet. I've only just got him. If he's the deliverer, we've got to give him time to deliver us.'

'This island needs no deliverance that he can bring,' rasped Smokewreath, 'except by his death. I can make such magic from his death.'

'He can deliver us from poverty first,' argued the king. 'I know, I know, we're *not* poor. But I want so much silver that we never *will* be, and I'm sure he has the gift of finding it. *That's* the deliverance he will bring us. He's going to find wonderful silver for us and make us rich and powerful.'

There was a throaty growl from Smokewreath. 'My magic has found silver for you,' he muttered. 'And it can do more. All you want. *All*, Your Majesty. I can give you the thing you want most in the world, but I must have the body of the Marked Squirrel.'

'Yes, I know,' said the king, and to Urchin he sounded greedy. 'I can have my heart's desire. But I want to make the most I can of him first.'

'Have you considered,' asked Smokewreath, 'that he may be here to deliver the island from *you*?'

There was a shrill giggle from the king, quickly muffled. 'Oh, silly Smokewreath! Why would the island need delivering from *me*? I'm the one who started the silver mining. Everyone loves me.'

'And the *other* prophecy?' said Smokewreath.

'Oh, *that*,' said the king petulantly. 'You mean the one . . .'

'*He will bring down a great ruler*,' said Smokewreath. 'Just look at him. Look at that colour. It may well be him.'

'And it probably isn't,' said the king. 'There are islands everywhere. Some of them may be full of Marked Squirrels, so why should this one be *that* Marked Squirrel? I think that one probably died. Anyway, if it is him, he's already brought down a great ruler, because he brought down Lord Husk. So I'm safe. Wouldn't it be funny if he brought King Crispin down, too, without even meaning to!'

Urchin bit his lip hard and imagined wringing King Silverbirch's neck. The king giggled again.

'You can have him, Smokewreath, but only when I've finished with him,' he said.

'Oh, what I could do with the body of a Marked Squirrel!' whispered Smokewreath. 'The power of sorcery! Those ears, that tail! That fur! And . . .' he drew out the words in a hungry whisper, 'what I could do with his heart! Let me have him for death.'

'Not yet,' said the king irritably. 'Yes, yes, you can have him, but not yet.'

'When, then?'

'Next summer.'

'Too long,' hissed Smokewreath.

'Spring, then,' said the king.

'Next moon,' said Smokewreath.

'Oh, snowfall, then,' said the king firmly. 'You can have him at the first snowfall. Isn't that a good time for killing? All right, if he's no good at finding silver you can have him before that. But I promise you can have him at snowfall if not before. Isn't he sweet when he's asleep?'

With a stale whiff of burning and vinegar, they slipped away. Furious at being bargained over, Urchin sat up. The king was deranged. So, probably, was Smokewreath. He couldn't go back to sleep, so yet again he examined his cell for a way out.

By morning, rain was drizzling steadily. Urchin was still trying to scrape the window bars free – unsuccessfully, he knew, but it passed the time – when Trail, Bronze and the guards arrived to march him down to the High Chamber. Trail and Bronze were surly this morning, with Trail insisting haughtily that she was in charge and Bronze refusing to cooperate. Two hedgehogs carried a basket of logs into Urchin's cell, muttered something nervously about it being somebody or other's orders, and glanced over their shoulders as a female squirrel in a helmet walked briskly along the gallery. She had a very upright way of walking with her head held high, and her tone was crisp and commanding.

'Prisoner to the king,' she ordered, and turned on Trail and Bronze. 'Don't you dare keep the king waiting! Get him moving!'

In the High Chamber Granite stood behind the throne, and though he wore his grim helmet Urchin could feel the grin on his face. The squirrel in the helmet had followed them and took her place beside the dais. Leaning back in the throne, King Silverbirch flexed his gleaming claws.

'Dear Smokewreath's ever so busy dismembering something,' he drawled. 'Now, Freak, tell me all about yourself. Who are you, exactly? No, I know you're Urchin of Mistmantle, but who are you really? Who are your parents? You don't really come from Mistmantle, do you?'

'He was found, Your Majesty,' said Bronze. 'They said –'

'Shut up, soldier,' growled Granite, and Trail smirked with pleasure. 'Yes, Your Majesty, I can vouch for that. Found.'

'Found?' asked the king, leaning forwards with interest.

'I was found in the water when I was newborn,' said Urchin. He didn't want to be helpful, but he could safely tell them this much. 'Nobody knows anything about me.'

'So you're not from Mistmantle?' purred the king.

'With respect, sir,' said the squirrel in the helmet, 'we're wasting time. It doesn't matter where he comes from, so long as he can find silver for you. And he can.'

'Oh, thank you, Commander!' said the king, flourishing a paw at her. 'That's what I need to know. So you do have a gift for finding silver, Freak?'

Urchin didn't like to say so. He had no idea about finding silver, but it might be safest to pretend he could.

'I might have, Your Majesty,' he said.

'He has, Your Majesty,' said the squirrel Commander.

'How do you do it?' asked the king. He laced his claw tips and leant forwards with glittering brightness in his eyes. 'Do tell me. What do you need? Anything magical? Wires, powders? We can kill something for you, if you like.'

He was saved from having to answer by the Commander. She seemed to know a lot more about the subject than he did.

'The best just do it by instinct, Your Majesty,' she said. 'They don't really know how. But he'll need to get outside and see the island, so he can get his bearings.' Urchin's ears twitched hopefully.

'Is that right, Freak?' asked the king.

'Oh, yes, Your Majesty,' said Urchin earnestly.

'There's foul weather coming,' observed Granite. 'Still, it won't matter if the Freak gets wet.'

'It most certainly does matter!' insisted the king. Bronze grinned, and Granite glared at him. 'We'll arrange a tour for you, Freak. In the meantime, Bronze will take you back to your chamber.'

He was marched back to his room and pushed in by Bronze. The door clanked shut. He was about to have another go at the window bars when something moved.

He whisked round. The logs in the basket were moving. Urchin sprang back, reached for a sword, remembered again that he didn't have one, and retreated as far as possible from the basket, watching.

'Urchin!' said a voice from somewhere under the logs, and the sound of his name made his heart leap. Firewood spilled out. There was a gleam of dark red fur that Urchin found impossible to believe.

'Juniper?' he whispered.

Juniper's head bobbed up from the basket. He shook sawdust from his ears. 'Found you!' he said as he climbed out.

Speechless, Urchin leapt forwards and siezed Juniper's shoulders, astonished at the delighted smile and the bright, almost too-bright, eyes. But under his touch Juniper was shivering, and after the first great surge of joy at seeing a Mistmantle face, he felt desperately sad and sorry. Juniper had ended up in this wretched place, too.

'How did you get here?' demanded Urchin. He kept his voice down to a whisper, and glanced warily at the door.

'Followed you,' said Juniper.

'But it was –'

'I know,' said Juniper. 'I'm all right with water, I grew up with otters. I wanted to rescue you. I'm sorry I didn't. But I couldn't leave you.' Urchin tried to say the right thing, didn't know what it was, and hugged him. Juniper coughed, still trembling.

'You're ill,' said Urchin. The surprise had left him shaking almost as much as Juniper. 'I'm surprised that journey didn't kill you.' There was still wine and bread on the table. He put a drink into Juniper's trembling paw, folded the claws around it, and pulled a blanket from the bed to tuck tightly round Juniper's shoulders, noticing that his paws were still wrinkled

134

from the water. 'Juniper, don't you realise? We're beyond the mists!'

'I know,' said Juniper, and sipped the wine. 'I knew I'd have to do that. I could have swum back. But you didn't have anyone else.' He looked up into Urchin's face. 'You're Urchin of the Riding Stars and you're my friend. I wasn't going to leave you.'

Urchin's heart clenched. Mistmantle had adopted him, Apple had raised him, Fir, Crispin, and Padra had protected and encouraged him, but never in all his life had anyone done anything like this for him. A few days earlier, he had thought of Juniper as a younger brother, perhaps the sort of little brother who had to be looked after and rescued. It left him ashamed now. He wondered if any of the heroes in the Mistmantle Threadings had done anything so noble.

'Are you all right, Urchin?' asked Juniper.

Urchin squeezed his shoulders. 'I'm all right. I'm just amazed. And I'll get you home somehow.'

'I was thinking of doing that for you,' said Juniper. 'I've found out a lot already. There are good animals here, who want to help you. To help both of us. They found me and looked after me when I was soaking wet and a stranger. They know about you. They got me in here.'

Urchin looked anxiously into Juniper's feverishly

bright eyes. He gave him some dried fruit from the table, but Juniper coughed as he ate and this time they both glanced nervously at the door. Juniper lowered his voice to a whisper.

'Listen,' he said. 'Are you listening? This is important. They told me all about the island, and you need to know it, too. King Silverbirch isn't the real king at all. He was the last queen's husband, and when she died there was only her little niece, Larch, to become queen. Larch was just a child, so he became Regent. He was only supposed to look after the island until she grew up, but gradually he took the power for himself. He has bouts of dangerous madness, and he's getting worse. He's so obsessed with silver that the island's riddled with mine workings, and the dust makes the animals ill. When Silverbirch first took power he was mostly all right, and there were enough sensible creatures around him to keep him under control, but he takes sudden dislikes to animals. Lots of islanders left Whitewings. Some just disappeared and nobody was quite sure whether they'd fled the island or he'd had them killed.'

'Did he have Larch killed, too?' asked Urchin.

'No,' said Juniper with a twitch of a smile. 'Everyone thinks she left the island in secret, but she's still here. One day she'll be the real queen again, when they're strong enough to overthrow the king.'

He glanced at the door again and whispered even more quietly, 'It was Larch who found me. Her supporters are the Larchlings. I think all the islanders would support her, but they're terrified of the king's archers, and a sorcerer called Smokewreath.'

'I know about Smokewreath,' said Urchin. 'Was there no good priest on the island?'

'There was,' said Juniper. 'There was a wonderful young priest, Brother Candle, but he was found dead at the foot of a cliff, though by that time he'd already trained another priest, Brother Flame. It was as if Candle knew that Silverbirch would have him killed and was training Flame to take over. Then Brother Flame disappeared, too. Everyone who opposed Silverbirch and Smokewreath disappeared, or were accused of some terrible crime and shot by the archers. But Brother Flame survived. He's in hiding with Larch.' Juniper smothered a coughing fit, sipped the wine and swayed.

'You really are ill!' whispered Urchin, catching him.

'Then I'll tell you the important things now,' said Juniper. 'Pretend you can find silver. If the king thinks you can do that, he won't let Smokewreath kill you. And don't try to escape. Cedar has plans for you.'

'Who's Cedar?'

Juniper's eyes were puzzled and half closing. 'But you've met her!' he said. 'She's the . . .' and he slumped to the floor in silence.

Chapter 11

'Ooh . . . ooh . . . ooh!' said Needle, and stood on her hind paws with her mouth open, unable to say another word.

They had reached Sepia's song cave, high and arching, shining with spindling waterfalls and the bright stones that glittered in the walls. A hole in the hillside above them let in a little daylight, and the rays of late afternoon sun brought flashes of gold.

They had explored all the other caves, nearer to the shore and the waterfall, and Fingal had found any number of flat stones for skimming. There were some very beautiful translucent pebbles that Sepia liked, and Hope had put the nicest ones in a satchel to take home. If Needle tried to remind them that they were supposed to be looking for the Heartstone, Fingal would say cheerfully, 'Yes, in a minute,' and

Sepia would calmly say, 'Don't worry, Needle, I *am* looking for the Heartstone.' She was mildly surprised that they hadn't had a row, but Fingal and Sepia weren't the sort of animals you could have a row with. Fingal was too easy-going, Sepia was too calm, and you couldn't have a row in front of Hope.

Needle wished Urchin had been there. She and Urchin always made a good team. Fingal had been a bit disappointed because the rowing boat wasn't there and he'd meant to row them around the bay, and Needle had muttered that he'd have to find another way to show off and then wished she hadn't said it, but Fingal had only laughed and turned somersaults. Hope was trying very industriously to find the Heartstone, but being short-sighted didn't help.

'I've found lots of stones that could be the Heartstone, but when I look more carefully they're never the right one,' complained Needle, sitting down wearily. 'They always stay in my paw. I don't think we'll find it in here.'

'There are stones in the walls,' said Sepia. Needle sprang up again.

'That could be it!' she cried. 'Run up the walls, Sepia!' There was a splash behind her. 'Fingal, now what have you found?'

'Water, of course!' said Fingal. 'A slide!'

Near the cave entrance he had found a spring

which gushed down a sloping section of the wall to make a waterfall, ran down into a channel and disappeared under the ground. Fingal swam straight into it, vanished and bobbed up again.

'There's a river under there!' he said, beaming. 'It's snaky at first, then it whooshes down and there's a lake. It must be the one that joins up with the tunnel network.'

'Can I come too?' piped up Hope.

'Certainly not,' said Needle quickly.

'It might be a bit dangerous for somebody your size,' admitted Fingal. 'I'm a natural swimmer, so I'm always falling into rivers.'

'I'm always falling into everything,' said Hope.

'All the same, it's different for hedgehogs,' said Fingal, sounding almost grown-up for once. 'We don't want you to slip into deep waters. You can go down the slide and I'll stand here and catch you so you won't go underground.'

He sprawled in the channel while Hope clambered up the rock, sniffed the air and launched himself down the slide on his back with all four paws outstretched. With a cry of 'oof!' he landed in Fingal's paws, scrambled out and ran to do it again.

'Have a go, Needle!' he cried. 'Sepia! You have to try it!'

Needle decided the Heartstone could wait. There

was a lot of splashing and shrieking before she and Sepia shook themselves dry and reminded each other that they should be searching.

'Just a bit more?' said Hope.

'Go on, then,' said Fingal. 'Shout when you're ready, and I'll catch you.'

For a while there was nothing to be heard but the clink of pebbles and the scrabbling of paws, and the occasional cry of, 'Ready, Fingal?' followed by a splash and a giggle. Outside the sky clouded and the light dimmed, but Needle had brought flints and lanterns and they searched on until Sepia climbed down the walls, stretched, rubbed her eyes in tiredness, took a deep breath and sang.

She sang so that the notes rang and danced from the sparkling walls and hung in the air. Her song made Needle imagine springtime, and the breath of primroses on the air, and Fingal thought of enchanted kingdoms under the sea, and Hope . . .

. . . nobody knew what Hope thought. Whether he forgot to call for Fingal, or whether he did and Fingal didn't hear him, never became clear. There was a sudden splash and when they looked round, he wasn't there.

'Whoops!' said Fingal and dived underwater. There was a muffled cry of, 'Don't worry!', then nothing.

Needle and Sepia dashed to peer down into the darkness, soaking their fur and whiskers. Over the swishing of the water, they strained to listen. They could hear a few squeaks from Hope, then Fingal's voice – 'got you . . . hold tight . . . not that tight . . .' – then his voice carried further away until they could hear nothing but the waterfall. They sat and looked at each other, realising suddenly how dark it had become.

'They'll be all right, won't they?' said Sepia anxiously. 'I mean, Fingal did have Hope when we last heard him,' said Sepia.

'Fingal seemed pretty certain that the lake linked with the tunnels,' said Needle. 'Oh, but Hope can't swim much!'

'He can ride on Fingal's shoulders,' suggested Sepia. 'All the otters give rides to small animals.'

'Then Fingal will probably carry him to a tunnel, and look for the nearest way out,' said Needle. 'It would be easier than climbing back up a waterfall with a hedgehog on his back.'

'Yes,' said Sepia, but she still felt uneasy.

'I know,' said Needle. 'I'm not happy about this either. But I suppose there's nothing to be worried about.' She curled up. It was getting colder. 'Where would the tunnels take them? D'you think they could get back up here?'

'I've no idea,' said Sepia. 'I don't do tunnels much. But I suppose they must be linked with the caves.'

'I thought you knew these caves,' said Needle, trying not to sound grumpy.

'Not underwater,' said Sepia reproachfully. 'But they can't be far from dry ground, and when they find a tunnel, somebody will meet them. There are always moles about. We'll try shouting again.'

They leant as close to the gap as they could, and called Fingal and Hope's names into the darkness.

'Ouch!' said Needle. 'You yelled right down my ear.'

'Sorry,' said Sepia. 'I'll try not to this time.'

Their cries hung and echoed, clear and loud, in the cave. There was no answer.

'They're sure to be all right,' said Needle. 'But I think I should go to the tower. I should let them know what's happening.'

'I'll go,' said Sepia. 'I'm quicker.'

'No, I'll go because I'm slower,' said Needle. 'They're almost certain to get back here soon, and then you can run and catch me up and tell me, if you can. Mind, I know all the short cuts. If I meet anyone around while I'm still near here, I'll ask if they've seen an otter and a small hedgehog. I'm sure they'd look out for them.'

'And if anyone else comes to the caves I'll get them

to search,' said Sepia. 'It should be all right. Animals are always splashing round and exploring caves and they always come back in one piece.'

'Will you be all right here on your own?' asked Needle.

'Oh, yes,' said Sepia. 'I've stayed here alone for hours.'

She didn't add that she'd never stayed there alone at night. It was harder to feel confident without Needle. She went on with a half-hearted search for the Heartstone, not expecting to find it, and the lamp was low. Now and again she called for Fingal and Hope, but there was no reply. She began to wish she'd insisted on going instead of Needle. She told herself not to worry, and worried all the same. In the deepening dark she sang to pass the time and keep her spirits up, and when the lamp became only a pale flicker and then nothing at all, she made herself a nest out of her cloak. If only Hope had a cloak. Finally, she said a prayer for them all and for Urchin, and settled down to sleep.

She tried very hard to fall asleep. If she lay awake she would imagine all the worst possible things that could happen to Fingal and Hope, and Hope was so little, but after a long time wriggling in the nest she stopped trying to sleep. At times like that, her mother used to tell her to 'think of something lovely', because it may not send you to sleep but it would give you something worth staying awake for. So what was the loveliest thing that could happen? She imagined King Crispin being crowned in the Gathering Chamber with all the animals around him, and Brother Fir in a neat new tunic limping down to the throne to offer him the Heartstone and put the crown on his head. Urchin would be there, groomed and carrying a sword, in a deep red cloak to match his ears and tail tip, and Fingal and Hope would be with them. Hope would sit at the front so he could see. Her parents would be there, and they'd hear her singing and playing with the musicians, and there'd be a party. She might play there, too, or even dance with the king. A banquet . . . new Threadings . . . perhaps, perhaps, even a night of riding stars . . . she slipped into a dream. Stars above her, stars around her, stars at her paws, stars to dance on, she was dancing with stars in the mist . . .

Something had woken her. Something was moving. She opened her eyes and sat up, shivering, wrapping herself in the cloak and trying to ask who was there, but found she was too frightened to do more than squeak. By the time she could falter a few words, all was silent again. She sat wide awake, telling herself not to be silly. Hadn't she been hoping Fingal and Hope would come back, shaking their wet fur and gabbling about all their adventures? She whispered their names in a voice that sounded strangely thin. There was no answer. She lay down in a tight unhappy huddle, still listening.

Sunlight falling through the hole in the cliff side woke her and she jumped up and shook herself. Were they back? But the cave was reproachfully silent. Fingal and Hope had not come back. They might have found another way out. They were probably playing by the shore already. They might have emerged into the cave and gone home, not knowing that she was asleep in the corner.

Look for pawprints. She followed the scuffed trails from the previous day, and at the sight of fresh ones her heart lifted with joy, then fell again. She could see hedgehog prints, but these were too big for Hope. That explained what she heard last night. Hedgehogs must have been sheltering in here.

No Fingal, no Hope. *I should never had stayed here. I should have gone straight to the tower. They could have drowned, they could be lost underground, they'll be cold, they'll be starving, they could be trapped, they could be hurt, they might have become separated, if anything happens to Fingal little Hope will be all alone in a strange place, he might be crying . . .*

Furious with herself, she left her cloak and sprang through the caves until the sound of the waterfall grew louder, swung herself on to an ash tree growing out of the rock, and was about to scramble up the rocks when she saw Sluggen and Crammen of the Hedgehog Host on the shore below.

'Can you come up here, please?' she called down, and waited impatiently while they looked past her and from side to side before catching sight of her. 'Will you look out for an otter and a hedgehog? I'll explain later. Thanks.' Sluggen shouted something about the caves not being a safe place for youngsters, but Sepia was already leaping away.

With weary paws, Needle watched dawn spread through the sky. It should have looked beautiful, touching the wave tips with pink, shedding a soft grey light on the boats as they waited patiently by the mists, their lights pale and steady in the dawning. But Needle was too agitated to care about anything but Hope and Fingal. She had expected Sepia to have caught up with her by now to tell her that they were safe, but it hadn't happened and, running through the wood alone at night, she had imagined the worst. Drowning, an injury underground . . . *oh, please, please, Heart keep them, please, and I'm sorry for all the times I've been snappy with Fingal, oh, please*

148

keep them safe, please look after them . . .

Would Crispin be awake yet? Clambering on to a rock by the spring that ran down from the castle to the shore, she remembered too late that Padra lived at the Spring Gate. He glided through the water, saw her and scrambled up.

'Needle! How's the treasure hunt going?' And when she hunched her back and turned her face away, he asked in concern, 'What's the matter, Needle?'

She tried to find the right words, but there weren't any. Finally, she managed a hoarse whisper. 'Please, Captain Padra, sir, you're going to be very angry.'

'I doubt it,' he said, and leant over to see her face. 'Angry with *you*?'

She nodded miserably.

'But you're going to tell me what it is anyway?'

She nodded again.

'Then you're a brave hedgehog,' he said. 'And I'll try not to be angry. What have you done?'

Looking down at her paws she told him everything, her voice quavering, stopping now and again to dry her eyes when she thought of Fingal and Hope alone in the dark. When she finished she felt a warm and comforting otter hug.

'Ouch,' said Padra. 'I'd forgotten how sharp you are. Needle, you mustn't blame yourself. You and

Sepia did exactly the right thing.'

'It wasn't Fingal's fault, sir,' she said. 'We were all there, and Hope just jumped or something and Fingal tried to get to him in time, and went straight in after him.'

'Fingal comes out of most things all right,' said Padra. 'And as for Hope, I think the Heart takes special care of that one. I'll send a search party, and I'm taking you to Crispin. He won't be angry either, but he should know. Oh,' he added with a frown, 'and Docken's on guard at the Throne Room.'

'Hope's daddy!' cried Needle in dismay.

'Could be awkward,' admitted Padra. 'Leave it to me.' He waved at a passing otter. 'Get a search party of moles and otters together and report to me outside the Throne Room, sharpish.'

Needle trotted up stairs and corridors after him. Normally she enjoyed the sight of the Threadings she had helped to make, but this morning she couldn't enjoy anything and after her long journey she struggled to keep up with Padra. As they turned along the corridor to the Throne Room, she stopped with something between a gasp and a squeak.

Hope was standing on his hind legs, his paws on his father's knees, his little short-sighted face turned up, his nose twitching as he gabbled his adventures. Docken, bending over him, was occasionally saying,

'Did you?' and 'That was brave,' as Hope rattled through his story. It was all too much for Needle. She rushed past Padra and hugged Hope so hard that his hind paws were left kicking in the air.

'Hope, you're all right!' she cried. 'Where's Fingal?'

'Yes thank you, he's with the king thank you, please will you put me down now?' gasped Hope. 'Thank you. Have you got the Heartstone?'

Padra had already swept past her to the Throne Room door. It was opened by Fingal, wiping butter from his whiskers with a broad grin on his face.

'Oh, it's you,' said Fingal brightly, and stood back to let him in. 'Hello, Needle, what are you doing here? May as well come in. And you, little Hope. I mean,' he looked over his shoulder, 'is that all right, Your Majesty?'

'I do apologise for him, Crispin,' sighed Padra.

The Throne Room smelt pleasantly of fresh bread, and Crispin himself buttered a roll for Needle. She bowed as she thanked him, noticing that he looked happy for the first time since Urchin went away.

Padra took Fingal's shoulders in both paws while he looked him up and down, and finally said, 'You seem to be in one piece, and so's the little one. Before we leave, and if His Majesty permits, I'll teach you the correct way to answer the door of the Throne Room.

Crispin, who's going to tell the story, you or Fingal?'

'Go on, Fingal,' said Crispin.

'It was like this,' said Fingal, nearly sitting down then standing up again as Padra raised his eyebrows, 'we went to look for the Heartstone – didn't find it, by the way –'

'I know what happened until you and Hope vanished down the waterslide,' said Padra.

'Ah,' said Fingal. 'Well, when Hope fell down the waterslide he curled up, being a hedgehog, and the water swept him all the way down and by the time I caught up with him he was bobbing about in the underground lake like a chestnut shell. I swam out and got him back, but there was no way he could climb back up. Tried it. Too hard. I tried carrying him on my back, but he fell off. I told him to hang on tight, but either he fell off or he knocked me off balance and we both fell down and he wasn't going to let go of his bag of pebbles, so I looked for another way. He rode on my back, or on my chest depending on which way up I was, and I swam across the lake.'

'Didn't he fall in?' asked Padra.

'Oh, yes,' said Fingal. 'I just scooped him up and told him to hang on a bit tighter.'

Padra turned Fingal round. There were two rows of gashes on his shoulders that made Needle flinch to see them.

'Go on,' said Padra quietly.

'It was a long swim,' said Fingal. 'And it brought us to a tight, squeezy place through the rocks and a cave and another squeeze, and then we were so dead-beat we had a sleep. When we woke up we went on because we knew we'd find tunnels sooner or later, and we did – at least, Hope did. That little hedgehog was off and into that tunnel like a squirrel up a nut tree. I couldn't keep up.'

'Excuse me?' said Hope.

'Yes, Hope?' said Crispin.

'I slowed down for him,' said Hope. 'And I looked after him in the tunnels, Captain Padra, sir.'

'Thank you very much, Hope,' said Padra. 'He needs looking after. Go on, Fingal.'

'It was a long, straight tunnel,' said Fingal. 'Dead boring. It sloped uphill a long way and widened out, and then we heard voices.'

'Whose voices?' asked Padra. 'Saying what?'

'Something about "chuck the water out and scrub those pans",' said Fingal. 'We were under the tower scullery! There was a winding stairway further on so we went up it – we thought it must go halfway to the moon, there must have been miles of it. We could smell breakfast, too, and we were starving, weren't we, Hope? We thought the stairway must lead to the main kitchens so we followed it, but after all that it only led to the door of a tight little chamber with a ladder leading to an opening above it. Not much of an opening, but we squeezed through – an awfully tight squeeze for an otter, just as well I hadn't had any breakfast, really. And when we got through there, we were in a narrow slit of a gap between the ceiling of the lower room and the floor of the one above. This one, in fact.'

'This one!' Padra looked at Crispin in horror. 'The Throne Room!'

'Yes, but I didn't know that at the time,' said Fingal. 'It was dusty and I sneezed and hit my head on the floorboards, and ouched, and then I heard the king ask who was there . . .'

'. . . and I got the floorboards up with my sword and got them out,' said Crispin, smiling. 'They've had a wash and breakfast.'

'Nice breakfast, thanks,' said Fingal.

'But, Crispin,' said Padra, 'anybody could have got under the Throne Room!'

'Good thing it was only us,' said Fingal.

'And a good thing they did,' said Crispin. 'I'll tell Gorsen to get it sealed.'

'It might be useful to keep it open, Your Majesty,' said Needle, 'in case you ever need an escape route.'

'I'd rather His Majesty jumped out of the window and ran down the walls as usual,' said Padra. 'Your

Majesty, I think Fingal could do with a swim.'

'Yes, please,' said Fingal.

'Well done, Fingal,' said Crispin. 'You've looked after Hope commendably.'

'Is that good?' asked Fingal.

'It's very good,' said Crispin. 'You may go.'

'And if the salt water doesn't ease those gashes,' said Padra, 'go and ask Arran to put something on them.'

'What gashes?' beamed Fingal. He bowed and left the Throne Room.

'He seems to have muddled through,' said Padra. 'Needle, find someone to get a message to Sepia. Her brother may be about.'

'And go down to the kitchens for something to eat,' said Crispin.

'What's happened to you?' said Padra to Crispin as Needle hurried away. 'You look a lot better than you did. Is that just because of Fingal and Hope?'

'The moles,' said Crispin. 'They should reach Whitewings tonight.'

By the time Needle and Sepia had met, exchanged stories, jumped a few streams and pattered round the north side of the tower, they were ready to stop for a snack. Sepia was nibbling blackberries and Needle had just swallowed a worm when a squirrel hurried past.

'Hello, Gleaner!' called Sepia.

Gleaner glanced over her shoulder, hesitated as if she might say something, and ran on. Needle shrugged.

'Let her go,' she said. 'She's dying for us to ask where she's going.'

Gleaner ran on. They were looking for the Heartstone. Let them look. She knew more about it than they did, but they wouldn't dream of asking her.

They forgot that she had been an animal of some importance in the tower, not so long ago, when she had been Lady Aspen's maid. Whatever Husk had done, whatever anyone said, none of it was anything to do with Lady Aspen. You only had to look at lovely Lady Aspen to know that none of it was her fault. She was so charming and beautiful, she couldn't do anything bad. It was all lies.

With any luck, Needle and Sepia would get stuck in a bog looking for the Heartstone. Serve them right.

Chapter 12

For three days, King Silverbirch did not send for Urchin. Trail, when she brought food, said that the king was deciding on his strategy, and Bronze said smugly that the king and Smokewreath were still arguing about what to do with him. Apart from that they barely spoke to him and nobody came into his cell, which was what Urchin wanted. He needed to be left alone to attend to Juniper, and Juniper was desperately ill.

Urchin had hidden him in a deep nest of cushions in a corner where he lay tightly huddled and shivering, though his paws were hot. When the guards brought food, Urchin would sit on the window sill kicking his paws restlessly to conceal any rustlings from the nest, and as soon as they had shut the door he would force water between Juniper's clenched teeth. Juniper was far too ill to eat anything, but Urchin knew he should drink.

In a hushed voice he whispered to him, telling him stories of Mistmantle, singing their homeland songs, and wondering what he would do without Juniper to look after. Go mad, probably, shut in a stone cell in the long summer days. Looking longingly down from the barred window he saw animals trundling barrows about, exchanging brief chats about their work – he knew they weren't happy or free, but at least they were outside.

In the days when Husk had controlled King Brushen, Mistmantle animals had been burdened with long hours of hard work, but it had never been as bad as this. Mistmantle animals had never been so miserable and dispirited. The idea that they might have been, if Husk had finally triumphed, was a thought that chilled his skin. Angrily, he kicked the window seat and promised himself that he would go home.

He promised Juniper, too, as he whispered into the nest. The Heart would bring them home, and home was worth staying alive for. He talked to him of Mistmantle, of the woods in autumn and wriggling through fallen leaves to gather up baskets full of nuts. He talked about gathering round fires with scalding soup and hot walnut bread, and of brilliant winter mornings when the snow dazzled, icicles hung like a necklace round Fir's turret and there were snowball fights in every clearing and slides on every hill. He talked of spring, with the first breaths of warm air ruffling the fur and primroses in the wood, and summers when high colour was everywhere and the woods were full of sweet soft berries that looked like jewels and tasted of sunshine.

He felt the dryness of Juniper's paws and nose and wished there was somebody like Mother Huggen or Fir, who would know how to look after him. 'All this about the mists not letting anyone go back,' he said, thinking aloud, 'it can't be that simple. Brother Fir says the mists are there to protect Mistmantle, so if you have to get back for the sake of the island, surely there must be a way. The Heart must have made a way. I could get us home with swans again. That was what they suggested, when they were pretending they cared what happened to me. But it's a long way, it may be too far for swans.'

In the silence that followed, Juniper's breathing seemed slow and wheezy. It sounded like a struggle. Every breath was harder, and after each one was a long and terrifying pause as if the next would never come. Urchin found he was holding his own breath, too.

The wheezing grew longer and louder, and Urchin

heaped the cushions more tightly round Juniper, glancing nervously at the door. When Bronze opened the door to bring in food, Urchin leapt to the fireplace and scratched at it noisily. Bronze grinned.

'No good sharpening your claws,' he said, and banged down the tray. 'You've had it. The wind's changed.' He clanked the door shut behind him, and there was nothing for Urchin to do but watch Juniper, tip water into his mouth, and pray.

'Come on, Juniper,' he whispered. 'Please. Just keep breathing. Oh, Heart help him, *please*.'

The shadows grew longer. The light faded. The day cooled. *Just take the next breath. And the next.*

A thundering from beyond Urchin's cell made the room shake. Urchin flung himself over Juniper. Another crash followed with the ringing of iron, the splintering of wood and the king's voice in screaming rage.

'Kill who you like!' he screeched. 'Kill anyone! Plague and pestilence on Crispin of Mistmantle and his minions! Get that filthy freak squirrel down here and cut him into little pieces!'

Paws were running upstairs and along the corridor. Urchin snatched the log basket, his ears sharp, his claws flexed. If he could heave the table and the log basket against the door, it would at least hold them off for a while – but as he barricaded the door he heard more animals running, dozens and dozens of them, in all directions. Some were running to his cell. They were louder, faster, nearer. He heard the clank of bolts and locks on the cell door, and nothing else.

Nothing at all. There was no wheezy breathing.

The cell door crashed open with a force that flung the furniture spinning across the floor. In the doorway stood the helmeted Commander.

'Whatever you're planning,' she snapped, 'forget it.' She stepped in and banged the door shut behind her.

Padra returned to the tower from patrolling the shores as the night air grew cool and the waves hushed softly on the shore. Far away, near the mists, lanterns glowed from sterns and masts. That was the watch for Urchin. *Urchin's lights.* A lamp moved in a high corridor, and he mentioned it when he reported to Crispin in the Throne Room.

'That'll be Tay again,' said Crispin. 'She's educating the Whitewings prisoners in the laws and the histories. They need to learn that we're reasonable animals with good laws. But Lord Treeth won't let her anywhere near him. We've had to take everything breakable out of his room.'

'Which must be practically everything,' said

Padra. 'Aspen did like delicate things. What about Scatter?'

'She loves it,' said Crispin. 'I'm sure the law bores her, but she soaks up the stories.' He picked up a dish of blackberries from the table. 'I'm going with her this time.'

'I'm relieved to hear it,' said Padra, and walked with Crispin to the well-guarded corridor where Tay waited, stroking her whiskers, and Gorsen stamped to attention. He had groomed himself until his fur gleamed, and smelt of spices.

'His Majesty King Crispin and Mistress Tay to see the prisoners!' he barked out. From Lord Treeth's chamber came a curse and a crash as something hit the door.

'Have fun,' said Padra as he bowed and left them. When Gorsen unlocked Scatter's cell she sprang up, her eyes wide, and curtsied deeply.

'Your Majesty!' she gasped.

'Mistress Tay has kindly allowed me to help her tonight,' said Crispin. 'Would you like some blackberries?'

Crispin perched on the bed. Tay drew herself up to give a long explanation of when prisoners were allowed out of their cells, and how much they should be guarded, and and in what circumstances treats, such as blackberries, could be brought to the cell, and Scatter's eyes strayed constantly to Crispin's face.

When Tay was about to start on another subject, Crispin said, 'Thank you, Tay. Now, Scatter, what sort of story would you like? A squirrel, a mole, a hedgehog or an otter?'

The night before, Tay had told Scatter a terrifying story about a monstrous mole called Gripthroat. She hadn't slept after that. But she liked otters. There weren't any on Whitewings.

'An otter, please,' she said.

'There was an otter called Arder,' began Crispin. 'He had three daughters, and his wife was dead. Many otters from other islands swam under the mists to Mistmantle, and Arder's two older daughters had married two of these otters and left the island with them. Poor Arder only had his youngest daughter left. Her name was Westree. He fretted and worried when he saw the handsome male otters swimming to the island and the young girl otters flirting and falling in love. He was desperate to keep Westree on Mistmantle.

'He tried to get her to marry a Mistmantle otter, but she didn't like any of them enough. So he ordered her to have nothing to do with the visiting otters, but she couldn't help meeting them when she went for a swim, and, as she said, it was only polite to talk to them. After that, Arder said Westree should never go anywhere without him. Father and daughter had such terrible rows that they could be heard by the squirrels on top of Falls Cliffs, who complained to the king.

'Westree had always done as she was told, but she felt her father was being unreasonable. If he made her stay in their home, she would find a way out as soon as his back was turned and run away along the shore to meet her friends. When they went swimming, she was fast enough to leave him behind and hide under the nearest boat until he swam away to look for her. If they went out in a boat, she'd slip over the side, tip it over with him in it, and escape. He even made a cage for her at night so that she couldn't escape while he slept, but she bit through the bars and ran away.

'Finally, he went to see Sister Tellin the priest and begged her to help him. And Sister Tellin said, *She must have her freedom, because her life is her own, not yours. If she leaves us, she must leave for love. If she stays with us, she must stay for love. If you force her to stay you take away her freedom and the choices of her love, and love will die in her, and you will see her grow miserable. Let her be free.*

'It was not the advice that Arder wanted to hear, but in his heart he knew that she was right. So he gave Westree her freedom, though the thought that she might leave him hurt him deeply.'

'And did she leave?' asked Scatter anxiously.

'No, she didn't,' said Crispin. 'She was free to go. And because she was free, she lived happily on the island for the rest of her life.'

'But . . .' began Scatter, and stopped.

'Is there something you want explained, Scatter?' asked Tay.

'No, it's all right, ma'am,' said Scatter quickly.

'Then goodnight,' said Crispin. 'Tay, we are keeping Scatter up very late.'

Scatter hadn't quite understood that story. Why would Westree want to leave Mistmantle? Why would anyone? But as Crispin rose to go, she remembered the other question she wanted to ask.

'Excuse me,' she said, looking nervously from one to the other and not sure which to ask, 'what does "expendable" mean?'

'Expendable,' said Tay, 'means "unnecessary, not needed". If something is expendable, it is something you can do without.'

'All right, Scatter?' said Crispin.

'Yes, Your Majesty,' she said quietly, and when the door shut she sat down miserably on the bed. So that was what Lord Treeth thought about her. *Scatter is expendable.* She curled up in a lonely knot of fur.

* * *

Urchin only stared. There was no escape, no time even to think of it. The squirrel Commander pulled off her helmet to reveal red-gold fur and a face that didn't go with the helmet and the sharp voice at all, and said softly, 'Where's Juniper?'

She didn't wait for an answer. She whisked the covers from the bed and, not finding anyone, pushed aside the cushions and snatched up Juniper. Urchin darted forwards, but he stopped suddenly. Juniper was breathing again, and the squirrel was looking down at him with such concern that he knew he had to trust her.

'How long has he been like this?' she demanded, pressing her ear to Juniper's chest. 'I'm Cedar.'

Cedar! It was the name Juniper had told him, and the relief flooding Urchin was almost as good as freedom. But he had only ever seen her as a Commander who advised the king.

'I know you've seen me in the High Chamber,' she went on, speaking quickly and quietly. 'I'm a Commander of the Inner Watch, yes, and the king thinks I'm his loyal servant. I'll explain it all later, but you have to trust me. All you have to know is that if anybody hears a word about Larch, Flame or anyone to do with them, we're all dead, do you understand?'

'I understand,' said Urchin, watching her. 'Juniper's been ill since he got here, but he told me I had to meet you.'

'I would have come before,' she whispered, 'but I never had the chance, with the king being –' She stopped suddenly and sat up, her ears twitching. Paws were still scurrying about, dozens of them in all directions. From somewhere in the gallery, Granite was barking out orders. Cedar let go of Juniper, leapt past Urchin to the door, and stood with her back to it.

'Filthy Freak, you're crawling, you're verminous!' she screeched. 'Even your lice have got lice!'

'*What?*' said Urchin.

'Don't answer back, you lousy Freak!' she snarled.

Urchin didn't know what this was about, but he was insulted. 'I haven't got lice!' he said.

'I'm very pleased to hear it,' said Cedar quietly. 'But as long as the guards think you have, they'll stay out.' She flung open the door, yelled, 'Bring me my satchel!' and banged it shut again. Then she knelt beside Juniper and cradled his head in her lap.

'They'll think I've sent for my satchel to get the stuff that repels lice,' she whispered. 'Really I want something for Juniper. All that time in the sea must have made him seriously ill. You've done well to keep him alive.'

It was a long time since anyone had told Urchin he'd done well, and the words warmed him. 'I know all about you, Urchin,' she said, and glanced towards the door. 'I'll have to do a bit more shouting, so they don't get suspicious.'

She stood by the door again, yelled, 'Stand still in that corner, you freak, and don't come near me with your vermin!', then darted back to kneel quietly beside Juniper again. Though she held Juniper's wrist, she was watching Urchin, studying his face as if she were searching for something.

'I don't know if you really are the one to save this island,' she said at last. 'It certainly needs saving. But you shouldn't have been dragged here like this. You're in great danger, and it's up to me to get you home.'

'Home?' said Urchin gladly, his ears twitching. 'When?'

'Don't raise your hopes,' said Cedar. 'We've had a setback. The king's raging and both ranks of the Fortress Watch are on alert, so there's something going on, but I don't know what. We wanted to get you out tonight. The king was planning a party to celebrate capturing you, so I thought the Outer Watch would all be too drunk to notice anything. But all that's changed. Suddenly the tunnels are crawling with guards, and the Outer Watch are everywhere. I'm sorry, Urchin, we can't get you out tonight.' She looked at him with a kindness and understanding that reminded Urchin of someone, but he didn't know who. 'But we will get you out.'

Somebody knocked at the door, and Urchin pushed the cushions round Juniper again. Cedar marched to the door, snatched a battered old satchel from whoever was there, and exchanged a few low, urgent words with the guards. He heard her ask, 'Where?' and 'How many?' before the door banged shut. From the satchel she lifted a glass phial, unstoppered it so that Urchin caught a scent of something sweet and spicy – there must be cinnamon in it, and ginger and something peppery – and mixed a few drops with water.

'Be brave, Urchin,' she said. Urchin saw the frown on her face and heard it in her voice. 'I've just found out why we're all on alert. There was a rescue attempt by some Mistmantle moles. They'd used the old tunnels, and reached Whitewings tonight.'

'Crispin sent them!' cried Urchin. Crispin had tried to rescue him, even if he hadn't succeeded. He'd try again.

'If I'd known the Mistmantle moles were coming, we needn't even have escorted you home,' said Cedar grimly. 'We could have just passed you over to your own animals. But I didn't know.'

'That wasn't your fault,' said Urchin.

'But the king and Granite knew!' she said fiercely.

'There were armed moles ready to meet your rescuers.'

'Oh,' said Urchin, and almost wished he hadn't known any of this. To be so close to rescue and still be here was too hard. 'The Mistmantle moles – did they get away?'

Her solemn face warned him of the worst. 'The Mistmantle moles were few and brave,' she said. 'The first of them ran straight on to the swords of our soldiers. Hopefully the rest got away, and are on their way home.' She laid a paw on his shoulder. 'Don't lose hope. I've heard about King Crispin. And your Captain Padra. They won't abandon you.'

'But how did the king *know*?' demanded Urchin fiercely. 'How did he know about the Mistmantle moles?'

'I wish I knew,' she said. 'Hold on, Urchin. Unfortunately the king is having one of his bad times now. Because of the Mistmantle mole attack he's screaming for your death, but it's just one of his tantrums. We can weather it, but you'll have to trust me, and be guided by me. I think I've convinced him that you can find silver. He has to believe that. He's so greedy for silver he'll keep you alive while he thinks you can find it. And remember, when any other animals are around I'm Commander Cedar, and you're in awe of me. I think they'll send for you tonight, so I'll put some of this on your fur. Sorry, but they think I'm treating you for lice, so you have to smell like it.'

She pulled the stopper from a bottle, and from it came a pungent smell that had a strange, unsettling effect on Urchin. He suddenly felt as if he were a very small squirrel in the woods again, in the days before he went to the tower, when he would climb his favourite tree or play on the forest floor with Needle and his friends, with Apple never far away. Cedar was rubbing it vigorously into his fur.

'You won't like the smell, but neither do lice,' she said. It was so strong it made Urchin's eyes water, and he was about to ask her what was in it when there was a sharp rapping at the door.

'Urchin the Freak to the king!' shouted Bronze with a grin in his voice.

Cedar put away the bottle. 'Don't be afraid,' she whispered. 'I'll be there. And if you want to get out of the king's presence quickly, scratch. He hates lice.'

'What about Juniper?' he whispered.

'He'll be safe in here,' she said. 'Nobody will come in when it smells like this.' She tucked her helmet under her arm and marched Urchin to the High Chamber.

Urchin steeled himself. Nobody must see the fear that made his heart pound and his legs feel wobbly.

He glanced at the first mirror and was dismayed to see a scared and wide-eyed squirrel staring back at him. That was no good. He had crossed the ocean alone, flown on a swan, and rescued a hedgehog from armed moles. In the next mirror was a squirrel putting a brave face on things. *I am a Companion to King Crispin*, he told himself, and approached the High Chamber with his face set, his shoulders squared and his chin high.

He ducked only just in time as a table hurtled past his head. A silver cup flew towards him next, and a bowl which shattered on the door frame.

'Prisoner Urchin of Mistmantle, High Splendour!' announced Cedar as she stamped to attention.

By night, the High Chamber looked far worse than it did by day. Torches blazing on the walls cast a livid light on the glaring eyes and bared teeth of King Silverbirch. Around him, armed and helmeted guards stood to attention, and a small hedgehog with a smug and unpleasant smile on its face crouched by the throne. Two tall guards stood in the shadows beyond the king – they seemed to be holding something between them, but he couldn't see what it was. Granite was behind the throne, and in the flickering light of a torch Urchin saw grim satisfaction on his face.

Something in a dark corner shuffled. It was

coming towards them, a bent figure that stopped, crouched, raised its paws, shook its outspread claws at Urchin and hissed, and before he could see it clearly Urchin knew who this was. He bit the inside of his lip. At last, he would get a good look at Smokewreath.

Smokewreath wore a grey robe hung with some sort of decorations that dangled on cords all round him. The fur of his tail had been closely trimmed so that the tail looked unnaturally thin, and on his head was a grey triangular cap which sat between his ears and trailed into a long cord hanging down his back. He growled softly, and as he stepped nearer Urchin saw what was hanging and swaying from the cords. There were twists of fur, there were claws, teeth, pieces of bones, birds' feet, feathers – Urchin looked up into the sorcerer's face instead. He must not show fear, and it crossed his mind that Smokewreath couldn't be much of a squirrel if he needed all those charms and cords to impress everyone. Brother Fir had the respect of all Mistmantle without having to dress up.

Smokewreath stared fiercely into Urchin's eyes, looked him up and down, hopped back and muttered under his breath, and in spite of fear, darkness and danger, or even because of them, Urchin wanted to laugh. He bit his lip harder.

'He is priceless,' hissed Smokewreath. 'I want winter. Kill.'

The king's eyes glinted with malice. With a swing of his cloak he turned to the two guards in the shadows.

'Bring him here!' he ordered, and as the two guards dragged someone forwards Urchin could feel the king's eyes resting on him in triumph. The king was waiting to see his reaction. Whatever was about to happen, he must remain calm, but when they hauled a small, dark figure into the firelight his heart twisted, and it was all he could do to keep the dismay from his face. They had caught Captain Lugg.

With a swirl of his robe the king strode to Urchin, towering over him so closely that Urchin had to lean back to look up into his face. 'You know this mole, don't you, Freak?' he snarled. 'Stood and fought when he didn't have a chance, to let his troops get away. You may call it noble, but it was just stupid, stupid, stupid!'

The king had his back to Lugg, and didn't see him wink at Urchin. Urchin didn't dare wink back.

'Do you wonder why he's still alive, Freak?' spat the king. 'He's alive because we want to send him back to Mistmantle. He can tell King Crispin that you're staying here. Don't argue, Granite. King Crispin might not believe it from one of our moles, but he will from this one, even though it lacks the brains of a slug.' He turned sharply on Lugg. 'This Freak will bring us silver, and if there's silver on Mistmantle...' He left the sentence unfinished. With a yelp of laughter he swooped on Lugg, snatched him up in both paws and lifted him high from the ground. Urchin darted forwards with rage, but Cedar caught his wrist and forced him back.

Grinning with glee the king held Lugg high above his head, then let go. Urchin lunged forwards again as Lugg thudded to the floor, but Cedar's paw tightened.

'Behave, Freak!' she barked, then bent to whisper, 'He's all right.'

Lugg was picking himself off the ground with surprising dignity. He didn't even seem to have noticed what had happened.

'I see you've got old Granite here,' he remarked. 'How's the bad paw, Granite? Just remind me what happened to it?'

'The Lord Marshall,' said the king haughtily, 'was injured in battle. He was treacherously stabbed by your Captain Padra.'

Urchin tried to protest, but Lugg got in first. 'Is that so?' he said. 'And here's me thinking he was bitten by a girl hedgehog. Well, well, I always thought he was a claw thug with the brains of a bucket, and look at him now. Lord Marshall of the Hedgehog's Toothmarks.'

In the silence that followed, Urchin felt that the stale air of Whitewings had been made clean by a Mistmantle voice. The king glared down at Lugg as Lugg gazed back up at him, clear-eyed, without blinking. When the king spoke it was in a harsh growl forced out through his teeth.

'Go back to that little squirrel,' he said. 'Tell him we will keep the Freak until the first snow, then everyone will see what Smokewreath's magic can do with him. Oh, and I demand the safe return of my ambassador.'

'Are you sure you want him, Your Silver Majesty?' asked Lugg politely.

'Go!' screamed the king. 'Take him away! Cram him down a tunnel and point him to Mistmantle!'

'Well done, Captain!' yelled Urchin as Lugg was hustled out of sight. 'Take my greetings to King Crispin and . . .'

Cedar grabbed him by the throat. With bared teeth, she rammed him against the wall hard enough to knock the breath out of him.

'Look as if I've hurt you,' she whispered, and Urchin slumped to the floor. The king strode towards him, his eyes bright with fury.

'Get up, you,' he ordered. 'Cedar, don't damage

176

him, I need him. Freak, do what you're here to do. Find us silver. Deliver us from fear. Deliver us from poverty. Then when you've done that, deliver yourself, Freak, to Smokewreath, and when you're dead he'll turn your body into magic. The strongest magic! Snowfall, I told him he can have you at snowfall. Sooner, if I'm disappointed in you. Don't want the expense of keeping you alive through the winter, do we?'

Urchin didn't know if he was meant to answer and stood helpless and uncertain until he remembered Cedar's advice. He scrabbled at his ear with his right paw and scratched his side with his left, and the king leapt backwards.

'Take him away!' screamed King Silverbirch. 'Filthy, verminous beast, out, out! Go! Get him out!'

Cedar dragged him away. 'Well done,' she whispered as soon as they were safely out of the chamber. She hurried him back to his cell, locked them both in and rubbed pungent oil into Juniper's fur.

'So far, so good,' she said.

'Good?' said Urchin, and lowered his voice as she put a claw to her lips. 'They caught the moles, they caught Lugg –'

'And they've let him go,' said Cedar, 'and you and Juniper are still alive. The king is trying to get as much out of you as he possibly can. As long as he thinks you can find silver we have until snowfall, which gives King Crispin time to make another rescue attempt, and for us to try to get you off the island in case he doesn't succeed.'

'But Crispin can't send moles again,' said Urchin miserably. 'They'll guard the tunnels more than ever now. Why can't you just rally the animals against the king now? Surely they'd rise against him, if they knew Larch was alive and on the island?'

'They're not ready,' she said. 'They're too frightened of the king and Smokewreath, and they're so used to having a raging king, they'd have to get used to the idea of a quiet, sensible queen. If we tried and failed, there'd be terrible loss of life, and we wouldn't have the chance to try again. We can only do it once.'

'Like Crispin and Lugg and the mole tunnels,' said Urchin.

'If Crispin's half the king I think he is, he'll find a way,' said Cedar, and sat back, rubbing oil from her paws. 'Mistmantle!' she said with longing. 'When we have more time to talk, Urchin, will you tell me about it?'

'I'll tell you now, if you like!' he said hopefully. 'And I'll tell you what might be useful. When Padra had to gather the animals together against Husk, my friend Needle and I were always going to the woods on errands, and we made sure animals knew what was really going on at the tower. The Larchlings could do that.'

'They could,' she said. 'I'll have to leave you now, I'm afraid. It might look suspicious if I stay much longer, but I'll be back in a day or two.' She dropped her voice. 'I want you to meet the rest of the Larchlings. In the meantime, give Juniper plenty to drink, keep him warm, and keep rubbing this into his fur. Unfortunately it smells strong, but the lice treatment is even stronger so that will hide it. It's no good pulling faces, you have to put up with it. Here, I'll spread it around the room.'

Cedar shook the bottle and sprinkled drops of the sharp-smelling oil on the cushions. Unpleasant though it was, it gave Urchin a lurch of homesickness that tightened his throat.

'It's got some very strong herbs in it,' she said. 'It frightens everything off.' She pressed the stopper into the bottle and looked at him searchingly, as she had before. 'Urchin, do you really have no idea where you came from?'

'None,' said Urchin. 'They never found my mother, only me.'

'I'd better go,' she said reluctantly, as if she'd rather stay, and Urchin nodded. He didn't trust his voice. Then somebody shouted along the corridor that Mistmantle moles were savage fighters and they needed a healer and somebody should fetch Commander Cedar, and she left with a last glance at him over her shoulder.

Urchin settled the cushions round Juniper. He sniffed once more at the oil on the cushions, and with a pang of pain and longing, he knew why it had stirred him.

There was a secret joke on Mistmantle. Apple made apple and mint cordial which she seemed to think was extremely nice, and nobody had the heart to tell her it tasted appalling. It was popular in summer, though, because flies and biting insects wouldn't go near it. Whatever Apple put in her cordials, Cedar must have used it in this, and the sharp, strong note of it struck Mistmantle into his heart. Sunlight dappling through the forest, ice-cold water splashing from springs, the giggling of small animals and the swish of autumn leaves, Apple telling him to drink up his cordial to make him strong, and while she wasn't looking he'd tip it down a mole hole. Mistmantle rushed on him with memories of Apple holding on to her hat, Padra's laughing, whiskered face, fresh, warm walnut bread, the wise, kind eyes of Brother Fir, his own nest in the little firelit chamber – he struggled to keep the tears from his eyes, but it was too hard. He crossed to the window, clutched the bars with both paws and looked out. At least he could see the stars and the sea. Tide and starlight were part of Mistmantle, too.

He swallowed hard before he could get the words out, and spoke to the stars. 'I'm . . . I am Urchin of the Riding Stars. Do you remember me?' Then he wrapped himself in a blanket, curled up beneath the window and sobbed as quietly as he could, so Juniper would not hear him.

Chapter 13

On a warm, early autumn morning at Mistmantle Tower, Needle waited unhappily outside the Throne Room holding a carved wooden plate of hazelnuts with blackberries, fir cones, and walnut and hazelnut bread. Beside her stood Sepia with a cup of a strong, spicy cordial that wafted a scent of orange and nutmeg, but nothing smelt nice to her today.

The attempt to rescue Urchin had been a wretched failure with the loss of Mistmantle lives. Gorsen, who stood on duty and smelt of pine oil, made things worse by lecturing them again on how dangerous the caves were, and how if he'd known they meant to go there he would have warned them not to. It was a relief when a small mole opened the Throne Room door and invited them in.

Padra and Arran stood gravely on either side of the throne where Crispin sat, his back very straight and his face solemn. Needle shared his disappointment, and hurt for him. Kind, sensible Mother Huggen the hedgehog and Brother Fir were side by side at the empty fireplace, and Lugg stood before Crispin, his blue cloak over his shoulders and his captain's circlet held out in both forepaws.

'I won't have this, Lugg,' Crispin was saying. 'Put your circlet back where it belongs. Nobody has served Mistmantle more faithfully than you, and if anyone could have rescued Urchin, you could. It's because of you that we didn't have more casualties. If you hadn't been ambushed, he would have been home by now. I don't want your resignation, Captain Lugg, and I won't accept it.'

'Permission to try again, then, Your Majesty,' said Lugg gruffly.

'You're as brave as your ancestors were, Lugg,' said Crispin, 'but we can't try the same thing twice. And if there's a traitor on Mistmantle keeping King Silverbirch informed, we need to find out who it is before we make another move. That's what we need to talk about now.'

'Before we do, Your Majesty,' said Padra, 'you've been so involved in the aftermath of the rescue and planning the next one, you've hardly eaten for two days. Needle and Sepia have prepared this specially.'

Crispin drank the cordial and said it was perfect, and Arran sent Sepia straight to the kitchens to order another one for midday. When she had gone, Padra turned to Needle.

'You're a Companion to the King, and should hear this,' he said. 'The secret counsels of the Throne Room have been betrayed. Either one of us is a traitor, or there's a spy somewhere.'

'Oh!' said Needle, because the answer seemed obvious. 'There's that place under the floorboards that Fingal found!'

'That's been sealed up now,' said Crispin. 'Gorsen saw to that. But even if any animal had been listening down there, they'd still have to get off the island. All the Whitewings animals are accounted for, including the ship's crew.'

'Mistress Tay's been visiting them,' said Needle, and wondered why Crispin laughed.

'Mistress Tay is giving Scatter lessons in law and history,' said Padra, 'while Lord Treeth yells curses and throws things. She's doing no harm.' He winked at her from behind Crispin's back. At least, thought Needle, she'd made the king laugh.

'I don't like to think ill of anyone,' said Mother Huggen, 'but we still don't know what happened to that new friend of Urchin's, Juniper, who disappeared at the same time. There's no sign of him anywhere on the island, living or dead, and why would he leave?'

'Hadn't he disappeared before Crispin ordered the moles to go?' asked Arran.

'Might have hidden on the island, then run off through a tunnel,' said Mother Huggen. 'Not that I'm saying it's him, but the king said we had to talk about it, so I'm talking.'

'He's young,' said Padra, 'and he seemed to be making good friends. I hope very much that it isn't Juniper, but it's possible.'

Needle was about to say that she had her doubts about Gleaner when Crispin sprang up from the throne and banged his paw on its arm.

'I hate this!' he cried. 'The idea of going about the island, even the tower, knowing that anyone I meet could be a traitor! I don't want to doubt my friends! Look at us, huddled up, choosing who to spy on! We'll end up with an island that's perfectly safe, but nobody can pick up sticks for firewood without being watched. Is that what we want?'

He turned his back to them and stood without speaking, gripping the arms of the throne with both paws. Everyone watched him except Fir who, in spite of Crispin's outburst, sat very still on the floor with his back straight and his eyes shut. Crispin turned to face them again.

'Bear in mind,' he said firmly, 'that none of our plans must ever be discussed outside our councils. Watch for anyone behaving strangely, anyone listening at doors, anyone disappearing underground. There may be tunnels we don't know about, so Lugg, get your best moles on to it. And I want you all to pray. Thank you all, and unless anybody else has any comment to make, you may go.'

Arran and Mother Huggen bowed, though Arran, who was with young, couldn't bow very far. Needle curtsied and was about to ask Crispin to eat when there was a 'Hm!' from somewhere near the floor.

Everyone turned to look at Brother Fir. He was still sitting absolutely straight, but his eyes had opened. Needle was afraid he might be ill, but when he spoke his voice was clear and strong.

Over the water
The Secret will bring them
Moonlight, Firelight,
The Holy and the True,
The Secret will draw them home.

Needle didn't know what was happening, and looked at the others for help. They were all watching Brother Fir intensely.

'Tell it again, please, Brother Fir,' said Crispin urgently.

Slowly, steadily, Fir repeated it. He said it a third

time, and this time Crispin, Padra and Arran said it with him, paying great attention as if they were committing a lesson to memory. Needle suddenly realised that Crispin was looking at her.

'Have you learned it yet?' he asked.

She found she could repeat it by heart. Mother Huggen had to say it, too. Then Crispin asked, 'What does it mean, Brother Fir?'

Fir blinked, stood up and shook his ears briskly. 'Dear King Crispin,' he said, 'it's quite enough to receive a prophecy without being expected to understand it. There it is.' He smoothed down his old tunic which, Needle noticed, was looking more frayed and threadbare than ever. 'We must be alert, of course, but I do hope that we're not all going to go off looking for traitors. The king was quite right. Mistrust is poisonous.'

'You may all go,' said Crispin, 'except you, please, Padra.' It seemed to Needle that there was a new brightness about him. The prophecy must have given him hope. She pushed the plate firmly towards him before trotting from the chamber.

'Will you please finish the royal breakfast?' said Padra. 'Or do I have to cram it down the royal throat?'

'I'll eat it,' said Crispin, taking a pawful of hazelnuts. 'A prophecy, Padra! What do you think it meant?'

Padra shrugged. 'If Fir doesn't know, you can't expect me to. But it makes me sure that Urchin will come back. *Over the water.* Do you suppose "the Secret" is Urchin? It might be, as we don't know anything about who he is.'

'Or could it be Juniper?' said Crispin. 'But if we knew what it was, it wouldn't be a secret. I've had Russet and Heath organising searches for Juniper, but he's not on the island. I hope he's not a traitor, but he's another one we know nothing about. A mystery, like Urchin.'

Needle liked to be busy, especially now, as it took her mind from Urchin. She hurried down to the shore, accompanied by Gorsen's friend Crammen who insisted on telling her again that the best kings were always hedgehogs.

After a little beachcombing, she would need to speak to Thripple. She wanted her advice about a sewing project she had in mind. Sooner or later there would be a coronation, and Fir couldn't possibly crown Crispin wearing that shabby old tunic.

And what about Gleaner? She felt extremely curious about Gleaner, and more than a little anxious. She had to protect the king, and Gleaner could be dangerous.

Chapter 14

After the night of the failed rescue, Urchin's spirits lifted. Juniper recovered slowly. His voice was still no more than a croak and his pointy face looked hollow, but he was awake, conscious and able to eat and walk. Each day he became a little stronger, making a patch of gladness in the long, frustrating days. They talked of Mistmantle, of the waterfall and Anemone Wood. They carved pictures on firewood, flipped plum stones into an upturned bowl from as far a distance as possible in a small cell, and made plans for escape, all of which were impossible. And they played endless games of First Five, a Mistmantle game to do with getting five pebbles into a pattern in the middle of a grid while preventing your partner from doing the same. (Cedar provided the pebbles.) The king, who was making a tour of the mineworkings and silversmithies, had not sent for Urchin again.

'His Majesty doesn't want to see you, Freak,' said Bronze, grinning as he brought bread and water. 'Not bothered about feeding you very much, either, by the look of things.' The bread and water wasn't much between two of them, but at least they were left alone, and Cedar smuggled food to them on the rare occasions when she saw them. The hardest thing was knowing that summer was over, autumn was blowing in, and they were still held in a small cell smelling of lice lotion with nothing to explore, nothing changing, and nothing to climb but the walls.

'We should be bringing in the hazelnut harvest,' said Urchin restlessly.

'I hope Damson's all right,' said Juniper. 'She'll be making cordials from the rose hips, and it's hard work. I should be there to help her.'

When the king finally did send for Urchin, his mood had changed again. Summoned to the High Chamber, Urchin saw a small hedgehog curled smugly by the king's throne. He knew he recognised that hedgehog from somewhere, but it took a minute to remember that this was the one who had appeared on the night when the Mistmantle moles had attacked. He was small, but his face was adult and cunning. The king was speaking to him as Smokewreath huddled in a corner, his arms folded and a scowl on his face.

'You've done ever so well, Creeper,' the king was saying to the hedgehog. 'For now, I think you should just enjoy the fun.' He looked at Urchin, stood up, and held out his paws with a frightening smile. 'Dear little Freak, you're going to come with me round the island. Let me show it off to you? Won't that be lovely?'

'Yes, Your Majesty!' said Urchin, and his ears twitched with anticipation. At the thought of fresh air he wanted to leap from the nearest window and race the wind.

'Yes, it'll be such fun!' gushed the king. 'And you can tell me where all that lovely, lovely silver is hiding!'

Oh, thought Urchin, and hoped he could bluff his way through convincingly. The king swept towards him and placed both silvered paws on his shoulders.

'Smokewreath's such a crosspatch today,' he said. 'He's jealous because you might be better at finding silver than he is.' He called over his shoulder to Smokewreath. 'I've arranged a lovely little killing for you!'

He clapped his paws twice, sharply, and four

nervous squirrels shuffled into the chamber carrying something in a blanket. They laid it before the king, and stood meekly back, their paws behind their backs and their heads bowed. Smokewreath edged forwards.

Urchin didn't want to look, but he had to know the worst. He forced himself to look down at what lay in the blanket.

For one horrible moment, he thought it was Cedar. When he gathered himself together he realised it was nothing like her, but it was still the body of a young squirrel with an arrow wound staining her fur. It was a young life, somebody's daughter, somebody's friend, who would never go back to her nest.

With a clatter of bones and a stale smell of smoke, sweat, and vinegar, Smokewreath bent over the body. His gnarled front paws clutched at the dead squirrel's ears and heaved her up, sniffing her face, forcing her mouth open to squint at her teeth, tugging at her fur. Urchin turned his face away in disgust and pressed down the churning in his tomach.

'What's the matter with you?' demanded the king.

Urchin's paws tightened. He had to hold himself back from seizing Smokewreath and wrenching him away from the body.

'Don't you mind that she was killed?' he asked. 'She was one of your islanders.'

'As you say,' answered the king. 'She was one of my islanders. Mine. Mine to dispose of. Mine, mine, silver mines!' He laughed hysterically and threw an arm round Urchin. 'She had to die one day, didn't she? Oh,' he went on as Urchin flinched from his touch, 'are we cold? Lord Marshall, fetch a warm garment for our honoured guest!'

'Bronze, get a cloak for the Freak,' grunted Granite. Urchin didn't want one, but he couldn't afford to annoy the king. He fastened it at his throat as, surrounded by guards and attendants, he followed the king from the palace. It was reassuring to see Cedar take her place among the guards.

His prison was at the opposite side of the Fortress, so he stepped out into part of the landscape he hadn't seen since he first arrived. Gladly he took a deep breath of cool air, but it tasted of dust and made him cough. The leaves had started to twirl down, but like everything else on the island, they lay under the fine grey powder of dust from the mines. As they marched from the Fortress and passed scrawny woodland, he saw that even the fruit and nuts on the trees shimmered with it. Still, after all this time in prison it was wonderful to be outside at all. The king was watching him with a smile of pride.

'Isn't it beautiful?' he said. 'My lovely island! And there's something you simply must see.'

He led them far away from the Fortress and along a steep path that wound up a hillside, and the further they walked, the cleaner and kinder the air became, with a sniff of the sea in it. The fallen leaves were deeper here. If he hadn't been with the king he would have leapt into them and rolled. As it was, he reminded himself to be alert, his ears twitching, his eyes wide with attention, looking for anything at all that would help when the time came for escape. He needed to find places that would provide cover after leaf-fall. The trees grew more thickly here and there were times when he was very tempted to make a dash for it, but it was far too risky. The archers were proud of their skill, and they'd be glad to show it off. He did his best to take in everything he saw in the hope that he'd remember it, but it wasn't easy with the king distracting him, throwing an arm round his shoulder or slapping him on the back, and saying, 'What do you think? What do you think? Have you smelt silver? Can you feel it? Do you want to stop and have a little search? You do have the gift for finding it, don't you? Commander Cedar says you have, don't you, Cedar?'

'Your Majesty,' said Urchin, 'do you really think silver is what your island needs? Animals can't eat it. The dust from the mines is in the soil, it's everywhere. I think that's why the trees don't thrive.'

'Aren't they healthy trees?' asked the king in alarm. 'Don't you think so? We need trees! We refine the silver in furnaces, and we need trees for the fuel! And coal, of course. We have mines for that, too.'

'*More* mining!' said Urchin. 'Your Majesty, you don't *need* silver! You need good, soft earth where things can grow, and healthy plants to grow in it!' The king was gazing into the distance and might not be hearing a single word, but Urchin went on, quickly thinking of all the things hedgehogs like to eat. 'Your Majesty, if your soil is good it'll be full of slugs and worms and beetles, and you can grow berry bushes . . .'

'Good soil,' murmured the king. 'Good earth, with fresh green grass and moss, slugs and beetles . . .'

'Yes, that's what you need . . .' urged Urchin.

'. . . fruit and flowers . . .'

'Yes!' said Urchin.

'Mmm,' said the king thoughtfully. But Urchin, looking up at his face, saw a gleam of greed and menace that made him shudder from ears to tail tip.

'Nice,' said the king softly. He was almost purring. 'Yes, I think so. Yes, I have thought of it. Yes, I want an island like that!'

Urchin didn't want to guess at what the king meant, but he had a horrible suspicion. *I want an island like that* . . . it was a good thing Mistmantle couldn't be invaded. Then the king flung an arm about him with a force that knocked him paws first into a puddle.

'Come on, little Freak!' he cried. 'Up the hill! It gets harder after this!'

Urchin allowed the king to do the talking as they marched and climbed up the long, steep hillside. Long before they reached the top he had noticed how much fresher and saltier the breeze had become. A gull wheeled overhead, a far-off swishing of waves reached him, there was sand mixed with the earth – it took all his self-control to keep from dashing ahead over the thick, shrubby bushes and bounding down to the sea. Forcing himself to stay at the king's pace he trudged to the top of the dunes – and there he stood and gasped, forgetting all about captivity, feeling a leap of joy in his heart.

He looked down on a small, curving bay of silvery sand. Gulls swooped. Gentle waves washed themselves to nothing on the shore. A wooden jetty extended into the water, small boats were tied up and two tall ships stood at anchor. Beautifully and painfully, it reminded him of Mistmantle. Perhaps this was the way Whitewings used to be, the way it could be again if Queen Larch and Brother Flame were in their rightful places. Curled asleep on the water, their beaks under their wings, were two swans with something gleaming on their necks. Did even the swans here wear silver? This was not only the loveliest sight to meet him since he arrive on Whitewings. This bay offered the best chance of escape so far.

'Aren't you simply thrilled?' cried the king. 'Isn't it just delightful? Look at the view! I knew you'd be impressed. We're so high up, we can see all the way past the Fortress!' He took Urchin by the shoulders and turned him round. 'There's the forest with the Fortress in it,' he was saying. 'You can see the battlements from here, do you see? Smokewreath could stand up there and wave at us! You can see it far better in winter, when all the leaves are down – as long as you're still with us, of course!' He gave a shriek of laughter which Urchin found intensely irritating. 'And you can see all the way across to the mountains,' he went on proudly. 'Do you see the three in a row? Eagle Crag, Claw Crag and Beacon Top. Isn't it simply stunning?'

'Oh, yes,' agreed Urchin, surveying the view. He

took in the flat surface of Beacon Top, Claw Crag rising steeply beside it in the shape of a curled claw, and Eagle Crag towering above them both.

'Now,' said the king. 'Now that you have a good view of the island, you can tell me where we can find more silver. Can you feel it yet? Do you need to do any magic? We can find something to sacrifice, if you like.'

'No, thank you,' said Urchin, and thought quickly. This bay with its swans and boats looked the best place to escape from, so he had to keep the king and his guards away from it as much as possible. He stretched out a claw confidently towards the mountains and with a firmness that surprised him said, 'It's in there.'

'I knew it!' cried the king, and hugged him tightly. 'I always thought so, you know. Smokewreath wouldn't have it, but what does he know? I always *knew* there was silver there! Whereabouts *exactly*? Tell me, tell me.'

Urchin opened his mouth to speak and shut it again, realising that he could have made a terrible mistake. For all he knew, Larchlings could be hiding in those mountains, or under them.

Make time, he thought. *Don't tell him anything until I've talked to Cedar.* He looked about for her, but she still wore her helmet and her expression was impossible to see.

He rubbed his eyes. 'I can't tell yet,' he said. 'I'll need time.'

'How much time?' demanded the king.

'I can't tell,' repeated Urchin, struggling to think one step ahead. 'It could be days, I don't –'

'Oh, just have a teeny peek at the mountains today, then,' said the king. 'I'm sure it'll help. We'll go straight there now. March!'

All day, the king and his guards marched Urchin from one part of the island to another. The grim, gaunt mountains were much further away than he had realised, and the king insisted on leading him up and down the foothills and showing him every path and every boulder. Urchin could only hope that as there were so many of them, and making such a noise with the clanking of their weapons, any Larchlings in hiding would hear them far off, and vanish. He tried hard to remember everything he saw, but long before the sun was setting he had decided that one bit of rock was much the same as another. Even the guards were slow and grumbling about their sore paws. Trail was struggling and fell behind, and Bronze, teasing her at every step, made sure everybody noticed it.

Exhausted, with aching paws, Urchin returned to his cell that night and was about to flop on to a cushion when he saw Juniper's ears sticking up from underneath it.

'Hello, Juniper!' he whispered, and lifted the cushion. But Juniper didn't wake up. In that appalling second, Urchin saw that he lay absolutely still. His eyes were closed and his whiskers drooped.

Urchin seized him by the shoulders. Frightened, he gave him a swift, sharp shake. 'Juniper!'

Juniper felt cold. He didn't wake.

'*Juniper!*' whispered Urchin.

Juniper snuffled and wriggled, then opened his eyes wide and shut them again. Urchin sat back, angry with Juniper for the scare and wildly glad to see that he was, after all, only asleep. Juniper muttered something.

'I beg your pardon?' asked Urchin.

'Firelight and moonlight,' said Juniper. 'The secret.'

'Oh,' said Urchin. Lots of animals talked in their sleep, and none of them ever said anything sensible. Juniper sat up and shook his ears.

'Firelight, moonlight,' he said firmly. 'And a secret.'

'You've been dreaming,' said Urchin. 'Listen, I need to tell you what I've been doing. And we need Cedar. And I'm starving, is there anything to eat?'

'Moon—' began Juniper again, but the sound of

paws and the rattle of dishes outside meant that the guards were bringing food. Juniper disappeared under the cushions again while they placed covered dishes on the hearth, and a jug and a beaker on the table.

'Thank you,' said Urchin, and waited until the door was locked before whisking the cushions off Juniper and the covers off the dishes. Steaming vegetables and bowls of nuts and warm bread wafted an aroma that sharpened Urchin's hunger.

'You must be in favour again,' said Juniper. After that they were too busy eating to talk about anything, but the food was finished all too quickly and they were licking crumbs from their paws when they heard Cedar's voice outside.

'Freak's lousy again,' she said. 'They must have lice as big as earwigs in that place. And his paws are too soft for all this walking.' Presently she was admitted to the cell, where she offered cough medicine to Juniper and rubbed lice lotion into Urchin's fur, 'so you smell right,' she said.

'Juniper keeps talking about moonlight and a secret,' said Urchin.

'I don't know what it's about,' said Juniper with a twitch of his ears. 'It was just there, when I woke up, something about moonlight, firelight and a secret, in my head. It was really strong, and I know it's important but I don't understand what it means. And when I was ill, I sort of saw something, remembered something, and that felt important, too.'

'What did you sort of see?' asked Cedar. Juniper's ears twitched again.

'I'm not sure,' he said. 'Something to do with when I was very small.'

'If it happens again, tell me,' she said. 'It may be that you have extra sensitivity – you're aware of things that the rest of us don't notice. Some animals are just born that way.'

'Like feeling sick when I saw the Whitewings ship?' asked Juniper.

'Exactly like that,' said Cedar, and turned to Urchin. 'Urchin, you did well today. If the king wants silver from the mountains, he can mine at Beacon Top all he likes. He'll be out of our way there.'

'I wanted to keep him away from the bay,' said Urchin, and his face brightened when he thought of it. 'You should see it, Juniper! There's a ship! And swans!'

'Swans!' said Juniper, with shining eyes. 'Do you think we could fly home?' But Cedar's face was sad and kind, and Urchin's heart sank.

'Didn't you see, Urchin?' she said gently. 'I suppose, if the swans were asleep, you couldn't tell.'

'Couldn't tell what?' he said, and tried not to resent her for spoiling his hope.

'The collars,' she said. 'All the swans have silver chains round their necks and they're tethered to the jetty. They can't fly away.'

Urchin took a deep breath as if it could arm him against his disappointment. 'Then they need to be set free,' he said.

In his dark cellar, Smokewreath chewed at his claws. *Marked Squirrel. Marked Squirrel.* It wouldn't be safe until the thing was dead. Who cared what the magic did? Whether it worked? The king would believe anything. But that squirrel was a threat. It was dangerous. It had to die. He would take pleasure in killing it. There was a quality about it that disturbed him deeply.

And there was worse. Smokewreath sensed something. He had a talent for sensing things that could not be seen, and he had used this talent in his rise to power as the king's sorcerer. He could tell when there was something close that threatened him, the sort of simple goodness and honesty that he could not control. Something of the kind hung about the Marked Squirrel. It was as if there were two of them. He'd only ever seen one Marked Squirrel, but it was as if there were another one with a rare, true quality that threatened him and made him shudder. If he killed the Freak, the other thing might go away.

Trail knocked quietly at the Lord Marshall's chamber door. When it creaked open she slipped into the chamber which, with its rows of weapons, looked more like an armoury.

Lord Marshall Granite sat at a table examining a small iron dagger, turning the blade towards the lamplight.

'It's Bronze, sir,' she said. 'It's not easy to talk about him like this, but you should know, sir.' Granite gave no answer, so she went on. 'He's always tried to imitate you, but now he wants to take over. He sneers about you, sir, behind your back, he's not content to live in your shadow any more. He's ambitious, and he thinks it's his turn to get to the top. He thinks he'd be a good Lord Marshall, and there's only room for one.'

Granite ran a claw along the dagger blade and grunted. He didn't want to admit that he hadn't noticed Bronze making a bid for power, but that didn't matter. He never trusted anyone, especially young animals seeking promotion.

'We know he doesn't have your experience, sir,' Trail went on, 'and he'd never be the soldier you are. He seems to think the king would favour him because – well, sir, because he comes from Whitewings, and he's a hedgehog, the same as the king.'

Granite grunted again and jerked his head at the door, but Trail smiled inside her helmet as she left, closing the door behind her. She'd had enough of Bronze. Getting on the wrong side of the Lord Marshall was about the worst thing that could happen to anyone, and Bronze had been asking for it.

Chapter 15

Day by day on Mistmantle, the autumn grew cooler and the nights longer. Younger animals rustled about through the curling leaves, gathering nuts and playing. The older ones grumbled about the cold and their ageing joints. Little boats came and went as far as the mists, their lights bobbing above the water all night as Mistmantle watched for Urchin.

In the tower, Arran arranged and rearranged the chamber she shared with Padra by the Spring Gate. Restlessly she aired blankets and smoothed them over fresh heaps of moss and leaves, sprinkled the floor with rosemary, and swept ash from the hearth. When she had finished with their own chamber, she would open the door of the room next to it, which, this autumn, was always empty. But she liked to keep

206

it dusted, with fresh moss in the bed and kindling in the grate, even though it hurt her to see that room always empty, and Urchin's bed not slept in. She wanted it to be ready for him coming home.

In the workrooms, skeins of wool and reels of thread were heaped up on shelves. Rolls of canvas and fabrics leant against the walls, rough homespun cloth the colour of stone and rich scarlet and purple velvets. On the grimmest days, when autumn rains fell relentlessly and it was hard to keep hoping that Urchin and Juniper would come back safely, those brightly coloured wools and satin ribbons gleaming like jewels seemed the only cheerful things on the island. Needle, Thripple and the other workroom animals stitched and painted faithfully, finding work to do although everything for the coronation had been finished long ago. On the days when she felt most forlorn, Needle would sort out the ribbons because playing with the colours seemed to cheer her up a little.

Docken was an excellent tower hedgehog, but he looked as if he belonged in the wood even when he stood faithfully to attention at the Throne Room door. However, Gorsen seemed at home absolutely anywhere, on duty in the Throne Room, sharing hot cordials with the hedgehogs on night patrol, or reminding Needle not to play at the caves. Gorsen,

Lumberen and the rest of the Hedgehog Host would gather together and tell old stories of Mistmantle kings, usually hedgehogs. They often attracted young female hedgehogs who decorated their spines with beech leaves and sat gazing at Gorsen.

'About time we got Gorgeous Gorsen married off,' observed Mother Huggen. 'There's no getting any sense out of the girls these days. If they're not watching him they're staring at their own faces in the pools, turning this way and that and preening their prickles. And don't tell me he hasn't noticed, because he has.'

Delightful young female squirrels still turned up at the tower, their fur scented and gleaming, often carrying messages from Apple to the king. All were pleasant, many were bright and gifted, some were beautiful. King Crispin always received them politely, but that was all. Padra, reporting to the Throne Room after a swim on the first breath-misting morning of the season, saw Sepia's sisters Lichen and Auburn curtseying their way out of the Throne Room.

'There can't be many left,' he observed when they had gone. 'You shouldn't be so gallant about it, Crispin, it only encourages them.' He looked down from the window. 'There's Needle and Sepia trotting down to the woods. Give those two half a chance and they'll rule the island. I wonder what they're up to now?'

'Singing, I should think,' said Crispin. 'According to her sisters, Sepia's training a choir. She's teaching them a new song to sing for Urchin, when he gets back.'

Where rocky ground sloped away from the tower, bushes sprawled down to the woods. Their branches were wild and trailing, and at this time of year, gold and scarlet mixed with the deep green. Two hushed voices whispered from the undergrowth.

'I *can't*!' whispered Sepia.

'Why not?' Needle whispered back.

'Because it's a thorn bush!' said Sepia. 'I'm not hiding under a thorn bush! It's all right for hedgehogs.'

Needle tried not to sigh dramatically, but she felt like it. Urchin wouldn't have complained about a thorn bush. She had promised to help with Sepia's choir, and in return Sepia had offered to help her find out exactly what Gleaner was up to. Needle wasn't at all convinced that she could sing at all, whatever Sepia said, but she had agreed, though it meant she had to keep a lot of little squirrels in order when she'd rather be curled up with her own small brother. It was for Sepia's sake, and Urchin's. But for the moment it was much more important to find out what Gleaner was doing, and whether she was meeting a spy from Whitewings – and here was Sepia, complaining about a pleasantly dark, cool hiding place under a perfectly good thorn bush.

'I'd be much better hidden in a tree,' whispered Sepia.

'The leaves are falling,' said Needle. 'You wouldn't be hidden at all.'

'Yes I would, because lots of leaves are still up and they're squirrel-coloured,' said Sepia. 'There's something sharp sticking into my paw.'

'That'll be me, sorry,' said Needle.

'No, it's a bramble,' said Sepia, and hopped away to run up a tree trunk before Needle could argue. Needle was peering up into the branches trying to see exactly where Sepia had gone when the rustling of leaves nearby made her crouch in absolute stillness, her bright black eyes watching the forest floor as Gleaner ran into sight.

She came rather slowly with a lopsided tilt, carrying something in one front paw. It was affecting her balance and slowing her down, but in her face there was fierce determination. Whatever she planned, nothing would prevent her from carrying it out. She paused to look back along the way she had come, glanced round in all directions without seeing

Needle, then hopped under the twisted thornbushes called the Tangletwigs.

Keeping a distance, Needle trundled after her. Thorns tugged her spines in a way that didn't hurt but was furiously irritating. When she glanced up, she saw Sepia springing lightly from one treetop to another. That was annoying, too. She had expected Gleaner to jump over the bushes, being a squirrel, but she was threading her way underneath and Needle, huddling her spines close to her body, shuffled on after her and found the path leading under the Tangletwigs was well worn. Gleaner must come this way frequently.

She had imagined Gleaner meeting a Whitewings spy. What if it wasn't just one? There might be a whole pack of them, waiting at the heart of the Tangletwigs, plotting against the king! Inside her spines, Needle tingled with fear. Well, she'd come this far. If she was caught, Sepia could run away and raise the alarm. She hurried on, biting her lip when a thorn caught in her paws, squeezing under impossibly low branches, running further into a place completely unknown to her until she found herself in the open so suddenly that she had to shrink quickly under the nearest bush and hope that she hadn't been seen.

Following Gleaner had brought her to a clearing of uneven, mossy ground with a small cairn of stones in its centre. Dead flowers lay before it and something gleamed among them. Needle couldn't see what it was, but she had seen enough to know what the cairn must be. Gleaner was visiting a grave. Needle shrank back, watching.

Gleaner trotted to the cairn, laid down the parcel she carried – it was something wrapped in leaves – and, with her paws on the cairn, pressed her cheek against the stones as if she wanted to hug them. With a sniff she sat back, rubbing tears from her face.

That moment of tenderness was soon over. Gleaner scrabbled at the moss, tidying away dead flowers and shrivelled berries and opening her parcel of leaves to reveal fresh rowans, autumn daisies and oak leaves. She arranged them fussily, talking to herself all the time. Burning with curiosity, Needle inched forwards.

'That's better, my lady,' Gleaner was saying. 'You're all nice now. I've brought you fresh flowers and tidied up.' She picked up the gleaming object and Needle thought – though she couldn't be sure – that it might be a badly dented bracelet. 'Let me polish up your bracelet, my lady.'

Needle crept nearer. Gleaner rubbed the bracelet hard on her fur, held it in both paws and pressed it against her chest.

'I'm sorry I haven't been for a while, my lady,' she

said. 'You know how it is, this time of year, winter coming. I've brought you something special, though it's only your due.'

From the parcel of leaves she lifted something else that glittered. As Needle stretched forwards to see, Gleaner looked up.

'You!' she cried tearfully. 'What are you doing here? Spiky fleasy pincushion!'

With a flash of fur and outstretched claws she sprang at Needle, who tucked in her head and curled up. There was a squeal of 'Ow!' from Gleaner as she struck out, then Sepia's calming voice.

'Sh, sh,' Sepia was saying to Gleaner. 'We didn't mean any harm. We were worried about you.'

'There's nothing to be worried about,' snapped Gleaner, nursing a prickled paw. 'Go away.'

'Yes, yes, we'll go,' soothed Sepia as Needle uncurled. 'But I don't like to leave you so unhappy.'

Gleaner tilted her chin proudly. 'My Lady Aspen should have been buried in the tower vault with the queen,' she said. 'She was the queen's best friend, and she was beautiful. Whatever Captain Husk did, it wasn't my lady's fault. She was buried out here in the Tangletwigs, and who comes to visit her grave? I do. I'm the only one who cares about her. I won't forget all about her, like everyone else!'

She bent her head over her paws and rubbed her

eyes, but when Sepia reached out a paw she pushed her away.

'Go away!' she snarled tearfully. 'This is my queen's place!'

'Your *queen*?' said Needle, and glanced again at the grave where something sparkled with a glint of gold thread.

'My *queen*,' insisted Gleaner, 'and yours. You didn't know that, did you?' She lifted the bright object so that Needle and Sepia saw it at last. Green stems and rowans were woven with gold and silver threads into a crown – a lopsided crown, but made with great care.

'It's beautiful, Gleaner,' said Sepia. 'Did you make it yourself?'

Gleaner seemed a little soothed. 'Of course I did,' she said. 'Nobody else would, because nobody else ever knew she was a queen.' With all the dignity she could gather, she placed the crown on top of the stones, stepped back as if paying her respects, then turned to them with a smile of triumph.

'You think you know it all,' she said. 'You and your hunt for the Heartstone. I can tell you something about the Heartstone, something you didn't know, cleverclaws. Do you want me to tell you?'

'Oh, yes, please,' said Sepia.

'It was one morning shortly before the Spring

214

Festival,' said Gleaner haughtily. 'I'd polished my lady's jewellery and I was bringing it back to her, but when I knocked I didn't get an answer, so I opened the door anyway, to go and put it all away, but there she was, and she hadn't heard me. She was sitting on the little chair by the fire, looking at something in her paw. And the thing in her paw was a very pretty pinkish stone with gold in it, sort of heart-shaped. I didn't know then what it was. Then . . .' she widened her eyes and slowed down, 'I swear to you that it lay on her paw perfectly still as anything could be, all that time I was watching. It was such a beautiful sight that I forgot to tell her I was there.'

Needle opened her mouth to comment and shut it again when Sepia stepped on her paw.

'And then what happened?' asked Sepia.

'Then she looked up and saw me and wasn't a bit cross, she just smiled, sweet as ever,' said Gleaner. 'She popped the stone into a little bag and never mentioned it again. But when you started talking about the Heartstone going missing, when the tower animals were all strutting about telling us what it looked like, I knew that was what I'd seen in my lady's paw. I saw it with my own eyes, how still it lay on her paw. I know what that means,' she finished triumphantly. 'It means she was the true queen of Mistmantle.'

Sepia pressed Needle's paw as a warning to stay quiet. 'Thank you so much for telling us,' she said. 'Do you know what Lady Aspen did with it after that?'

'I never saw it again,' said Gleaner. 'Suppose it might be in her chamber, though nobody would think to look in there, would they?'

'Oh, but that's where –' began Needle, and stopped as Sepia pressed harder on her paw.

'Where what?' asked Gleaner. A suspicious light had come into her eye. 'What have they done with it?'

'Nothing!' said Sepia.

'Nothing?' repeated Gleaner. Her eyes gleamed.

'Well, the thing is,' said Sepia carefully, 'it's such a lovely room, and you and Lady Aspen kept it so beautifully, they only use it for very special guests.'

'What guests?' demanded Gleaner. 'That lot from Whitewings?'

'Only for the Lord Ambassador himself,' said Needle. 'Lord Treeth. So –'

'Lord Treeth?' spat Gleaner. 'He throws things around and breaks them! Everybody knows that!'

'But I'm sure they're not –' began Needle, but Gleaner elbowed her way past and sprang away through the bushes.

'Oh dear,' said Sepia.

'Let her get on with it,' said Needle. 'She can go and storm about it if she wants to. There's no point in trying to keep the truth from her. Lord Treeth is in Aspen's old room and that's that. Brother Fir's always telling us we should learn from our past. We shouldn't let her go on thinking Aspen was so good and sweet, and as for holding the Heartstone . . .'

'Yes,' said Sepia. 'We haven't found the Heartstone, but now we know who made the fake one. Aspen had probably just finished smoothing it down, and was admiring it when Gleaner saw her. We should go and tell the king.'

Suddenly they both felt cold and uneasy, standing by the cairn with Aspen's old bracelet and the twisted crown. Without another word they hurried back to the tower. They had learned something useful, but neither of them felt any better for it.

Chapter 16

U rchin was still in the king's favour, but he
knew it wouldn't last. Autumn grew colder.
Bare trees reached up empty branches to a
colourless sky, and Urchin raged in his heart against
the lost summer. Winter was coming too quickly.

There was always a basket of firewood in his cell,
and whenever he was returned there after a long day
at the silver mines with the king he would find a fire
already flaring brightly in the grate. Wine, fruit and
biscuits were always left for him, even on the days
when he was ordered to eat with the king in the High
Chamber.

Juniper took care to stay hidden. Alert to every
sound outside the cell, he made sure he stayed close
enough to the bed to jump into it and hide if he
thought anyone might come in – Cedar's rumour that

Urchin had lice meant that no animal would go near his bedding. Food and drink were always left in the cell, but Juniper had decided never to eat or drink anything until Urchin came back – he felt it wouldn't be right to.

'You should have had something to eat,' Urchin would whisper, stretching his chilled paws to the fire on his return from the mines. 'At least I'm allowed outside. I don't know how you can stand the boredom.'

Alone all day, Juniper would remember the animals and places he loved and hold them before the Heart. He was learning to find quietness inside himself. He was learning to pray.

Every day, Urchin was marched to Beacon Top to watch the search for silver, and he could never have imagined anything so tedious. It should be the time of year for storing nuts, building warm nests and playing games with fallen leaves, not for standing at the foot of a mountain watching hedgehogs hack it with axes and dusty moles bobbing in and out of tunnels. Sometimes a group of them would mutter together and look accusingly in his direction. So far, they'd found nothing. Urchin tried to look keen and confident but it wasn't easy, and when the king hugged him or threw an arm round him he had to force himself not to cringe. Bronze took every chance to tread on his paw or tweak his fur when the king wasn't looking, which annoyed Urchin more than it hurt him.

Smokewreath was the worst, shuffling and sniffing with a rattle of bones and claws as he made magic passes at the nervous animals. Sometimes he made a jabbing movement at Urchin, but he didn't seem quite sure of how to cast magic at the Marked Squirrel. He contented himself with sniffing the air and muttering, 'Chill, chill. Winter comes. White wings in the sky.' The king would laugh loudly.

'Isn't he hilarious!' he said, one chilly morning when Smokewreath was squinting up at the sky. 'He can't wait for the first snowfall. Never mind, Urchin. We won't let him have you yet.'

Urchin felt a change in the air as they returned to the Fortress one evening. The shivering wind which had been in their faces on the way to the mountains had turned on them again and rushed against them, spitting icy rain into their faces. Smokewreath muttered. The king wrapped himself in his cloak and snarled. Animals scurried past, heads down, hunched against the rain as they trundled barrows and ran for cover. Earth and sky were hard iron-grey, cloaks were damp and whiskers were drooping long before they reached the Fortress and Granite pushed

Urchin through the doors.

'The Freak's unlucky for us,' snarled Granite. He took off his wet cloak and swirled it so that water sprayed in Urchin's face. 'You're useless, Freak! You're worthless!'

Grinning unpleasantly, he looked around to see if he had an audience. Bronze, Trail and more of the Fortress Watch were there, standing around, waiting to see what would happen. After a long hard day, this could be entertaining.

Urchin steeled himself. He mustn't react, mustn't make trouble. It would make life worse and escape harder, and not only for himself.

'Everyone on Mistmantle wonders what happened to the Freak's mother,' said Granite, looking round. 'Never a sign of her. Took one look at that thing and scarpered. He probably takes after his father, whoever that might be.'

Urchin whirled to face him, but Bronze and another guard grabbed his wrists and held him back, laughing. 'I'll teach him his manners, Lord Marshall!' called Bronze.

'He's mine, runt,' growled Granite. Slowly, flexing his claws, he advanced towards Urchin.

A sudden flash of silver sent Granite reeling sideways so that he fell with a thud against the wall. Bronze bit his lip and looked at the floor, grinning helplessly. The king stood among them, lifting a hind paw to kick Granite hard in the shin.

'I'll decide what happens to the Freak, not you, Lord Marshall!' he screamed, and stretched a silvered talon at Urchin. 'Where's the silver, Freak? If I find you've sent us searching in the wrong place I'll send you back to Mistmantle one paw at a time! Why did you come here? You're after my crown!' His voice rose to a screech. '*My* crown! You think you'll sit at table with me tonight, don't you? Well, you won't! Take him to his cell! You needn't wait for snowfall! I'll kill you tomorrow! Do you hear? Tomorrow!'

Bronze pushed Urchin into his cell and banged the door. He would have loved to stay and taunt the prisoner, but he was due to take guard duty on the battlements. He stamped up the stairs, begrudging every step. Worst posting of the lot, the battlements, nothing between your fur and the winter, and these days he was always being sent to the battlements when he wasn't trudging off on a fool's errand to those miserable mines. The sooner they killed the Freak, the better. He strode along the battlements, barking out orders to shivering guards, kicking the ones who were falling asleep on their paws from long hours on duty, scowling at the rain. And that spoilt

Freak had a comfortable cell, with a fire! With any luck it wouldn't be for long. Commander Cedar had personally arranged the deliveries of firewood when he first came . . .

. . . Bronze paused in his marching, and leant his elbows on the battlements.

Commander Cedar was taking a great interest in the Marked Squirrel. Interesting, that. Worth thinking about.

Bronze had always known that there were two kinds of animals on Whitewings. There were the ones who just got on with the work, kept their heads down and stayed out of trouble, and there were animals like himself. Animals with ambition, determined to be in power, and ready to destroy whoever got in the way. Commander Cedar was in a powerful position already, but did she want more?

You never could tell what she was up to, thought Bronze. Snobby madam, kept herself to herself, too good to speak to the rest of us except to give orders, but she was up to something now. Taking so much trouble over the Freak, you might almost think she was helping him.

You might almost think she was helping him.

So that was it. The two of them were in it together, Cedar and the Freak. Maybe she wanted to overthrow the king and make herself queen and she'd promised to save him if he'd help her, something of that sort.

There was a grim smile on Bronze's face. He'd tell the king, but not just yet. The king wouldn't believe anything against Cedar without evidence. He'd wait and watch her, catch her out. If he didn't succeed in bringing down the Lord Marshall, he wouldn't mind being a commander. It would only be a matter of time, and not much time at that.

Urchin felt he'd barely fallen asleep when, long before dawn, he was woken again for the cold, weary trudge to Beacon Top. He wished he'd told the king to search somewhere nearer. Frost made the bare earth harder and crueller under the paws, and the march seemed to go on for ever. The working animals built shelters and fires, and he was at least able to get warm when Granite was too busy to order him away from them. The rough wind blew dust from the mineworkings and cold soot from the furnaces. It was a day Urchin felt would last for ever, a day of cold, damp and boredom. The animals with their barrows and pickaxes shivered, their shoulders huddled, misery on their faces. Long before they reached the Fortress that night his bones were chilled to the core, his hind paws throbbed, and every step on the frozen ground hurt his paws as the Fortress loomed before them.

He was falling asleep on his paws, then suddenly jolted awake. He seemed to be swaying, then there was a terrible moment when everything was moving, and he wasn't sure if it was himself losing his balance, or the ground was moving beneath him – nothing was still and he found he was looking for a tree to climb up, a branch to spring to, but there was nothing in this desolate place –

Somebody grabbed him, dragged him aside and ran to safety. All around him animals were running, shouting, looking over their shoulders, and the ground was shaking and rumbling, there was nowhere to climb, nowhere was safe . . . Granite was shouting orders.

'All of you, crawl!' he bellowed. 'Two groups, spread out, spread your weight!'

Face downwards on the icy ground, Urchin crawled. From the corners of his eyes he saw animals around him creeping like insects across the grey, dusty surface. Shivering, he was wondering exactly what had happened and how long this would go on when Granite's voice barked out again.

'On your feet, all of you! No fussing, it's just a little earth tremor. Bit of shaking underground, nothing for anyone to bother about, except for the Freak, because he's a coward. Move on!'

Urchin turned in rage. He wasn't going to let that

remark go. But guards were grabbing him by the arms and hurrying him forwards, and there was no choice to go on, step by step, aching with cold and limping with sore paws over the frozen ground.

At least the Fortress was in sight, and he had a warm cell to look forward to. He had never thought he would find the hall of mirrors welcoming, but the torches flaring on the walls at least warmed his fur. Hedgehogs marched him to his cell, forcing a pace that he struggled to keep up with. Holding his head high, he saw their grins and the way they glanced at each other as they reached the gallery. Bronze was shouting orders.

'Everything out! All of it!'

Urchin stared in horror and disbelief. The cushions from his cell, the table and even the curtains were being flung along the gallery. They were ruthlessly emptying his cell. There was nothing left for Juniper to hide behind.

Could he have escaped? Was he hiding in the chimney? Had they found him? 'Best bedchamber for the king's freaky friend,' announced Bronze, and grinned as he pushed open the door.

A blanket and a small heap of leaves lay in one corner. On the cold hearth stood a beaker of water, a plate of dry bread and the empty log basket. Ashes lay in the grate. There was no trace of Juniper.

He could feel Bronze watching him with that smirk on his face. Either Juniper had somehow escaped and they knew nothing about him, or they'd found him and taken him away, and were waiting to see Urchin's reaction. Careful not to give anything away, trying not to limp, he walked to the leaves and flopped on to them.

'Sleep well,' said Bronze with a bristle of spines, and was pulling the door shut when along the corridor came the marching of paws and the clang of weapons as animals stamped to attention. King Silverbirch was coming.

Urchin was too tired to care and his eyes were already closing, but with a bark of, 'Get up, Freak!' Bronze strode into the cell, dragged him to his paws and gave him a push that lurched him out of the door. It was only by keeping his balance with his tail that he was saved from sprawling at King Silverbirch's paws. The king sneered down at him.

'Bow, Freak!' he ordered.

I have had enough of your tantrums and your scenes, thought Urchin. *You're no sort of a king, and I don't see why I should bow to you.* A stinging blow from Granite's sword against his shoulder sent him flat on his face, and amid the laughter that made him burn with humiliation a guard stepped forwards and hauled him to his paws.

Her lips brushed his ear. 'Don't worry!' she whispered.

It was so soft and quiet that he couldn't even be sure he'd heard it, but he saw the gleam of Cedar's red-gold fur. He didn't dare risk looking up at her, so instead, as he found his balance, he glanced around the crowd. There, among the mailed and helmeted guards, he caught a glimpse of dark fur and a paw with a familiar twist to it.

He'd know that fur and that paw anywhere. He didn't dare look directly at Juniper, but he had to bite the inside of his lip hard to fight the smile.

'Stand, Freak!' ordered Cedar, and took her place dutifully behind the king.

'This time,' snarled Granite, 'bow to the king.'

Cedar was just behind the king. Urchin put his paw to his heart and bowed.

'That's better,' snarled the king. 'We had begun to think, Freak, that you'd sent us looking in the wrong place. We were minded to give you to Smokewreath already. I'm sure the snow will start soon. But they've found a seam of silver, Freak, at Beacon Top!' He turned to the guards and raised a clenched fist. 'Do you hear? A seam of silver!'

He waited for the cheers to die down, then turned to Urchin. 'Smokewreath says it was his magic that found it, but we'll give you the benefit of the doubt and keep you alive to see how it progresses. It had better be a good seam. Where's Smokewreath?'

With the usual clatter of bones, Smokewreath shuffled along the gallery.

'It was I who brought you the silver,' he hissed. 'My magic made the earth shake to open the seam. I found it.'

'But you never found it before the Freak came, did you?' said the king petulantly. Smokewreath continued to clatter along the gallery.

'It is a dangerous thing to question –' he began – then suddenly, barely two paces from Juniper, he stopped. His eyes narrowed. As Urchin watched, Smokewreath tipped his head like a bird, and sniffed.

Urchin forced himself to look straight ahead, but his skin prickled. It was as if Smokewreath knew about Juniper, could sense his presence. Smokewreath growled deep in his throat, and shuffled backwards.

'What's the matter with you?' snapped the king.

'Something . . .' rasped Smokewreath. 'Something . . .' He was breathing heavily. His ears were flattened against his skull, his coat bristled and, to Urchin's astonishment, his eyes were terrified.

'Strong magic!' wheezed Smokewreath. 'I will make stronger magic! Strong!' Shuffling backwards, almost tripping over his own paws, he retreated into the shadows. The king snapped out an order and a rough shove from Bronze sent Urchin staggering back into his cell with the lock clanking behind him.

After the torchlit corridor, the cell was dark and bitterly cold. Urchin sipped at the stale, metal-tasting water which made him even colder, and didn't feel like nibbling at the hard bread. He wrapped himself in the blanket and huddled among the leaves, wondering what had so alarmed Smokewreath. He had been alarmed himself when the sorcerer had stopped so close to Juniper. The presence of threatening evil made Juniper feel sick. Could it be that Smokewreath felt the same in the presence of someone as good and brave as Juniper – and was Juniper more than just good and brave?

The important thing was that Juniper was safe with Cedar. He was glad of that, in spite of the dull emptiness of the cell on his own.

There was still the faintest trace of lice lotion on his fur, and again it reminded him of Apple. He was coming to like it, as a reminder of Mistmantle. 'Winter drill,' Apple would have said at a time like this. 'Wrap up, curl up, settle down.' That was what most animals did in the coldest and hungriest of winters. Keep warm, and sleep as much as possible. There was a method to it, to retreating deep inside yourself and closing down every thought. There was nothing to do now but sleep. Urchin curled up tightly, pretended he was on Mistmantle, and was falling asleep when the door banged open. There was laughter in the corridor. Urchin closed his eyes tightly, desperate to sleep again.

'Commander Cedar of the Inner Watch for the Freak!' called Trail. Reluctantly, wearily, Urchin opened his eyes as Cedar dragged him to his paws.

'King's orders,' she snapped. 'You're to come with me.'

She dragged him through the gallery where guards laughed loudly and exchanged comments – 'Did you hear? She got permission to bath him. Yes, from the king. They must have fifty kinds of lice on Mistmantle that we don't have here. Not even Commander Cedar can finish them off.'

Cedar opened a side door, led Urchin quickly down a staircase, unlocked a door and hurried him through a maze of corridors with twists, turns and stairs. Finally she said, 'Now, Urchin.'

As he realised that he was fully awake and not dreaming, Urchin felt his ears twitch with excitement. 'Is this it?' he asked eagerly. 'Time for escape?'

'Not yet,' she said softly, and Urchin tried not to look disappointed. 'But there are animals you should meet, and I had the chance to get you out of the cell tonight. Hopefully, the king might let me make a habit of it. In the meantime . . .'

She bent to pull at a ring in the floor, and opened a hatch. Urchin looked down into blackness, and before he could ask what was down there, Cedar had jumped and disappeared. There was a soft thud, and her voice carried up to him.

'Jump!'

Not knowing what he would find, or even how far it was, his paws tingling, Urchin jumped. Torchlight in his face made him blink.

'This way, sir,' said a mole, and led Urchin along a tunnel so low that before long he had to crawl. He had never liked tunnels much, least of all tunnels that made him duck, and the tightness of this one was new and frightening. He concentrated very hard on putting the next paw forwards, then the next, trying not to think of the roof against his fur, and the weight of the Fortress above them. He mustn't think about not knowing how long this tunnel would last, and being trapped with a mole in front of him and Cedar behind him . . . his chest tightened. He tried to breathe deeply, but the air was warm and stale . . . *I need to be out, out, let me out . . . how do I know I can trust Cedar? Has she brought me here to kill me?* . . . Then, just as he had to fight against panic, the tunnel widened, the mole unlocked a door, and he was met by a wave of light, colour and brightly chattering voices.

He stood in the doorway of an underground room bright with torchlight and firelight. Wooden tables to right and left of him were heaped with food – plain, but plenty of it – and coloured cordials that made him fiercely thirsty just to look at them. Then he realised that every animal in the room had turned to face the door and was watching him with bright, hopeful eyes.

There were squirrels, all shades and sizes of moles, and keen-eyed hedgehogs, and with a heart leap of happiness he saw Juniper. Many animals had cups in their paws, but they had stopped drinking and fallen silent apart from whispers – *'That's him! The Marked Squirrel!'* Some bowed or curtsied politely to him, and he bowed back as a young female hedgehog and a male squirrel made their way towards him and the crowd parted for them.

The tall, lean squirrel stopped, folding his paws behind his back. He was dark with a deeply thoughtful look about him, and wore a plain brown tunic with damp marks on it as if he had just been drying his paws. He waited respectfully as the hedgehog stepped forwards with a smooth firm step and her head held high. She was small with a grave and plain, pointy face, but her eyes were bright. There was a sharp, alert quality about her, as if she noticed everything that was happening, that reminded Urchin of Crispin and Padra. She must have been taught to keep her wits about her. Urchin waited to be introduced, but he knew who they were.

'This is Queen Larch,' said Cedar, 'the niece of our late queen, and the true queen of Whitewings. And our priest, Brother Flame.'

'You are most welcome among the Larchlings,' said Larch, and her voice was low and grave. 'I must apologise for the ill treatment you have received here. Whatever we can do to help you, we will.'

Brother Flame darted forwards, seized Urchin's paw and shook it. He smelt of unpleasantly sharp herbs.

'Please excuse me,' he said briskly. His manner was nervous and intense, but he spoke to Urchin as if they'd known each other for years. 'I've just been treating a young mole who had difficulty breathing, and I fear I still smell of the infusion. Whatever else is wrong on Whitewings, we still have skilled healers.'

'And we need them,' said Larch. 'All this mining for silver and coal makes dust that gets into our eyes, our throats, our lungs and our fur. It makes us ill, and every season the plants we need for healing are harder to find. The smoke and dust are killing everything.'

'I'm so sorry,' said Urchin. With so many hopeful eyes fixed on him he felt he would gladly deliver the island, if only he knew how to. 'What do you want me to do to help you?'

Larch looked surprised. 'Urchin of the Riding Stars, we are here to help *you*,' she said. 'We will do all we can to get you home to Mistmantle. You have been treated shamefully by Silverbirch and his court.'

'But I'd like to do something for this island,' said Urchin. His mouth felt drier all the time, and in his own ears his voice was hoarse, but he saw the longing and hope in the faces around him and said what he needed to say. 'I mean, yes, I want to go home. I want it so much I try not to think about it. King Crispin wants me home, I know that. But he wouldn't want me to abandon you if I could give you any help.'

'The help you can give us is this,' said Larch, her solemn little face looking up into his eyes. 'When the silver frenzy is over and Silverbirch is overthrown, we will seek help from Mistmantle. Not soldiers, not jewels. Just some good Mistmantle soil to replace the earth that's been wrecked by mining, and something to grow in it.'

'That's exactly what this island needs,' said Urchin.

'Just what I said,' said a gruff, familiar voice.

'Lugg!' cried Urchin. Grinning broadly, Captain Lugg pushed through the crowd towards him.

Larch clapped her paws together and suddenly everyone became busy, pouring cordials, moving chairs, gathering into little groups as if a party might be beginning. To Urchin, the lopsided grin on the mole's familiar face was better than a party and more welcome even than the cup of cordial Lugg put into his paw.

'How did you get here?' gasped Urchin.

'Drink that,' ordered Lugg. 'Come 'ere.' He jerked his head towards the fire where Juniper waited. 'Glad he's turned up. Thought he would. Good lad, that.' A procession of hedgehogs with bowls of hot water and sponges made their way towards them, and Lugg nodded at them. 'Here comes your bathtime.'

'My what?' said Urchin.

'Mistress Cedar said she was taking you out of your cell to wash you, so you have to look washed,' he grinned, as the hedgehogs left the water and sponges beside Urchin. 'Don't mind me, and be sure you do your ears.'

'But what are you doing here?' demanded Urchin as he washed.

'Getting you out, what d'you think?' said Lugg. 'The king was against sending another rescue party until we could be sure of not getting the same

236

welcome as last time. But time went on, and I said to the king, I don't want to risk anybody else's hide but I wouldn't mind risking my own, digging an extra tunnel or two that the Whitewings lot don't know about. So, I'm here. May as well get you out.'

'When?'

'How do I know?' said Lugg. 'Only just got here. Funny place, this.'

'But we thought all the tunnels were guarded,' said Juniper.

'They are,' said Lugg. 'All the ones they know about. So I made some more. That's what kept me. Mind, them old tunnels under the sea! Beautiful arches, lovely work. Good as the tower. Just big enough for small squirrels. We'll have to get back that way.'

Urchin and Juniper exchanged glances. Neither of them much liked the idea of several days' travelling far underground, but it was the only way back to Mistmantle.

'Lovely work, in these Whitewings tunnels,' went on Lugg, and nodded his thanks at the young hedgehogs who laid baskets of bread and fruit at their paws. 'They've got lovely tunnels all over this island, but they've dug too many of 'em. Not good for the land. Weakens it. And what's more, as I just told Larch and the rest of them, there's a whacking great fault line right under this Fortress. Takes a mole to find things like that. I had to work out the tunnel network, make a few byways of my own, not get caught, and all without the whole lot caving in. Nice work, though I shouldn't be the one to say it.' He gave a smile of satisfaction as he warmed his paws on his beaker of steaming cordial. 'Very neat.'

Urchin was enjoying the clean feel of his fur now that the dust was washed out. Lugg passed him a towel.

'I reckon we'll have a chance to get you out when winter really bites and it's too hard for mining,' he said. 'Then time will be tight, because we have to get you both out before Smokewreath claims his kill. Can't promise, mind. Do my best.' He stretched and smiled approvingly as musicians piped up music and Larchlings joined paws to dance. Urchin watched and wondered whether he was supposed to invite someone to dance or whether somebody would invite him and what he would do if he did have to dance, because he didn't know the steps, and besides, he was still damp, when he felt whiskers against his face. Cedar was behind him, bending to speak.

'You and Juniper, come with me,' she said quietly. 'There are things you need to know.'

Still holding their beakers, Urchin and Juniper followed. Cedar wove her way through the crowd, up a few shallow steps cut into the rock, and through a doorway so low that he had to duck before he found himself in a small round chamber with an arching ceiling, decorated with larches.

Even before he saw Brother Flame, he knew they stood in a priest's chamber. It had the quiet, prayerful feel of a priest's room. Baskets of leaves were stacked on top of each other, neat rows of tiny bottles stood on a ledge and a low fire murmured in the hearth. Lanterns glowed gently.

Brother Flame welcomed them to the hearth with an outstretched paw, and they sat closely round the warmth. A small wooden table stood by the hearth, empty but for a small polished box, and Urchin was wondering what might be in it when Brother Flame sat down and said quietly, 'Cedar. You should tell this.'

The power in the moment reached Urchin. It was solemn and significant. His ears twitched.

Cedar opened the small box and held it out to him so that he saw a woven bracelet, old, and a little worn-looking. It looked as if it might be made of squirrel fur, but – and Urchin's heart beat a little faster as he looked more closely – it was pale fur. It might be darkened a little with age and wear, but without that, it would be as pale as his own. She laid it on the floor in front of him, her paws shaking a little.

Urchin shivered. The intensity of the moment hummed and pulsed around him. His life was about to be changed, deeply and for ever. His heart told him so.

Chapter 17

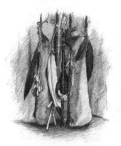

S epia had just woken up.

'That's where it is!' she said.

For days she had been nagging herself about a missing cloak. She couldn't think where it would be, or exactly where she'd had it last. She hadn't missed it before. But now there were mornings of bright white frost and cold winds that made her long for her warm green cloak. She had gone to her nest thinking of it, wishing she could spread it over the moss and leaves as the nights grew colder. And, as often happened with Sepia, she had slept deeply and woken early knowing the answer to her problem.

'It's still in the song cave,' she said. She had left it there after the night when Hope was missing. She sprang up, fluffing up her fur for warmth. Her winter coat was growing in thickly and she was glad of it, but she thought of Urchin and hoped he was warm.

It would be lonely, going to the song cave and back by herself. It wasn't that she was worried by Gorsen's warnings about the caves – she'd been playing and singing there for years without harm – it was more that she'd become used to having company. Needle might come with her. At this time in the morning she was usually on the beach searching for the Heartstone, so Sepia bounded down to the shore where Needle and Fingal appeared to be having an argument. Sepia found a rock to perch on until they'd finished.

Fingal was saying that he couldn't see why Crispin shouldn't be crowned, Heartstone or not, and they could always have another celebration when Urchin got home, Needle insisted that tradition was important, and they needed the Heartstone to prove that Crispin was the true king, Fingal rolled in the sand and said that anybody with half an eye and most of a brain could see that Crispin was the true king, and Sepia watched the pattern made on the sand by the waves. Apple came to join her, and as usual they tried to reassure each other that Urchin would be all right, and would come home. Apple wondered out loud about Captain Lugg, who had suddenly gone away again, and his poor wife, Lady Cott, she's as good a mole as ever popped up, she says he's away on the king's business but if she knew what business she wasn't saying, and maybe she wasn't allowed to say, you never knew, did you, poor Lady Cott, isn't she brave. Finally, when Apple had to stop for breath, Sepia hopped down and explained what she wanted to do.

'Oh, are you going to the cave with the water-slide?' said Fingal. 'Can I come?'

'You'll only play on the slide all the time,' said Needle.

'Yes, please!' said Fingal.

'Oh,' said Needle, remembering, 'I promised Mum I'd help line the nests for winter this morning.'

'Tomorrow would do,' said Sepia, 'though I have to rehearse the choir then. Do you think we could take them all to the song cave, if their parents are all right about it? They'll love the song cave, and they'd sound so good in there. I'd love them to hear themselves in there. D'you think we could take them with us?'

'Gorsen says it's dangerous,' said Needle, 'but you've been there loads of times, haven't you?'

'Oh, Gorsen just says that,' said Fingal. 'I think he wants to keep the caves to himself. A romantic little meeting place to impress his girlfriends.'

Padra had never liked heights, but Fir's turret was different. Its airy simplicity, its neat hearth and its sense of holiness never failed to quiet him. Having escorted Fir up the stairs, he knelt to light the fire in the grate himself and sent the young squirrel Whittle to bring breakfast from the kitchens. He pulled a stool to the fireside for Fir.

'Heart bless you, Padra,' said Fir, settling himself down and stretching his paws to the warmth. 'I'm not quite in my dotage, but it's very gratifying to have my fire lit by a captain.'

'Fir,' said Padra in exasperation, 'can you explain to me about the mists? I don't understand at all. They're supposed to protect the island, but they just make it impossible for us to go to the help of our own.'

Fir closed his eyes, pressed his paws together and rocked gently back and forwards on the stool, not even noticing when Whittle returned with the breakfast. Padra was about to ask if he was all right when he opened his eyes, shook himself, and said, 'The Heart is wise and Mistmantle is small. Small and beautiful. The mists were put there to protect us from attack. Our own animals who leave by water cannot return by water. That means that exiles who brought war and misery to our island cannot recruit an army to return and do it all again. But the mists are not there to keep out the valiant and the true. Such as Lugg with his tunnels. Lugg has left twice. Nobody has ever left three times and returned. It may not be possible. But nobody fully understands the mists, let alone the Heart that gave them.'

'But Husk was able to bring in mercenaries,' Padra pointed out. 'The mists let those ships through.'

'Hm,' said Fir. 'That does puzzle me. Why do some ships get here, and most don't? The Heart knows. And the Heart knows Mistmantle can't live entirely cut off from the rest of the world, whatever it consists of.'

'But why Whitewings, of all places?' said Padra. 'Since Husk came to power, we've had more of their ships than we used to.'

'Hm,' said Fir. 'The Heart knows. But what a delightful breakfast, Whittle! That bread does smell delicious.'

'And I brought fish for Captain Padra,' said Whittle eagerly. He hadn't been sure how much fish to bring, so he'd made sure there was plenty. He quickly removed a squirrel hair from the butter and hoped they hadn't seen it.

'That's very thoughtful of you, Whittle,' said Padra, noticing that Whittle had brought enough fish for a whole family of otters. 'Perhaps I can take some to Lady Arran.'

'And how is she?' enquired Fir, pouring hot cordials into beakers.

'Cross, and longing for it all to be over,' said Padra with a shrug. 'Mother Huggen says it's twins, but Arran won't believe that till she sees it. Lovely hot cordial, Whittle.' When he had finished breakfast he wandered down to the Spring Gate and offered fish to Arran, but she turned uneasily in the nest and said she didn't want it.

'Go away,' she muttered, so he did. When he had gone, she sent for Mother Huggen.

Leaving the tower, Gleaner found a door to bang and banged it loudly, twice, hoping it would wake somebody up. She'd argued herself breathless with those guards and they wouldn't let her near Lord Treeth. They even said she wouldn't want to see what Lord Treeth had done to Lady Aspen's chamber, and she had hotly replied that they didn't want to see what she'd do to Lord Treeth, either.

She hurried round the tower, ignoring Mother Huggen and Lugg's daughter, Moth, who were bustling towards the Spring Gate. As soon as Lord Treeth was allowed out of that chamber, she'd be waiting for him.

Chapter 18

Urchin sat in the round, firelit chamber with Juniper at his side and Cedar and Flame facing him. Everything had become very quiet, but it was a humming quiet, like the vibration where a note has been struck.

'The first thing you need to understand,' said Cedar, 'is that I don't come from this island, but I can't remember the place that I do come from, not clearly. It was an island called Ashfire because the mountain at the centre of it was said to be a fire mountain, but everyone thought it was a dead one.'

'Excuse me,' said Urchin, 'what's a fire mountain?'

'It's a mountain that heats up inside until it bursts,' said Cedar. 'It's so hot it melts itself and pours down in boiling rivers, then there's ash everywhere. I can't remember much about it. I can only remember shouting and the red glow, and my father picking me up and running to a boat – we all left our island for ever, and settled in different places. Some of us came to Whitewings, which was all right in those days. The Ashfire squirrels tended to stay together, and there was one who became my great friend. I can't remember a time when she wasn't there. She was older than I was, and she was like a big sister to me. She used to help look after me when I was small, and I looked up to her. She was lovely. She was the kindest animal I ever knew, and the first to tell me about Mistmantle. She'd never been there, but she'd heard of it and she hoped she'd find a way to go there one day. Urchin, I caught that longing from her. I can remember the way animals would look at her and whisper, because she was Favoured.'

'I'm sorry?' said Urchin.

'She was – well, she was more or less your colour,' said Cedar. 'Here, they talk about a "Marked Squirrel", but on Ashfire, they called it "Favoured".'

Urchin gasped. His fur prickled.

'She wasn't exactly like you,' said Cedar. 'She had red squirrel colour down her spine and it faded into honey colour on either side, and there was more red on her ears and tail than on yours, but the rest of her was your colour. Her name was Almond. There was a lot of interest in her because of the prophecy about a Marked Squirrel being the island's deliverer. Most of the Wise Old Whiskers on the island thought the deliverer would be a male and many said that she had too much red about her to be a Marked Squirrel at all, but all the same, animals were watching Almond. A lot of the healing skills that I learned came from her and her family.

'When the queen died Larch was next in line, but she was a small child then and Silverbirch became Regent. At first, he wasn't too bad. He was temperamental and very keen on mining for silver, but nothing like the way he is now. But he grew worse and worse, and animals began to leave the island. Almond would have helped him – his mind needed healing – but he wouldn't have it. We had an excellent, gifted young priest. His name was Candle, and animals still talk about him. He was already training Flame, but the king wouldn't listen to priests, only to Smokewreath.'

'Excuse me,' said Urchin, 'but I don't understand about Smokewreath and his magic. I mean, is it really magic? Does he really have power, or do they just think he has?'

'It's a good question,' said Flame. 'Certainly he has that extra dimension – he's aware of things that most animals aren't. You could call it a sixth sense. But lots of animals have that, and it doesn't make them into sorcerers. In Smokewreath's case, it's enough to make the king think that he is. Whether his magic, and all his poking about with dead bodies, actually does anything, is difficult to prove. But I'll tell you what I do know. Firstly, the king believes in it, and that gives Smokewreath power over him. And I do know that evil is at work in Smokewreath and through him. But evil is at work through lots of animals, unfortunately, like Granite and the king, without anything magical about it.'

'I see,' said Urchin.

'The king was fascinated by the magic, and feared it, too,' continued Cedar. 'It's always the same with magic – animals think it's a power they can control, but they find out too late that the magic controls them. But you want to know about Almond. When the rest of her family left the island, she stayed. She could have tried to reach Mistmantle, but she stayed.'

Urchin was about to ask why, but Cedar went on.

'Smokewreath convinced the king that whenever all was well on the island, it was because of his horrible magic and if things were going wrong, it was because he needed to do more magic. Whatever else he was doing, he was destroying the king's mind. Brother Candle could have left the island, but he felt he had to stay and do his best to protect the animals from Smokewreath, and because Candle stayed, Almond stayed. Candle and Almond loved each other, and Flame married them in secret. It had to be a secret because the king already mistrusted them both, especially Almond because of her colour. When Almond told me she was expecting a baby we knew the king mustn't find out about it.

'Candle made a prophecy about the baby. He said, "*He will bring down a powerful ruler.*" He didn't know what it meant, but he was sure it came from the Heart. We kept it quiet, but somehow the king heard of it. After that, it was much too dangerous for Candle and Almond to stay any longer, and we had a boat ready for them to leave Whitewings.

'The night they were to escape, Candle couldn't be found. Almond, of course, wouldn't leave without him. Urchin, it was terrible. Candle was found dead at the foot of Eagle Crag next morning, and nobody ever knew whether he fell or was pushed. The islanders were already losing heart. They were the way you see them now, terrified of Smokewreath and the king's archers, with dust from the silver mines draining their health. They were too scared to ask how their priest died. Too many of the king's enemies were being found dead below cliffs, or floating on the water. Some were killed for magic, some escaped. It's all horrible, Urchin, I'm afraid.'

'Yes,' said Urchin, 'but what happened to Almond?'

'First,' said Cedar, 'we took Larch and Flame into hiding and let everyone think they'd escaped. That way, the king wouldn't hunt them down and have them killed. They could have left, but they both felt they had to stay with the animals who needed them. I was young but I was a good healer, so I was safe, and I've stayed safe by pretending to be on Silverbirch's side. I know what's going on at court, and all the time I've been helping the Larchlings. You could say, Urchin, that I'm a traitor.'

'Nobody could call you a traitor,' said Urchin. '*Please*, what happened to Almond?'

'After Candle died, she had to escape before Silverbirch could hunt her down. He wouldn't risk leaving her or her baby alive. When I met her for the last time, she brought me that bracelet. It was a thing that the girl squirrels used to do at the time, exchanging bracelets with our own moulted hair woven into them. She was stowing away on a ship that night. It had been to Mistmantle before, and she hoped it might go there again.'

With a delicate touch she picked up the bracelet, turned it over gently, and laid it down again. Her paw shook. She turned her face away, and there was a pause before she could go on.

'She'd been such a friend, a sister, almost a mother to me, and I wanted so much to go with her. I said she'd need me when the baby was born, but she said Whitewings needed me more. I went down to see the ship sail, and I still wanted so much to be with her.'

Urchin gazed at the bracelet in the box. It held him. His heartbeat quickened.

'The ship was already sailing,' she said. 'And I never saw her again. I never knew whether she got to Mistmantle.'

She did, thought Urchin, his heart beating hard and fast. *Please. She did.*

He gazed at the bracelet as if it had its own story, but it needed his voice to tell it. He imagined a ship arriving on Mistmantle, and a pale squirrel slipping away. His ears prickled. He longed to touch the bracelet, but it lay like a sacred object and the time was not right.

'But,' went on Cedar softly, 'the young who were born that year are about your age, Urchin. Perhaps she did reach Mistmantle.'

The tingling turned into a shiver. Urchin remembered everything he had been told about his coming to Mistmantle – how he fell from the sky, how Padra thought a gull might have dropped him, how his mother had never been found. He tried to speak, and couldn't.

Cedar held out the box to him.

'This belongs to you, Urchin.'

Very gently, with a shaky paw, he picked up the bracelet. It felt stiff with age, and he was afraid of damaging it. He wanted to press it against his cheek and feel that pale squirrel fur as close to his face as it could be – but as so many other animals were there he only held it to his mouth for a second. He thought of going to his nest tonight with the bracelet in his paws. Then he put it back.

'Please will you look after it for me?' he said. His voice was quieter than he meant it to be. 'Only, if I took it and they found it, they might take it away.'

'Of course I will,' said Cedar gently. 'And we'll get you home, Urchin.' Then, as Urchin was still very quiet, she added, 'Would you like to be alone now?'

'Yes please,' said Urchin. It was exactly what he wanted. He didn't even want Juniper's company, or Cedar's. For a little while, he needed to be alone with his own story. 'But perhaps I really am meant to do something for this island. Or perhaps I should, after what you've told me, whether I'm meant to or not.'

'You were brought against your will, by force,' said Brother Flame. 'Nothing good comes of forcing an animal against its heart. And we have a duty to protect you. And besides, Urchin, you need time to take all this in. Would you like to go back to your cell?'

'It's so cold up there!' said Cedar.

'I won't notice,' said Urchin.

Alone in his cell, he stood at the window and looked up into the sky. The moon and stars shone so brightly that the frost beneath them sparkled, and for the first time he felt a pang of love for this island. This was the hard ground his mother and father had walked. The tired, dispirited islanders were the animals his father had died for.

He held his paw to his cheek as if he could still feel the smooth fibres of the bracelet and the softness of squirrel fur.

'Candle,' he said out loud. 'Almond.' He knew their names. He was somebody's son. He remembered the thing that, apart from his colour, singled him out.

He had been born on a night of riding stars. Almond the Favoured Squirrel had come at last to Mistmantle, and the stars had honoured her.

It became too cold to stay at the window any longer. He went back to the nest, pulled the blanket round his shoulders, and snuggled down to sleep.

'Goodnight,' he said.

On Mistmantle Padra lay wide awake, folded round Arran as Arran lay folded round two tiny, curled baby otters. He couldn't help watching constantly, observing their tightly shut eyes, the soft paws pressed against small round faces, the thin down of their first fur. Now and again one of them would wriggle or rub its face or sneeze, and his heart turned over with love. Sooner or later he would have to sleep, but he couldn't sleep yet. He couldn't bear to miss a squirm, or a squeak, or the twitch of a whisker.

They hadn't yet named the little girl, but the boy would be Tide. It was a good water name for an otter and something to do with Urchin. The tides had first brought him to Mistmantle, and maybe they would turn his way again.

Needle, Fingal and Sepia herded the excited little choristers to the song cave. Needle was asking about Arran and Padra's babies, and Fingal said they were boring.

'*Boring?*' said Needle.

'They don't do anything. Except one of them hiccupped. When they're bigger I can take them down the waterslide.'

Sepia and the small squirrels were scampering ahead. There were squeals of delight as they made slides on the frost.

'Too cold for the waterslide today,' said Sepia.

Seeing her cloak, she pounced on it and hugged warmth into it as she waited for Fingal and Needle to catch up.

'It's never too cold for a waterslide,' said Fingal. 'Come on, squeakers, get inside where you won't fall over.'

'We never fall over!' squealed a young squirrel before hitting the ground with a thump. He was trying to explain that he did it on purpose as Needle and Sepia ushered them into the song cave and Needle called sharply, 'Stop!'

The little squirrels froze with wide-eyed fear on their faces and their paws pressed to their sides. Sepia stood still with her paws round the shoulders of the nearest ones.

'What is it?' she whispered urgently.

'Pawprints!' said Needle.

Sepia sighed with relief and bristled with annoyance. 'Is that *all*?' she said. 'Hedgehogs are always coming here.' She steered her choir round the pawprints as she looked down at them. 'There was somebody here the night after we came looking for the Heartstone. I heard something, and there were hedgehog pawprints when I came out. And Sluggen and Crammen were outside.'

'Please, Sepia,' said a small squirrel, 'Fingal says Captain Gorsen brings his girlfriends here.' There were spasms of squeaky giggles.

'It's true!' said another. 'My sister said she saw him coming here.'

Sepia shrugged. 'It's anybody's cave, not just ours. Now, choir. Low voices – that's you, Swish, and Fallow and Grain, on the left. Siskin . . . no, you don't have to stand beside Fallow. I know she's your best friend, but I need you on this side . . .'

It took some time for Sepia to organise the small animals, during which Fingal took to the water, and Needle, curious to know if Gorsen really did take his girlfriends there, explored a cleft in the back of the cave. There was a lot of twisting about and looking over shoulders, and squeals of 'what's she looking for?' and 'ooh, look, he's going in the water', and some squirrels begging to be allowed to play in the water and another one, called Twitch, crying because she didn't want to go in the water and her older sister snapping at her that nobody said she had to, and Twitch crying even more, and somebody asking if they could play 'Find the heir of Mistmantle'.

Finally Sepia tapped her hind paw on the ground for silence and raised a claw to conduct, but they had hardly sung the first note when Needle whispered urgently, 'Sepia! Come here!' She was half-wedged into the cleft in the rock, beckoning furiously.

Sepia sighed quietly. 'What *now*?'

'It's important! Fingal, you too! Quietly!'

She squeezed through an impossibly small gap, said 'Sh!' again, turned sharply right, left and right, and disappeared into almost total darkness. After that, she didn't say 'Sh!', but only found Sepia's paw in the dark and squeezed it, which meant the same thing. From an intake of breath behind her Sepia knew that Fingal was about to speak, so she felt for his mouth and pressed it shut.

She smelt earth, tree roots and stone. The caves must be linked to a tunnel network, and the tree roots had formed a narrow split in the rock ahead of them. Through it, she heard a hedgehog voice. At first it was impossible to understand any words, but from the tone of voice the hedgehog seemed to be giving instructions.

'Throne Room . . .' She heard that clearly, then something about 'attack'. But it couldn't be, surely? Then came the words that made her skin shiver and her fur stand out –

'. . . *when Crispin is dead.*'

She felt her fur bristle, and pressed a paw against her chest. Silently they slipped back the way they had come, back to the dimly lit cave with the chattering squirrels who were now chasing round the cave and daring each other to jump into the water.

'No!' commanded Needle so sharply that they

were instantly still and silent. 'Stay where you are and don't make a sound!'

Needle, Fingal and Sepia huddled together at a little distance. From Fingal's face, even he was taking this seriously. He looked like Padra.

'They're planning to kill the king!' whispered Needle.

'But who'd want to?' said Sepia.

'Whoever they are, they must have found a way to the Throne Room from there,' said Fingal. 'The tunnels must link to the one I found on the other side of the lake. I'll go by water and get to Crispin before them.'

'It would take too long!' said Needle. 'It took all night last time!'

'That's only because I tried to climb back up first, and Hope needed to rest and be carried. We're wasting time.'

'You might get caught,' warned Sepia.

'I might not,' said Fingal, and disappeared down the waterslide.

'I'll go through the trees,' said Sepia. 'I'll be faster than hedgehogs in tunnels.'

'And I'll go through the woods,' said Needle, 'but we should send this lot home first.'

Sepia clapped her paws together. 'No practice today!' she called. 'Something important has to be done. Never mind what, Siskin. Have a race home!'

There were a few squeals of protest, but soon Sepia had left them far behind. Needle bustled them from the cave and towards the wood, trusting the smaller ones to their older brothers and sisters and to Damson, who lived nearby and had come to see what all the squeaking was about. There were still squeaks from those who wanted to go with Sepia, but she was far ahead, bounding and leaping from one bare tree to the next, twisting and balancing with her tail as dry twigs snapped and branches bent and sprang, her breath in clouds of mist around her, stopping only when she absolutely must gasp for breath. The chill winter air hurt her lungs. Never had she flown through the trees so swiftly, never had she raced so furiously over the bare forest floor, never, never before had her paws trembled like this with exhaustion. By the time she reached the tower her throat rasped with thirst and her paws ached and shook.

In the winter afternoon, the light was already low. To exhausted Sepia the walls of Mistmantle Tower looked so forbidding that her courage failed her, but they were the quickest way to the corridor outside the Throne Room. She took a deep breath and gathered herself up for the climb. On the third attempt she managed the leap that sent her clawing and scrambling up the stone, tumbling in through a window and staggering to the corridor where Gorsen and Lumberen stood on duty. They weren't agitated, they weren't fighting off intruders! She wasn't too late!

Crispin sat straight-backed on the throne, his head and tail upright, his paws on the carved arms, his face stern. Brother Fir sat on a low stool beside him. A young mole page, Burr, stood on duty beside a table where wine and biscuits had been set out, a fire crackled low in the grate, and untouched on the hearth lay the sword the envoys had offered to Urchin. Tall, dignified and fierce-eyed, his silver chain about his neck, Lord Treeth stood before Crispin.

'So,' said Crispin patiently, 'you are still complaining of your rooms, your lack of freedom, and the visits of Mistress Tay. Your rooms are amongst the finest on the island. Of course you are not allowed your freedom, after what you did when you had it. As for Mistress Tay, she is a very learned and distinguished otter. You should consider yourself honoured by her company. Doesn't it while away your imprisonment?'

'That is hardly the point, Your Majesty,' said Lord Treeth sternly. 'We should not be captives here at all.'

'The point,' said Crispin, 'is that Urchin of

Mistmantle should not be a captive. Please don't tell me again that he went of his own accord.'

'Now slow down, little Sepia,' said Gorsen outside the Throne Room door, stooping over her with a waft of scented soap. 'Take a deep breath and start again.'

'But there isn't time!' insisted Sepia furiously. 'It's very urgent!'

'So you think you heard hedgehogs, Sepia? Tell me again – this is important – tell me exactly what you heard them say.'

'They said there'd be an attack, and something about "when Crispin is dead",' said Sepia. Lumberen laughed, and she wanted to hit him.

'You're sure of this?' asked Gorsen gravely.

'Yes, I'm sure!' she cried, and beat her paw on the floor.

'Then it doesn't amount to much of a plot, does it?' he said, and smiled kindly. He leant closer, and softened his voice. 'They must have been discussing what happens when His Majesty dies – he will one day, you know – and who would lead us if we were attacked. You've been a brave young squirrel, Sepia, but I don't think there's anything to worry about.'

Sepia burned with embarrassment. Gorsen might be right, and she was a silly young squirrel with too much imagination, turning snippets of gossip into a plot against the king. But it hadn't sounded like a chat between hedgehogs, and she knew every animal had the right to see the king.

'All the same,' she said firmly, 'I want to tell the king at once. We mustn't take chances.'

'No, we mustn't take chances,' agreed Gorsen as his paws closed on her throat.

Crispin offered wine to Lord Treeth and saw him look down his nose at Burr the mole as he poured it. Burr was nervous, and his paw shook so that the wine splashed a little. He mopped at it with a napkin as Lord Treeth gave a low sigh.

'Well done, Burr,' said Crispin to the mole. 'Lord Treeth, if you've nothing else to tell me, the hedgehog on duty will presently escort you back to –'

'My prison?'

'Your chamber,' said Crispin.

Treeth bowed stiffly. 'As Your Majesty wishes,' he said. 'Permit me to drink the health of my king.' He raised his voice. 'King Silverbirch!' With a flourish he drank the wine, then a swift movement of his paw made Crispin reach for his sword hilt.

With a swish and flash of silver Lord Treeth swept a dagger from inside his cloak and hurled himself forwards. A twist of Crispin's sword sent the dagger whirling across the room, but Treeth snatched Urchin's sword from the hearth.

Sepia fought, kicked, scratched, struggled, tried to scream and bit with all her might into the paw that covered her mouth until Gorsen curled over with pain and Sepia pulled hard at his ankle. Voices in the Throne Room shouted for the guards. Off balance, Gorsen fell heavily and Sepia scrambled over him to the door, but Lumberen was through it first. She tried to cry for help, and couldn't. Everything was happening at once. Gleaner was tearing along the corridor and hurling herself at the door, Fir was at the door, then at the window, shouting for help, Lord Treeth was on the floor, grappling with Burr the mole page, Lumberen had drawn a sword from under his cloak and was fighting with Crispin, and as Sepia threw herself biting at Lumberen's sword arm the floor seemed to wobble as if it would give way altogether. Gleaner was pulling Lord Treeth from Burr, digging her claws into his shoulders. Sepia was flung from Lumberen's arm, Crispin stooped to seize Lord Treeth by the scruff of the neck, and turned to aim a blow at Gorsen who had struck at him as Lumberen threw a sword to Lord Treeth. Burr was biting a hedgehog ankle, and from under the floorboards Fingal appeared with a cry of, 'Treason, Your

Majesty!' before launching into the fight. Brother Fir took the tablecloth and threw it over Lord Treeth's head. Fingal, having felled Lumberen with a swish of his tail, turned to the throne and was trying to drag it into place over the hole in the floorboards, but Sluggen was already clambering up into the chamber. Fingal knocked him on the head and he tumbled back down, but more came, some seeming to lose their footing. Docken and a company of moles had run in from the corridor crying, 'Treason! Look to the king!' There were cries and clashes, blood and fur – Padra hurled himself into the room – and suddenly it was over, with Docken, Padra and Crispin holding drawn swords to the throats of Lord Treeth and the rebel hedgehogs. Fingal picked up Gorsen's dropped dagger, looked to see what Padra was doing, and copied him. Brother Fir was attending to Burr the mole, who appeared to be injured and was shaking. Guards blocked the doorway and window, and two of them were struggling to hold back Gleaner as she screamed tearful insults at Lord Treeth.

'Quiet, Gleaner,' ordered Crispin, still breathless from the fight. 'You have done your part bravely, and may rest now.'

'I did it for my lady!' snarled Gleaner.

'I know,' said Crispin. 'Guards, take her and leave her with a sensible squirrel who can calm her down.

Take Lord Treeth, Gorsen and Lumberen here under guard to the Gathering Chamber, and put the rest in cells.'

Padra bowed and gave orders, and the rebels were taken away. Fingal mentioned that there were more of the vermin down there, then vanished down the gap, and bobbed up again to report that the ones he'd knocked down were still there, and a bit bruised.

'Then I will attend to them next,' said Brother Fir calmly, and patted the young mole on the shoulder. 'Bravely done, Burr. What a very good thing you spilt that wine. There was still enough left for the hedge-hogs to slip on.'

'Was that wine?' asked Fingal. 'I thought it was just wet floor from wet otter! Sorry I didn't get here a bit faster, Your Majesty.'

'Loyal and true animals, all of you,' said Crispin, throwing a paw across Fingal's wet shoulders. 'Well done, and thank you. I owe my life to each one of you, and the island owes you more than we can ever know. Burr, well done! Are you hurt? No? We'll have to make sure your family know how brave you've been. Moles, send some fast squirrels to gather together as many of the Circle animals as you can find and send them to the Gathering Chamber, and I need two good tunnelling moles to investigate under the Throne Room.'

Mother Huggen and a team of efficient hedgehogs and moles slipped quietly in to care for the wounded. A silent procession made its way to the Gathering Chamber – guards, Lord Treeth, Gorsen, Lumberen, Fir, Crispin and Docken bleeding from a cut to his paw but insisting that he didn't need help.

'I'll join you presently,' called Padra. Fingal, who hadn't been in the Throne Room often, was lying on his back under the throne to inspect it from underneath.

'Fingal, get out of there,' ordered Padra. 'You're in the royal Throne Room now, not a cave at low tide.' Fingal wriggled out. 'You'll be needed in the Gathering Chamber.'

'Good!' said Fingal.

'Well, move, then!' said Padra, and, as Fingal lolloped away, he added, 'Well done, you.'

Fingal grinned back over his shoulder. 'I enjoyed it,' he said.

Padra called back one of the guards. 'We'll need Mistress Tay,' he said, 'and that other Whitewings squirrel, Scatter, just in case she knows anything. And Whittle, as he's learning law and history. He should be there. Sepia, would you –' But as he turned he saw tears standing in Sepia's eyes, and knelt before her in concern.

'Sepia!' he said. 'You've been so brave, and I'm neglecting you! Are you hurt?'

Sepia put her hands to her throat.

'Can't . . .' she whispered hoarsely, and struggled painfully to swallow, '. . . he tried to strangle me, and . . .'

'You can't speak?' said Padra.

'Sing,' whispered Sepia, and sobbed with heart-break into Padra's shoulder.

The Gathering Chamber had hardly been used lately, and though somebody had hastily made up a fire the air was still forbiddingly cold. The gallery built for the Hedgehog Host was conspicuously new and empty. Dust sheets covered the chairs brought in for the coronation and the new Threadings, but a Threading of a young female squirrel with a circlet on her head hung uncovered outside the doorway, looking serenely across at them. Crispin's eyes flickered towards it as he took his place on the dais in a grim, cold silence. Tay had been sent for and stood rigidly upright with Scatter beside her. She glared across the room at Fingal, clearly annoyed at his presence. Whittle stayed two paces behind Brother Fir, to the right. Padra and Sepia arrived, Sepia trying not to cry, Padra stern and tight-lipped, slipping to the dais to whisper something to Crispin.

Before the dais stood Lord Treeth, Gorsen and Lumberen, their forepaws tied, each one attended by a guard with a drawn sword. The Circle animals, stern-faced, stood in an arc around them. Mother Huggen, having attended the wounded, took her place among them, and when all were gathered, Crispin spoke.

'Gorsen,' he said slowly, 'Lord Treeth, and the rest of you who took arms against me and my subjects today, you have endangered the peaceful animals of Mistmantle. Gorsen, you attempted the murder of our young and loyal Sepia. You were one of our most trusted animals, nurtured by Mistmantle all your life. Explain yourself.'

Gorsen cleared his throat and drew himself up.

'I am delighted to, Crispin,' he said. 'Pardon me if I don't call you Your Majesty, but, of course, you're nothing of the kind. You're only a twitch-tail squirrel. I believe in some places they're called tree-rats.'

Padra's paw was on his sword, but he watched Crispin.

'Go on, Gorsen,' said Crispin calmly.

'The only kings of Mistmantle are hedgehogs,' said Gorsen. 'For generations, we had hedgehog kings and the island was well-governed. King Brushen was the last. His son was murdered by a squirrel. Who brought King Brushen down? Husk and Aspen. Squirrels. And,' he raised his voice, slowing down the words for impact, 'Husk the Squirrel encouraged the king to cull the young! Husk the Squirrel forced us into underground labour in far corners of the island! All our woes have been caused by squirrels!'

'May I interrupt?' said Brother Fir mildly. 'They were caused by only two squirrels, Husk and Aspen. Crispin the Squirrel and Padra the Otter freed you.'

'They were only doing their duty as captains,' said Gorsen loftily. 'I have no complaint about that. They were adequate captains. But having freed the island from a tyrannous false murdering squirrel, they made another squirrel king.'

'You are at fault,' came a clear, stern female voice, and Tay stepped forwards with a frown that made her strong dark whiskers stand out more than ever. 'Nobody *made* Crispin king. Under the laws of Mistmantle, he was next in line to the throne. His suitability for the crown might be questioned, but his right to it cannot.'

'Thank you, Tay,' said Crispin.

Gorsen cast a glance of contempt at Tay. 'This is what I'd expect from an otter,' he said loftily. 'Otters are only fit for splashing about in streams, just as squirrels are only fit for fetching and carrying. Moles are quite happy if they're kept underground, and they don't talk much because no mole ever has anything worth saying. Hedgehogs are creatures of the earth. We take life at a sensible pace. We have dignity and understanding. King Brushen was a true king, a good king. Who can respect a king with . . .' he gave a snort of laughter, 'a bushy tail and tufted ears? A king who runs up trees? Those who fought against Crispin the squirrel today – myself, Lumberen, Sluggen, Crammen and our supporters – were sworn to a secret brotherhood of hedgehogs, and not even our closest families and colleagues knew our plans. You needn't think the rest of the Hedgehog Host had a look-in. We were a very select band, only ten of us altogether, but we swore we wouldn't rest until we had a hedgehog on the throne again. We were few, we were brave, we were determined, we were loyal to our own kind. We would have given our heart's blood for our cause.'

'And what cause was that, Gorsen?' asked Fir.

'Simply to kill the upstart Crispin and all who tried to defend him,' said Gorsen, and smirked. 'You gave me the most wonderful opportunity, Crispin, when you set me to guard Lord Treeth. Great lordly hedgehog that he is, he treated me like a brother. He told me about Whitewings, and that's a place where hedgehogs are given proper respect. I made a pact with him. I would be king of Mistmantle, under King

Silverbirch, and Mistmantle would become a sensible, well-run island, like Whitewings. We thought we might even send slaves to Whitewings, as a sign of our loyalty. You didn't have an idea, Crispin, did you? It's all your fault, of course. You sent me to guard Lord Treeth. I heard your conversations. You even put me in charge of blocking the space under the Throne Room!'

'We trusted you,' said Padra.

'Yes, that's what I'd expect from an otter,' said Gorsen. 'It's the water that gets to your brains. As for squirrels, I suppose it's all those fir cones that damage your thinking.'

Crispin rose and walked to Gorsen very slowly, looking the hedgehog in the eyes. Even Sepia, who loved and trusted Crispin, felt afraid.

'Gorsen,' he said very softly, 'you have betrayed your own islanders. You have sent our good and loyal moles to their death, and left Urchin of the Riding Stars in an enemy prison. You have harmed and endangered our young. You have betrayed the hedgehog kind and led your companions into rebellion. And all because you think hedgehogs are superior, and no kind on this island is superior. If you had succeeded, the creatures of Mistmantle would have hated all hedgehogs for generations to come just because of the bitterness of ten hedgehogs who wanted their own way.'

Gorsen tried to look Crispin in the eyes, and couldn't. Crispin stepped nearer, and he flinched.

'Take him away,' ordered Crispin, 'and Lumberen, and Lord Treeth. Put them in cells and keep them well guarded.' The guards bowed and led the procession away.

From the doorway came a last shout. 'Death to Crispin!'

'Oh, be quiet,' said Padra wearily. Docken remained on guard. Sepia stayed close to Padra, and Fir was saying something to young Whittle. Still in her place beside Tay, Scatter stood very still and tense with her eyes wide and her claws curled.

'We still don't know how they got their message to Whitewings,' said Padra. 'There are no moles missing. Nobody at all.'

'Except . . .' said Crispin.

'Juniper,' said Padra. Sepia tugged hard at his paw and shook her head.

'I hope it wasn't him,' said Padra. 'But we have to consider it.'

Scatter left Tay's side at last. She hopped shyly forwards, stopped at a little distance from Crispin, curtsied, and took a deep breath.

'Please, Your Majesty,' she said. She fidgeted a little, then put her paws firmly behind her back and stood up straight. 'I think I know how they did it.'

'Go on,' said Crispin gently.

'Your Majesty,' she said earnestly, 'I was the youngest court squirrel on our island. I thought it was such an honour to be sent with the ambassadors, and I was pleased with myself for lying to you, even though I thought I'd be found out. I thought you'd send me to some terrible dungeon, but at least I was serving my island! Whitewings isn't a bit like Mistmantle. If I'd known, I mean, if I'd known what you were all like, and what Mistmantle's like, I wouldn't have done it, and I wish you had Urchin back, and I'm very sorry for everything I did, but I thought it was the right thing to do.

'Lord Treeth and the others were all very important, but I wasn't. I was . . . what's that word? Expendable. They didn't tell me everything they planned, but I think I've worked it out now.

'There was a hedgehog on Whitewings called Creeper, and he was a spy. There were lots of rumours about him, and I don't know how much was true – about him creeping up on animals and stabbing them or pushing them off cliffs. He was strong, but what made him a good spy was that he was very small for an adult, with small bones, and he could squash himself into hiding places where nobody would think of looking. When we came here on the boat Lord Treeth insisted on having a cabin to himself so that three of us had to squeeze into a cabin for two. And when his chest was brought on shore, he was most particular about how it was carried, and he insisted on unpacking it, though he doesn't normally do anything for himself.'

'I remember seeing them struggle to carry it, Your Majesty,' observed Docken.

'So I think maybe Creeper was in there,' went on Scatter. 'He would have come specially to report to King Silverbirch if there was anything he needed to know. Oh.' She stopped suddenly. 'Only he couldn't have got back, could he?'

'From what you say, he could have got through mole tunnels,' said Crispin. 'But without our moles seeing him? And in time to warn the king?'

'Excuse me, Your Majesty,' said Fingal, 'but there used to be a boat by the waterfall and there isn't now. Sorry, I didn't think it was important.'

'There's no reason why you should have thought so, Fingal,' said Crispin. 'Nobody would have thought anything of it. Could Creeper have rowed all that way, all by himself?'

'I'm sure he could, Your Majesty,' said Scatter, and went on nervously, 'Please, Your Majesty?'

'Yes, Scatter,' said Crispin.

'You were good to me, even though you knew I

was lying. I had a nice chamber, and sometimes you let me out in the sunshine and I could see Mistmantle. Nothing on Whitewings is so beautiful – it's hard and dusty there, and miserable. Not like here, where animals can play in waterfalls, and whatever work they're doing, they seem to enjoy it. Mistress Tay came every day, and sometimes she just told me the laws, but other times she told me the stories, and they were such good stories, even . . . um . . .'

'. . . even the way Tay told them,' whispered Fingal to Sepia.

'. . . anyway, I don't know if you'll believe me, and I don't care,' she went on quickly. 'I never knew there was anywhere as wonderful as this, so green and leafy and free, and I never knew what that was like. And I swear if I'd known what they were planning, I would have told you.'

She stopped for breath, and knelt down.

'Please, I would like to stay, Your Majesty,' she said. 'Even if you put me in a cell for ever. Even if I'm given the hardest work and the loneliest, coldest part of the island. And I will be Your Majesty's faithful servant, but please, Your Majesty, let me stay.'

'I will consider it, Scatter, in good time,' said Crispin. 'In the meantime, you will be escorted back to your chamber.'

'Yes, Your Majesty,' she said, and was led away looking very small between two otters. Most of the remaining animals were dismissed. Crispin sent for drinks and sat down on the floor with Sepia, Padra, Fingal, Docken and Fir.

Sepia sipped at her spiced wine, but swallowing hurt and she tried to hold back the tears. She didn't want anyone thinking she'd cry over a sore throat.

'Sepia,' said Crispin, 'is something the matter?'

'Gorsen tried to silence the sweetest voice on the island,' said Padra tersely.

'Shall I take a look at it?' offered Mother Huggen, and ushered Sepia from the Gathering Chamber. Crispin turned to Docken.

'You fought against your own comrades to save me,' he said.

'No comrades of mine, Your Majesty,' said Docken gruffly. 'Your Majesty, most of the Hedgehog Host are true to you. It's just a few of them turned bad.'

'I know you for a loyal animal,' said Crispin. 'We had already considered you for the Circle. You will be enrolled when Urchin returns.'

'Oh, Your Majesty!' said Docken as a broad smile spread across his face. 'I hope it's all right to tell Thripple?'

'You may tell her now, if you like,' said Crispin,

and Docken bowed deeply and hurried away. 'Fingal?'

'Oh, hello!' said Fingal.

'Well done, valiant otter,' said Crispin.

'Any time, you're welcome,' said Fingal. 'May I go for a swim now?'

'Show respect to the king, Fingal,' said Padra quietly, but Crispin laughed.

'Go and catch a fish, Fingal,' he said.

At last only he, Padra and Fir were left.

'I'm glad Juniper's in the clear,' said Crispin. 'I wonder about Scatter. Is she telling the truth, or is she up to something?'

'I wish I knew,' said Padra.

'Give her time,' said Fir. 'We'll know. As to Gorsen and his friends, they had grown bitter in their long slavery and fed each other's resentment. It was easy for Lord Treeth to harness their bitterness. They needed a target for their hatred, and it was you, because you are the king.'

'May the Heart help me,' said Padra, 'but when he stood there, so cool and arrogant, I could have run him through.'

'But neither of you laid a paw on him,' said Fir. 'That's nobility. To be able to strike out in anger, and not do it.' He smothered a yawn, and limped to the window. 'Dark already. Urchin's lights on the water.

Hm. Moonlight, firelight, the secret.'

'Do you yet have any idea what that means?' asked Padra.

'No,' he said. 'But it's getting closer.' He leant closer to the window. 'Well, bless me!'

Padra and Crispin jumped to their paws. 'What is it?'

'Snow,' he said.

Chapter 19

Needle arrived when everything was over. Crispin told her all that had happened, and she went to find Sepia who was on her way out of the tower. In the twilight they huddled their cloaks around them and stood on the stair.

Snow. Sepia would not have said anything, even if she could. She felt the magic of snow in her heart, and held it. Against the violet sky with its mist and cloud, soft flakes of snow drifted lazily to the ground. They settled on ledges and rails, gentle as feather, silent as prayer. They touched fur and whiskers, paws and noses.

Arran left the babies curled in their own warmth in the safety of the nest and wriggled her way to the Spring Gate. Raising her head, she sniffed the air and watched the snow. Padra, on his way back from the Gathering Chamber, wondered where to start in telling her all that had happened. He stood still as the snow fell round him, and offered a prayer for Urchin.

At a high window, Scatter pressed her paws against the crisscross panes. Snow on Mistmantle. Perhaps she'd be allowed outside for a little while tomorrow. On an island like this, they might let you play in the snow. And perhaps she could find a way to make herself useful. Anything, if only they'd let her stay and not send her back to Whitewings. *Please, please, let me stay*, she whispered, though she didn't know who to.

Apple had spent the day with Damson, who was still fretting over Juniper. Now Apple was running home through the woods, pulling her old green cloak about her, head down against the snow, ducking into her tree-stump home, lighting a fire with shivering paws, opening a bottle of cordial.

'That's good strong warming stuff, though I say it myself, puts the fur on your ears,' she muttered to herself. She pushed the stopper back into the bottle. 'And may the Heart bring my Urchin home, before this weather gets any worse.' Gazing into the fire she hugged herself, praying warmth for Urchin.

With a lantern in his paw Whittle knocked at the chamber of Brother Fir's turret room, heard no answer, and looked in. The priest lay sprawled on his bed fast asleep, still in his old tunic. Whittle found a cloak and gently spread it over him. Every day he looked forward to his lessons. Brother Fir was going to tell him about the Old Palace of the moles, and how the old routes were being closed, and new ones made. Even more exciting, he was going to tell him stories of those rare occasions – so rare that most animals didn't live to see one – when the mists changed and moved, and all manner of wonderful things happened at such times. But it would have to wait. It had been a long and troubling day. Fast asleep, even Brother Fir looked vulnerable. Whittle said a prayer silently, tiptoed out, and slipped back in again to pick up his lantern, which he had forgotten.

At the Fortress on Whitewings, Bronze leant over the battlements and watched Cedar. It had been difficult to spy on her, as he had to traipse to the mines every day while she had a cushy posting at the Fortress. But sooner or later, she'd make a mistake and visit the Freak once too often. Surely he couldn't need washing that much? Next time she tried it, he'd catch her out.

He hoped it would be soon. He was looking forward to destroying her. It would be worth doing, just to see her disgraced and killed. And before long, he'd be Commander Bronze. Or Lord Marshall Bronze. Why not?

Urchin had been locked in his bare cell all day. Now that there was nowhere in there for another squirrel to hide, Juniper stayed with the Larchlings. To Urchin, the lonely days seemed everlasting. In spite of the discovery of silver the king seemed to hate the very sight of him, and usually went to the mines without him. Bored, restless and alone, he had scratched squares on the floor so he could play First Five, but he had to play his right paw against his left and pretend not to know what the next move would be. At least it distracted him from the window. Sooner or later it would snow, and Smokewreath would claim him.

Cedar had managed to convince the king that the Marked Squirrel was a delicate creature who would die if he became cold, leaving a curse on the island and depriving Smokewreath of the pleasure of killing him, so he was allowed a fire. Tired of feeling that window like a menacing ghost at his back, he put down his pawful of pebbles and crossed the room towards it. If it snowed, it snowed. The Larchlings might come for him . . .

The door banged open. Urchin whirled round.

It's too late. They're coming for me.

'The Marked Squirrel to the king!' shouted Trail, and Urchin was marched down to the vast, silvered chamber where flickering logs in the fireplace made the only brightness in the room. King Silverbirch sat proudly enthroned, with Granite and Smokewreath behind him on either side. It was reassuring to see Cedar by the fireplace, even though she wore her Commander's helmet and he didn't dare look at her directly.

The wild joy in the king's face was startling and appalling. He strode dramatically to the fireplace, swirled off his cloak and flashed a smile so bright it was terrifying.

'You did it, Freak!' cried the king. 'Such silver!' He rushed at Urchin and grasped his shoulders, beaming into his face. 'We'd nearly given up, but we kept following that seam you found. Oh, you wonderful Freak! Such silver! Such gleaming, glimmering, wonderful silver, the very best and finest silver, and so *much*! You must see it yourself, Urchin, you absolutely must! It's so beautiful!' He waved a paw impatiently at the servants. 'Fetch him wine! Fetch him cake! Fetch him a cloak, fetch him jewellery! You must see it, this lovely silver. Too dark now, too dark. But you will, you will.'

There was a rattle and a hiss from Smokewreath.

'Oh, yes, Smokewreath, you can have him,' he snapped. 'He's done what we wanted! He's found all that lovely silver for us. But the snow hasn't fallen yet, so you'll have to wait for him!'

Urchin curled his claws. It was bad enough that they wanted to kill him, without bickering like two small squirrels over a hazelnut.

'Shall I sharpen a sword for you, Smokewreath, so you're ready when the time comes?' said Granite, looking Urchin up and down. 'Or do you want an archer to follow him around?'

'We should kill him sooner, not later,' snarled Smokewreath. 'He's done all he had to do.'

'We could leave him on the battlements to freeze,' suggested Granite. He stood back with folded arms and regarded Urchin. 'He's only a runt, it should finish him off. But I'm sure you'd rather have the pleasure of putting a knife through his heart. Or would you rather have a dagger?'

Smokewreath hissed softly through his teeth. 'I need his heart whole, whole,' he said. 'Strong magic.'

'I do beg your pardon, sir,' said Granite. 'I was forgetting the strong magic. Did you hear that, O High Splendour of Silver? The sooner he gets his strong magic done, the sooner you can invade Mistmantle.'

Urchin gasped. He turned hot and cold and tried to say that Mistmantle couldn't be invaded, but his voice failed him. It was too terrible for words.

'Invade Mistmantle?' said Cedar sharply from the fireplace. 'Pardon me, High Splendour of Silver, I knew nothing of this!'

'Oh, Lord Marshall!' pouted the king. 'That was my tell! There you are, you see, not even Commander Cedar knew of it, only you and me and dear Smokewreath. But soon, everyone will know. Won't it be wonderful?' He turned his glittering eyes on Urchin. 'You said yourself that an island should have good earth and trees, and all those lovely things, and I'm going to have them. Smokewreath's magic will get me to Mistmantle! With a little help from you.'

Urchin started to say that he would defend Mistmantle and Crispin with every breath he took for the rest of his life, but Smokewreath hissed at him.

'Such strong magic, from the Marked Squirrel,' he rasped. 'From that fur, from those claws, from the bones, from the heart. Strong enough even to pierce those mists, oh, yes.'

Urchin's claws stretched and curled. His fur bristled. 'You're all wrong about that,' he said, and hoped with all his heart that he was right. 'Your magic isn't stronger than the Heart that gave us the mists.'

'Oh, what a pity you won't be alive to find out,' said the king, and gave a shriek of laughter. 'Isn't it delightful! Just think of King Crispin's face, when he sees the mists parting and my beautiful ship sailing to Mistmantle! And all my moles will run through the tunnels . . . what fun!'

'Even if you could get through the mists,' said Urchin, 'you wouldn't take Mistmantle. Every animal on the island –'

'Will support me,' said the king. 'I should think they already do. Creeper brought back such an interesting report from Mistmantle when he came to tell me about those little rescue moles. He said there were hedgehogs on the island all ready to turn on the king and kill him.'

'No!' cried Urchin.

The king waved a paw. 'They've probably done it by now,' he said with a shrug. 'Take the Freak away. Lock him up.'

'They'll never turn –' cried Urchin, and was dragged back to his cell. It had already been beautifully furnished again and he kicked the cushions, strode to the window and clutched the bars tightly, defying the threat of snow. Help from Crispin might be on the way, and Cedar must be planning something. There was still hope. There had to be.

Of course the Mistmantle hedgehogs wouldn't

turn on Crispin. Or would they? There must still be animals on the island who had supported Husk. Crispin could be dead or in terrible danger, and here he was, in a tiny turret room, surrounded by cushions.

Granite returned to his bare chamber, where swords and daggers hung on the walls and empty bottles littered the table. Creeper slipped in beside him.

'You wanted me, Lord Marshall?' he whispered.

Granite took a small silver dagger from the wall. 'Yours to keep,' he said, 'and a bottle of best spirit when it's done. I want Bronze out of the way tonight. More trouble than he's worth.'

The night on Mistmantle was still with the hush of snow as King Crispin knocked at the door of Fir's turret. There was no answer.

'Fir?' He knocked again, fairly certain that Fir was in there, but there was still no response. Cautiously, he opened the door.

The only light came from the bright fire in the grate, and there was a warm fragrance of spice and apple logs. The fire cast flickering, dancing lights on the bare walls, on the plain table with its beaker and plate, on the low stools, on the neat little bed, and on the figure of the priest at the open window as he leant out into the night sky, turning his head one way and the other. Crispin stepped in softly and shut the door without a sound.

Fir closed the window and hobbled to the next without a sign as to whether he had noticed Crispin or not. He leant out, looking at the stars, then pottered on to the next window, and the next. Finally he closed the last one, nodded at Crispin, and limped to the fire where he put a pan of berry cordial on to heat, and bent to warm his paws. He picked up a second beaker from the hearth.

'I want to ask you about our prisoners,' said Crispin. 'Gorsen, Lumberen, Sluggen, Crammen, the rest. What do you think is the best way to deal with them?'

'Hm,' said Fir, who appeared to be thinking of something else. 'Let them cool off.'

'And then?'

'Then we'll see.' He scurried to the window again, looked up, smiled as if he had recognised a friend, and came back counting on his claws.

'One, two, three . . . four . . . five?' he said as if he were thinking aloud. 'Four or five nights, and we shall have riding stars.'

A shiver of fear and hope ran through Crispin. However many of these nights he had seen, they still thrilled and fascinated him. But would the stars ride for good or for harm? It was no good asking Fir. Not even he knew that. But they always meant something, and now, there was so much for them to ride for.

'Moonlight, firelight, and the secret,' muttered Fir and knelt by the hearth, rocking slightly, his paws on his knees and his eyes shut. Crispin couldn't be sure whether he was thinking about the words or repeating them in a mystical state, or just an old squirrel drooping into sleep by a fire on a winter night.

Chapter 20

uard duty on the battlements again. Everyone else, including Granite, was celebrating finding all that silver, and Bronze was supposed to guard the battlements. He'd rather guard the Freak in case Cedar turned up. If she didn't, he could at least march about outside the door talking loudly about snow and rusty knives, and make sure the Freak didn't sleep well. As he was here, he may as well look for any sign of snow.

The hedgehog on relief guard should be here by now. He was late. When he did arrive, Bronze snarled at him.

'You're late, you useless idle scrubbing brush,' he said.

'Not my fault,' grunted the guard. 'Commander Cedar was giving orders about the Freak.'

'Cedar!' said Bronze. He took a step forward. His spines bristled.

'Yeah,' said the hedgehog. 'I had to cover for her while she went to his cell.'

In wild triumph, Bronze pushed past him and hurtled down the stairs, not seeing the small, sleek shadow of Creeper. There was a sharp cold pain in his neck, then a hot rush of blood. It was the last thing he felt.

On guard at the cell door, Trail paced impatiently about. She was on duty with an elderly guard who'd drunk too much and couldn't stay awake. When Commander Cedar came to see the prisoner, she didn't feel like being pleasant.

'The Freak needs grooming before Smokewreath gets him,' said Cedar.

Trail drew herself up. She was taller than the Commander.

'I've orders not to let anyone in,' she said. 'And if you could take him, you wouldn't be allowed to go alone with him. You should be escorted.'

'You should be demoted,' said Cedar, nodding at the drowsy guard. 'Trail, I'm doing you a favour. If Smokewreath comes up here – and believe me, he will, at the first trace of a snowflake – and finds the Freak isn't washed and ready for him, you'll be the next one for the knife. At the very least, you won't be in the Inner Watch any longer.'

Trail hesitated. 'Can't you bring everything up here and wash him in his cell?' she said. 'I can send someone for a tub of hot water.'

In the cell, Urchin stood with his ear pressed against the door, listening to the argument and biting his lip. There must be something he could do to make Trail unlock the door. The fire was still burning in the grate. If he could make enough smoke to convince her that the cell was on fire, she'd have to come in and rescue him – but she'd bring the whole Inner Watch running, too. Cedar was probably quite capable of overpowering Trail if she wanted to, but she wouldn't want to. It must be part of her plan to make it look as if she was meant to lead him from the cell, as she had done before, and nobody would question it.

They were still arguing, and it sounded as if Trail was weakening. If Cedar was trying to persuade her that he should be washed, it might help if he looked as if he needed it. He glanced sharply round the cell.

The ashes in the grate might still be hot. He hopped to the fire, and used a stick from the log basket to scrape them out in a thin layer. Warily he touched them and found them warm, but not too hot to touch. He dug his paws into them, rubbed his face, and in the most desperate, pleading and urgent voice he could, yelled, *'Help me!'*

The lock clanked. Trail and Cedar rushed in. Urchin stood before them, black and grey ashes smeared on his fur, his face, his paws. He coughed harshly.

'Fell in the grate,' he gasped.

'You lying little Freak, you've been trying to escape up the chimney!' snarled Cedar. 'Come with me!' She grabbed the scruff of his neck and dragged him past Trail. 'Trail, I'll be as quick as I can and get him back to you before they send for him. In the meantime, get this lot cleaned up, the filthy Freak's spread the soot everywhere. If the king sees this, he'll have your hide for a hearthrug.' Before she had finished speaking, they were out of the door.

She had dragged him halfway along the corridor before she whispered, 'Well done.' Then the sound they had both dreaded made them freeze. The doors of the High Chamber were opening. King Silverbirch laughed.

'Run!' whispered Cedar. She dashed for a door, pushed Urchin through it, and sprang after him as paws and voices sounded on the stairs.

In the Presence Chamber of King Silverbirch, heavy silver-grey curtains had shut out the night. Fire blazed in the hearth, crackling, leaping, casting an angry light into the shining floor and on the silvering of robes, furniture, goblets. Torches threw flame and shadow over King Silverbirch as he talked to himself and fidgeted.

A few senior animals were still there, growing drowsy among the remnants of a banquet and empty flagons. Lord Marshall Granite sprawled in a chair, called for more wine, and punched the hedgehog who brought it. Smokewreath hugged his knees as he sat by the fire, muttering. The servants stayed as quiet as they could. Late at night with the mad king, the evil sorcerer and the bullying Lord Marshall, it was best not to be noticed.

'Build with it,' the king was muttering. 'So much silver! Trade with it, buy weapons with it. Yes. Swords, make swords, buy swords, daggers, chairs, manacles, helmets. No, too good for helmets and manacles. Do you want an armoury, Lord Marshall?'

'I *am* an armoury,' grunted Granite.

'I want to see my new silver mine,' said the king again. 'I don't care if it's too cold to work. I just want to see it. I want to touch it.' He wriggled with impatience. 'I want it to be day!' Jumping from the throne, he strode to the window.

'Curtain!' he snapped. A squirrel darted forwards

to open the curtains and the king gave a gasp of joy.

'It's snowing!' he cried. With his ears pricked, Smokewreath leapt up. 'Snowing! Granite! Come here!'

Granite trudged unwillingly to the window. 'Plague and fire, so it is,' he growled.

'The sky is saluting me!' cried the king. 'I am the Splendour of Silver, and the sky itself honours me!'

Bones clattered as Smokewreath scuttled across the floor. He looked up at the king with a wild pleading in his face.

'Splendid Majesty,' he said, in a voice that was almost a purr. 'You promised me. You promised I could have him when the snow fell. I have waited so long.'

'Good idea,' said Granite. 'Your Majesty's not safe as long as that Freak's around.'

'Oh, but really . . .' began the king.

'Your Majesty is the Splendour of Silver,' purred Smokewreath, 'and with the magic I will work from his heart and blood, you will be the same for ever. The Everlasting Splendour of Silver. Undying Splendour. King of Whitewings and of Mistmantle, for ever.'

'I can't wait,' said the king. 'Oh, but I'll be so sorry to part with the little Freak. I'd become fond of it. But I did promise.' He strode to the doors, and barked with laughter as the servants flung them open. 'Follow me!'

Eager and fast, the procession made its way up the stairs. Smokewreath beat with his staff at every step, muttering 'Kill the Freak' with the rhythm of his footsteps. The other animals took it up, a quiet, menacing chant. They were Fortress animals. They had served the king well, and deserved a death. *Kill the Freak! Kill the Freak!*

Trail appeared at the cell door. She was rubbing ashes from her paws.

'Commander Cedar has just taken him for his wash, O High Splendour of Silver,' she said, bowing. 'She won't be long. She said Smokewreath wanted him washed before the sacrifice.'

Smokewreath said nothing, but gave a low, rattling growl and shuddered. Trail dared not look at the king.

'I did question it,' she said nervously, 'but she's a Commander and I had to obey orders. And he did badly need a wash.'

'Smokewreath,' snarled the king, 'did you order him washed?'

Smokewreath found his voice, low and menacing as the hiss of a snake. 'I did not. I said nothing to Commander Cedar. I smell treachery.'

The king spun round with his cloak swishing and mad fury in his eyes. 'Find him!' he screamed. 'All of you! Find him! And find Cedar! Bring her to me! I will tear her apart with my own claws!'

Cedar dragged Urchin on through tunnels, round corners, squeezing underground. From above them came sounds of running paws and shouted orders.

'The hunt is on,' she whispered breathlessly. 'But our route to the coast is quicker than theirs. Keep going.' They emerged at last in the underground chamber where Urchin had met the Larchlings. Larch and Flame were there with pale, set faces, and Lugg and Juniper, cloaked and ready for a journey.

Cedar threw a cloak round him. 'Pale grey for camouflage,' she said. We've made a small boat ready for you, next to the ship in the harbour.' She buckled a sword round his waist, and somebody hung a satchel over his shoulder. 'It's a fair wind, you'll have a swift run to Mistmantle. We'll get you to the shore.'

'What about getting through the mists?' asked Urchin.

'We did what you suggested,' said Cedar with a bright smile. 'A group of the Larchlings went down and freed the swans. They can go with you as far as the mists, then carry you over.'

'Cedar and I will go through the tunnels first,' said Larch. 'We know the routes. Then Urchin and Juniper, and Flame and Lugg will follow.'

'And defend you if need be,' said Lugg. 'Very good, Your Majesty.'

Following Larch and Cedar, they ran. Little was said apart from Lugg exclaiming about the size and structure of the tunnels and the Whitewings squirrels explaining that these weren't really tunnels, they were burrows.

'Nice burrows, then,' said Lugg, then stopped.

'Quickly, Lugg,' ordered Cedar.

'Sh!' said Lugg, and flattened himself on the ground, his ear down and his face grim with concentration. He scrambled up and listened at the wall. Urchin and Juniper glanced over their shoulders and curled their claws in impatience.

'Stand still!' said Lugg with a frown, then got to his paws and continued running. 'There's moles running along those tunnels like there's Gripthroat behind them,' he muttered. 'Wish I knew what was going on.'

'Are they following us?' gasped Cedar.

'No,' said Lugg. 'Heading east. Towards Mistmantle.'

Juniper was falling behind, his breathing coming in rasps and wheezes. Urchin reached for his paw and pulled him along as he ran.

'King Silverbirch sent the moles,' gasped Urchin, still running. 'He wants Mistmantle.'

'Well, he ain't getting it,' grunted Lugg. 'We can warn the king. The moles are on their way, but the boat can get there before them.'

The burrow widened into a network of tree roots where the air tasted fresher. They must be near the surface.

'Not far now, Juniper,' whispered Urchin.

'Spread out,' said Larch. 'It's safer to come out different ways. We won't be far from each other. Quickly!'

Urchin dived under a tree root and scrabbled forwards, hearing Juniper's struggling breaths behind him. Paw by paw he scrambled up through the tree roots, turned to extend a paw to Juniper, and finally stood up. He was far beyond the Fortress, under the icy sky. A pale arc of moon rode high above them, and starlight sparkled on a land already bright with snow and silver.

For the first time, the reality of the snow dawned on Urchin. Flakes tumbled softly, slowly to the earth. They melted on Cedar's cloak as she slipped from the burrow, on Flame's whiskers as he lifted his face to the sky. Watching from one side to the other, ears and nose twitching, Urchin and Juniper scurried forwards. Lugg came after and gradually they gathered together again, keeping their cloaks wrapped tightly about them for warmth and secrecy, pattering steadily up to the top of the dunes.

Somebody was moving nearby. Urchin didn't dare turn his head, didn't want to make himself conspicuous. There was somebody ahead of him, too.

'There are other animals about,' he whispered.

'I know,' said Larch, hurrying on. 'They're all on our side. They'll rally to us if we have to fight. Since you came, they've had hope. Partly it's because Cedar told me what you said, about how your captain on Mistmantle encouraged you to talk to the other animals and tell them what was really going on. We've been doing that, since you came. But more than that, it's you yourself, Urchin. Just knowing there's a Marked Squirrel on the island gives them courage, especially knowing that he might be Candle and Almond's son. It's not only the Larchlings. Most of the animals have only put up with Silverbirch and Smokewreath because they were terrified. You've given them hope.'

'It's getting lighter,' said Cedar. 'Faster!' Hushed and hurrying, helping each other up the stony and slippery paths, they finally struggled to the top of the dunes.

By the pale rising light, Urchin looked down on

the harbour and thought again that it was the loveliest place in the island. A stately ship still stood at anchor, tall and noble in the dawn. The small boat waited for them, very still on the water.

Our boat! thought Urchin with a thrill of excitement.

'Nearly there!' said Larch, and holding each other's paws for balance they rushed down the dunes towards the bay. Then a tug on his paw flung Urchin to the ground.

'They've found us!' gasped Juniper.

All of them lay flat in the sand and sharp grass. Urchin raised his eyes to see armed figures running on to the beach, lifting the bows from their shoulders, bending them, setting the arrows – he pressed his head down.

'Crawl backwards!' hissed Cedar. 'Burrow!'

Keeping his head down, Urchin crept backwards into the nearest burrow. Flights of arrows shrieked through the air. Juniper and Flame were on either side of him as they huddled as far back as they could in the shelter of a shallow, sandy burrow where Cedar was already prodding at the walls, searching for a tunnel and not finding one.

'The only way out is the only way in,' she said. 'Stay still and hope. Where are Lugg and Larch?'

Flame had flattened himself against the sandy

earth. 'Hiding in the undergrowth opposite us,' he said. 'They're safe.'

Voices were calling out, drawing nearer, barking orders, asking questions. Urchin drew in his shoulders as if he could make himself small enough to be invisible. Silently, they drew their swords and pressed backwards. The sound of his own heartbeat and Juniper's breathing sounded to Urchin as loud as a drum beat. Juniper stifled a cough.

As animals tramped through the dunes, swishing through coarse grass, calling to each other, sudden rage rose in Urchin, helpless simmering fury at the unfairness of it all. Why couldn't they all leave him alone? He never asked to come here. All he wanted was to go home!

He took a deep breath. There was no point in thinking like that. Never mind if this were fair or unfair, it was real, that was all. Vividly, he remembered something he had once said to Needle, on another shore.

'There's more that I have to do. And more that I have to be. It's not as if you can do one special thing, and that's it. It's what you go on being that matters.'

He was here. He couldn't change that. He had talked about doing something to help this island and Flame had said that he would, if he was meant to. Perhaps it was only by being here, hiding and hunted, that he could see what to do. His father had died for this island. He might be able to make a difference to it now, to continue the work his father had begun.

Paws hurried about above them. He heard guards calling to each other.

'If you find the Marked Squirrel, don't kill him,' said a voice. 'The king wants him for Smokewreath, then the king's happy, Smokewreath's happy, everyone's happy. Except the Marked Squirrel. Oh, and Commander Cedar. The king wants her alive. By the time he's finished with her, there'll be nothing left for Smokewreath.'

Urchin rolled over and hugged his knees, gazing ahead of him. There was only one thing to do. He stood up, taking off his cloak and brushing soot from his fur so his true colour would show clearly.

'Get down!' ordered Cedar.

Urchin took Juniper's paw. 'Thanks for everything you've done,' he said. For staying with me. I wish you were my brother – you *are* my brother, as far as anyone can be. Cedar, Flame, thanks for everything.'

'We're not beaten,' said Cedar. 'Get down.'

'They'll be here soon,' said Urchin. 'Sooner or later the chances are they'll find me, and that means they'll find you, too. I'm the one Smokewreath wants. If I give myself up, they won't come looking for you.'

Juniper gripped his paw. His eyes glowed with an intensity that astounded Urchin and frightened him.

'No!' he snarled. 'Don't you dare! I came all this way to save you, and you think you can just walk out and get yourself killed!'

'If I really am meant to do something for this island, maybe this is the way,' said Urchin.

'Don't be stupid,' said Juniper. 'How can this help anyone?'

'I just think it might,' said Urchin wretchedly. Juniper was making it much harder. 'This will give you a better chance to get away and save Mistmantle. Silverbirch's moles are on their way. If I go to the king, freely, now, you can slip down to the bay, take the small boat, and get home before the moles. Warn Crispin. You too, Cedar, it isn't safe for you here. They'll be so busy dragging me off to Smokewreath, they'll even forget to hunt for you, at least long enough for you to get away. You can have my place in the boat. Tell them what happened to me, and tell them what Whitewings is like. Give everyone my love – Crispin, Padra, everyone. Hug Apple for me, and tell her I said thanks for everything.'

Cedar looked beseechingly up at Flame. 'Tell him he's wrong!' she pleaded. 'Urchin, I won't let you.'

'You can't stop me,' said Urchin.

'I will,' said Juniper. He confronted Urchin with fierce eyes and outstretched claws. 'Don't you take one more step. I've seen that dungeon Smokewreath works in, and it's foul, and I won't let you go there. What if he really can make evil magic out of you? Magic that can endanger Mistmantle? Had you thought of that? Tell him, Brother Flame!'

But Brother Flame's eyes were heavy with sorrow. He laid his thin paws on Juniper's shoulders. He looked wise and strong, and reminded Urchin of Fir.

'Urchin is right,' he said sadly. 'I wish he wasn't. He has seen the thing he must do, and he will do it. Whatever Smokewreath can do, he can never make evil magic out of such a true heart. The Heart is stronger than all Smokewreath's sorcery. The Heart creates, evil can only destroy. Urchin, we'll give time for Cedar and the others to get away, then if the Larchlings can rescue you, we will. Perhaps this will make the islanders stand up to Smokewreath at last.'

'Thanks,' said Urchin, but there didn't seem much hope. He lowered his head. 'May I have your blessing?'

'The Heart keep you, warm you, and receive

you,' said Flame. 'And for ever may the Heart be with those you love, Urchin of the Riding Stars.'

Flame hugged him, then Juniper, and at last Cedar embraced him like a mother before she reached into the satchel under her cloak.

'Your mother's bracelet,' she said. 'Do you want to take it with you?'

He looked at the pale circle on her paw and touched it gently. It mustn't fall into Smokewreath's paws, but it was good to see it once more.

'Take it to Crispin, please,' he said. 'Ask him to keep it for me.'

It hurt that he couldn't say more. But there wasn't time, and no words were strong enough. Juniper could have become a tower squirrel too, and they could have worked together, taught each other new skills, skimmed stones and messed about in boats – that couldn't happen now. He wriggled to the burrow entrance.

'Heart keep me,' he whispered as he stepped from the burrow. 'Father, Mother, if you can see me, help me.'

He crept, staying close to the ground, until he was at a safe distance from the burrow where his friends sheltered and quite alone. Then he stood up, squared his shoulders, and lifted his head. Finally, he left his cloak lying on the ground and gave his fur one more brushing, so that everyone could see who he was. Climbing the dunes, he held up his paws. The singing of arrows stopped.

'I am the Marked Squirrel,' he called out, 'Urchin of the Riding Stars, Companion to Crispin the King. Do you want me alive?'

Chapter 21

Near the top of the dunes, he turned to look about him. At every second he had expected rough paws to grab at him, but nobody had touched him.

All about him, hedgehogs and squirrels stood and stared. Those who didn't wear helmets were glancing uncertainly at him, then at each other, as if they didn't know what to do. Wondering if this were all a dream, he marched on. He wished somebody would do something. It was as if they were watching to see if his courage would hold. It was almost a relief when two hedgehogs ran to his side and took hold of his arms and shoulders, but it felt as if they wanted to apologise for arresting him.

They marched him onwards. Other animals gathered around them and followed, but it seemed to

Urchin that he was the one leading the way until they stood at the highest point on top of the dunes, the point from which he could see as far as the Fortress and beyond it to the crags. On this bare winter day, the Fortress was clearer than ever.

The hedgehogs holding him were gaining confidence. They'd arrested the Marked Squirrel and he wasn't resisting, and, gripping his arms tightly, they quickened the pace. Archers and guards, keen to share the glory, ran to help them. Paws grabbed at Urchin, elbowing each other aside to reach him, pushing and dragging at him.

'To the Fortress!' shouted one, grabbing at his shoulder. 'Tell the king we've got him!'

Bundled across the landscape of the island, Urchin looked up to the Fortress. Dawn was spreading across the sky with an early, wide-awake light of pale gold over the bare trees and the harsh outlines of the battlements. Three figures stood there, and even at this distance their shape and size and their way of moving identified them. Granite, tall and broad in his armour, his feet apart, one paw on his sword. The king, swishing his cloak and raising his clenched paws in triumph. Smokewreath, hunched, darting and dancing. He'd be funny, thought Urchin, if he wasn't about to kill me.

For a moment he wished he wasn't doing this, but

then he was ashamed for wishing it. He was giving his friends the chance to escape and to warn Mistmantle, and if anything was worth dying for, that was. He walked on, not resisting the hedgehogs as they pulled him, his eyes now on the sky beyond the three triumphant figures on the battlements. This would be his last sunrise, and he was glad it was a good one.

Smokewreath was beating his staff on the battlements. The others were joining in, stamping, and armed animals and archers clapped their paws and took up the chant, louder and harsher. It carried in waves across the island until Urchin could hear the word clearly, and feel the pounding of the earth.

DEATH! DEATH! DEATH!

What have I done! What have I done, that they're all chanting for my death? thought Urchin, but he knew it wasn't anything he'd done. It was the wave of greed and fear that made them scream for his blood. But there were other voices, too, and a different chant that was hard to hear clearly. He twitched his ears.

He could hear his own name. Somebody was cheering, calling his name and cheering! He twisted and stretched to look over the heads of the animals dragging him onwards, straining to see what was happening.

The Larchlings were cheering him. Some he recognised from the underground party, but all were clear by the way they stood, more and more of them with their paws raised, some saluting, all calling out his name – 'Urchin! Urchin the Marked Squirrel! Urchin!'

DEATH! DEATH! DEATH! came the chant.

Run, Cedar, run, Juniper, he thought, and prayed with all his strength for them to get away. *Live. Get to Mistmantle*. The animals holding him were running him forwards now, hurrying in their eagerness to get their prize to the Fortress, and there was hardly time to see anything that was going on, but he could see enough. With cries of 'Urchin of the Riding Stars!' the Larchlings were running to help him. The animals dragging him turned, ready to defend themselves, determined to keep their prize as the Larchlings called out his name and rushed forwards.

They've found their courage at last, thought Urchin with a surge of joy *They've turned against the king!* But his next thought was a terrible one – *they're going to fight, the king's guards will destroy them, there will be a bloodbath, and all because of me.* Arrows sang, swords flashed, and from the Fortress the chant became louder, higher and wilder. The stamping was so hard, so rhythmic, so fierce that the earth shook. As Urchin looked up, the Fortress

314

seemed to be moving.

There was a noise like thunder, but it couldn't be thunder. It came from underground. Then from far off came such a violent splintering and cracking that Urchin ducked and wanted to run. Everyone was looking up in terror at the Fortress. The chanting and stamping had stopped. The hedgehogs holding Urchin let go and ran.

'The trees are falling!' screamed someone. The winter trees around the Fortress tilted stiffly, jerking, wrenched one way and then the other as if they were in pain. Animals ran for cover. Screams came from the Fortress, its doors were flung open, terrified animals ran and scrambled to escape. On the moving battlements, Smokewreath and the king clung to each other. Granite was trying to climb down the side, but the Fortress was rocking. Then an appalling cracking sound hit Urchin's ears like pain, and covering his head with his paws he tore back up the dunes. There was rumbling, creaking, screaming, and a furious rending crack that became a roar and thunder of falling stones. Then it was over except for some deep, growling rumbles from under the earth and the dust that filled the air as Urchin raised his head.

He coughed and squinted. Dust filled his mouth and stung his eyes. Clouds of it hung in the air, and slowly settled around the emptiness where the

Fortress had been. It covered the fur of animals with awed faces. It caught in his throat and made him cough until his eyes watered as he scrambled to the burrow, trying to call for Cedar and Juniper.

'Urchin!'

He heard the hoarse call amongst the cries and calls of frightened animals. Juniper was hurrying towards him, rubbing dust from his eyes with one paw.

'Juniper!' cried Urchin, stumbling forwards. 'Are you all right? Are you all all right?'

'We're all here,' said Cedar, and her eyes were pink with dust or tears. They all looked like that – Juniper, Cedar, Flame, Lugg, Larch – as they struggled towards the beach.

'We mustn't stop,' said Larch. 'There might be more quakes. We need to get everyone to the beach. If you see any animal that needs help to get there, help it.'

They coughed and staggered and slithered down to the beach, picking up and giving a paw to hurt and frightened animals on the way. Then at last they were on the beach, everyone seemed to be hugging each other and throwing down weapons, and Urchin's head was spinning. He couldn't really be free, the Fortress couldn't have just vanished – the only thing that made sense was the voice of Captain Lugg.

'Told you!' he said, and coughed. 'Too much

tunnelling, too much mining. Had to happen sooner or later. Watch them dunes don't go next.'

'We'll have to go back for the injured,' croaked Flame.

'Not yet, Brother, I wouldn't advise it,' said Lugg. 'Let things settle. Don't want you falling down a hole, they need you. And they're all looking out for each other.'

Animals were hurrying down to the beach, the walking supporting the injured. Larch was going from one group to another, giving orders – 'somebody go and help that squirrel, I think it's broken a paw – you, you and you, carry that hedgehog down here' – while helping Cedar and Flame to attend the wounded. Juniper and Urchin went with them to give whatever help they could, and Lugg organised the unharmed animals into bringing water from the nearest spring. Juniper and Urchin were just discussing the possibility that most of King Silverbirch's supporters must have been in the Fortress when it fell when the voices around them faded and stopped. Animals were watching them.

An old, grey-muzzled squirrel stepped forward and said in a deep, strong voice, 'Hail, Marked Squirrel, deliverer of Whitewings. Do you come to be our king?'

'Of course not!' said Urchin quickly. 'I mean, I'm

sure it would be a great honour, but you already have a queen. Queen Larch.'

A slow beam of joy spread across the old squirrel's face. His eyes brightened.

'Then it's true?' he said, and his voice trembled with excitement. 'What they've been saying, it's true? She's alive, and on the island? Little Larch?'

Urchin stretched up on his hind claws to survey the crowd, as Larch was too small to be found easily. He caught sight of her washing dust from a young hedgehog.

'There she is,' he said. 'Looking after that little hedgehog. That's Queen Larch. And you have a priest, and the animals who've kept them safe all these years.'

There was a lot of scurrying about and chattering amongst the animals, while everyone pointed at Larch and whispered and agreed that she had the look of the old royal family about her, and yes, this really was Larch. And was that Brother Flame? We always wondered what happened to him. Still white and grey with dust, still coughing, squirrels and hedgehogs knelt. On the sandy beach, on the snowy slopes, in the dust, bruised and dishevelled animals proclaimed Larch their rightful queen.

'Is it over?' said Urchin. 'Are they really dead?'

'Everything caved in,' said a breathless and very

dusty squirrel, wriggling through the crowd. She rubbed her eyes and blinked. 'They were all on the roof. I was in a treetop. Everyone was shouting and stamping, and it all caved in, and they just vanished, with everything falling on top of them – and I ran, sir. What do we do next?'

'Ask your queen,' said Urchin. 'I have a king to go home to, and my own island needs me. I have to go home.'

The snow had stopped falling, but leaves, twigs and dust still drifted through the air and settled on the shore. Juniper and Urchin picked their way through to Cedar.

'You'll have to go now,' she said, 'if you're going to catch the tide. They'll want to give you festivals and celebrations and goodness knows what if you stay any longer.'

Urchin sprang to his paws. All he wanted to do was to get home as quickly as possible, but the little boat at the jetty looked smaller than ever.

'Lugg will have to come by boat, too,' said Urchin. 'He can't go down a tunnel now, with the ground unsteady. And there's the swans. Will the boat carry us all?'

'Why take the little boat?' said Larch. 'Take the ship! There'll be no shortage of volunteers to crew it for you.'

'But there's a problem with the swans,' said Flame, 'something we hadn't thought of. Because they've been chained up all their lives, their wings aren't strong. I'm not sure if they can get themselves over the mists, let alone carry someone.'

'Well, they can try!' said Urchin. 'By the time they reach the mists, at least they will have exercised their wings! They could carry a message to Crispin, at least!'

'And Lugg didn't leave by water,' said Juniper. 'So if the rest of us can't go through the mists, he could lower the ship's boat, and try to row through. Please, we can't wait and talk about it now.'

Urchin gazed up at the ship. Proud and graceful on the water, she looked as lovely as an enchanted ship in a story.

'We'll send her back here,' he said eagerly, 'with a cargo of Mistmantle earth, to give the island a chance to be green again, as you wanted. And . . .' He hesitated. Knowing how much Cedar wanted to go to Mistmantle, he wanted to invite her, but he should ask the queen's permission first. 'Cedar always wanted to come to Mistmantle.'

'I can't leave now,' said Cedar, though Urchin had seen her gaze stray wistfully to the ship. 'You've only just come into your own, and there's so much to be done.'

'Cedar,' said Larch, 'you have taught me well, and you know the quality of the Larchlings. Flame and I can cope here.'

'And,' said Urchin brightly, as a thought occurred to him, 'if Lugg can't get through the mists, you might be able to. You could be the only one who can get through, and warn Crispin, and tell him where we are, so we can't go without you.'

'He's right,' said Juniper. 'We need you. And if there has been a rebellion against Crispin, we could do with someone like you on our side.'

'Now,' said Larch. 'This is my royal command. Go, Cedar, before you miss the tide.'

Cedar shared a few final words with Larch and Flame while Urchin looked with longing at the elegant ship. Snow still lay on the mast and the furled sails. To sail in that ship must be almost as good as riding on a swan.

'Come on, then, young 'uns,' said a voice behind them. 'Best get it over with. Time and tide.'

'Thanks, Lugg,' said Urchin, turning round, and stopped in surprise. He'd never seen Lugg look this worried before.

'What do you think?' said Juniper. 'Straight up the side?'

Urchin and Juniper hopped on to the jetty and measured the jump. Then they sprang to the side of the ship, scrambled up and tumbled on to the deck.

Organised by Larch, the Whitewings animals were escorting Cedar to the ship. A guard of honour hastily dusted itself down and lined up on the jetty. On the deck, Urchin and Juniper found cloaks to wrap round themselves and rubbed their paws against the cold.

'Heart be with you!' called Flame. 'May the Heart bring you all to Mistmantle!' Two swans, trying their wings, flew to the mast and circled it.

'You see!' said Urchin to Juniper. 'They're learning already!'

'We'll need more ballast,' said one of the hedgehogs in the crew, making Urchin bite his lip with impatience. 'We're too light without it. They're loading it up now.'

'Will that stop it rocking?' muttered Lugg. 'And it isn't even going anywhere yet. Moles aren't meant to be on boats.' He sniffed, and sniffed again. 'I can smell that stuff for killing lice.' He stepped a pace back from Urchin. 'You haven't caught lice here, have you?'

'Certainly not!' said Urchin. Cedar had warned him that it might take a while to wear off, and he hoped he wouldn't smell of it when he got home. He wouldn't want Crispin and Padra to think he was lousy.

Standing in the bow, he looked for the last time at the island where his parents had met, where his father had died. Finally the ballast had been loaded, the anchor was hauled up, the sails were unfurled, and the ship was moving – 'We'll take turns helping the crew at the oars,' said Cedar – there was clear deep water between the ship and the coast of Whitewings, animals waved, squirrels sang, and silver dust settled and caught the sunlight. Swans rose into the air. And when Urchin could see nothing more of Whitewings he turned his face to the horizon, pressed his forepaws against the bow, and prayed the ship to Mistmantle and to Crispin.

The sea breeze was sharp and chill, flapping his cloak about him. He felt somebody at his side and turned to see Cedar, with the little box in her paws. His heart thumped hard, and he held out his left forepaw.

'Tie it very tightly, please?' he said. 'So I never lose it.' And when Cedar had knotted the bracelet firmly on his wrist, he folded his right paw over it and pressed it hard against his heart under his cloak. Nobody could take it away from him now.

A harsh wind followed them, cruel with sleet, but it drove them hard to Mistmantle. They navigated by the stars at night and by guesses in the day, but in the deep winter the days were short and the nights were long. They helped at the oars, brewed up cordials for themselves and the crew, and slept by turns in nests beneath the deck. They kept their cloaks wrapped about themselves even in their nests, and in the night watch on deck Urchin and Juniper saw frost on each other's whiskers. When Urchin slept, huddled in a tightly clenched heap, he dreamed of roaring fires in Mistmantle Tower. He and Juniper talked of their childhoods, and Urchin realised that something in Juniper's story didn't quite fit. When he felt they understood each other well enough, he mentioned it.

'You're not that much younger than I am,' he said, 'and the culling didn't come in until Sepia was born. I think you're older than Sepia. So Damson must have hidden you before the culling law came in, before she absolutely had to.'

Juniper looked out to sea for a while. Then he said, 'I know. I've thought of that. She must have had another reason for hiding me, but when I've tried to ask her she changes the subject. I can't push her about it, can I?'

They talked a lot about what they'd do when they reached the mists. The swans were learning to use their wings, but the mists were long and it looked unlikely that they could fly all the way over them, let alone carrying a passenger. They were hopeful of

Lugg or Cedar at least getting through. If the rest of them were kept out, and there was no swan on Mistmantle to fetch them, they'd just have to return to Whitewings and go all the way back through tunnels. Nobody except Lugg liked the idea and even he admitted it would be a long way to go about it.

'We could climb the mast,' suggested Juniper. 'Then we wouldn't be coming by water. We'd be over it.'

'I think it would still count,' said Urchin. 'But if the mists are there to protect the island, they should let us through.'

'Firelight, moonlight, the secret,' said Juniper.

'I don't suppose you know what that means?' said Urchin.

'No idea,' said Juniper with a shrug. 'But I think it's something to do with getting back. And I don't feel sick.' Lugg trotted quietly to the side of the ship. 'I think, if the moles had invaded Mistmantle, I'd feel sick. Firelight, moonlight, the secret.'

When the sails needed to be furled or unfurled, the squirrels took turns to run up the rigging. Urchin could see that Juniper found it harder than he did, not because of his withered paw – that never seemed to bother him – but because he became breathless quickly. Urchin knew that Juniper had sacrificed his health by following him to Whitewings. He called up to Juniper that they could swap places if they liked, but Juniper shouted down that he could climb just as well as Urchin, and was soon pulling himself up into the crow's nest.

The trip was harder for Lugg, who endured it as best he could in spite of being seasick all the way. He persisted in calling the bow 'the pointed end', the stern 'the blunt end', the mast 'the sticky-up bit' (unless the sails were unfurled, when he called them 'the washing'), and the bowsprit 'the sticky-out bit'. As for port and starboard, he said it was all the same to him when he leant over it.

On the third night the sky was so cloudy that it was hard to navigate, but the wind still seemed to be set for Mistmantle. Urchin, yawning enormously, rubbing his eyes and huddling into his cloak, scurried across the deck to take over from Cedar. He hugged a beaker of hot cordial.

'Dawn takes for ever,' she said, chafing her paws against the cold. 'It always does when you're waiting for it. But it seems longer than ever tonight.'

'M – midwinter,' stammered Urchin through chattering teeth. 'Lugg's got the stove going and Juniper's heating up cordials.'

'Hot cordial!' said Cedar, and dashed away. She

was right about the dawn. Urchin stood at the wheel for what seemed like hours, and it was still dark. The cordial cooled quickly, and the heated core it had given him had faded before he noticed the sky seemed a little paler and greyer than before, but when Juniper came to take over the horizon still could not be seen. The chill had entered Urchin deeply.

'It's still grey,' he said, shivering.

'It's clearer behind us,' said Juniper, his fur fluffed out for warmth as he joined Urchin on deck.

Urchin looked round. Behind them the sky was pale blue, and the wave tips showed clearly.

'But it's foggy ahead,' he said, and suddenly he leapt across the deck, stumbling on numb paws, twirling his tail as he sprang down the hatch, shouting, 'Cedar! Lugg! We're in the mists!'

They stood on deck, all of them, their eyes shining, their ears pricked as they gazed at the white wall of mist. Lugg stretched up on clawtips, peering forwards with his nose twitching. Cedar pressed forwards over the bow, her chin tilted upwards, tears in her eyes.

'I've seen the mists,' she said in a shaky voice. 'Even if I never get to Mistmantle, I've seen the mists. I know it's in there.'

Juniper took her paw. 'The Heart won't keep us

out,' he said. 'There'll be a way.'

'Oh, good,' said Lugg, sounding unconvinced. 'Don't suppose you know what way? Should have gone by tunnels. Could have been hacked to death by mad moles, but better than a boat. Never again.'

'But we're moving,' said Juniper. 'We're in the mists, and we're still moving. So far, so good.'

Chapter 22

In the workrooms of Mistmantle Tower Needle stitched steadily, making Fir a new tunic for the coronation in hope that there really would be a coronation. A little heap of pebbles lay in front of her. Hope had not managed to find the Heartstone, but he had found any number of pretty pebbles to give to his mother and closest friends. Needle was neatly embroidering a pattern of leaves round the hem of a tunic, but on this winter day the light was poor and it was time to stop.

'You'll strain your eyes,' said Thripple. 'You've done enough for one day. Off you go.'

Higher up the tower, in Fir's turret, Padra looked down from the window with his son Tide in his arms. Fir sat on a stool by the fire with the baby girl otter in his lap. Bright brown eyes looked back up at him.

'She has your expression,' he said. 'One would think she's always going to laugh.'

'She is,' said Padra. The baby heard his voice, squealed with delight and wriggled as he turned Tide towards the window.

'Look, Tide,' he said. 'That's Watchtop Hill. No, not that way, that's Brother Fir. They're building a bonfire for the riding stars.'

'Does this young lady have a name yet?' asked Fir.

'We liked Swan, because of the way Urchin and Crispin came home,' said Padra. 'But we won't call her that, because she's not a swan, she's an otter. Then we thought of Swanwing. Then Swanfeather. We both really like that one.'

'Hm,' said Fir. 'Swanfeather of Mistmantle.'

'It's better than Wriggle, which is what we call her at the moment,' said Padra. 'It's what she does all the time.' He moved to the next window. 'And they're building another fire on the beach. They're going to make a great night of it.' With a sigh, he sat down opposite Fir. 'The fact is, Brother Fir, the whole island's desperate for a party. What they really want is the coronation. It's been a long hard winter and there's more of it to come, and they need something to celebrate instead of gazing into the mists watching for Urchin and Juniper. And Lugg – he may be a tough old soldier, but he's not invincible. Lady Cott and the family are being very brave, but my heart goes out to those two little grandsons.'

'Tipp and Todd,' said Fir. 'Yes.'

'They're always hanging around wanting rides in boats, and if any of us do take them out they're so desperate to see as far as they can, they're in danger of falling in. They're desperate to have him back. What will the riding stars bring, Brother Fir?'

'Ask Miss Swanfeather,' said Fir. 'She has as much idea as I have.'

'Look at me!' squeaked Hope on the shore. 'I'm climbing the bonfire!'

'What a big brave hedgehog!' said Sepia. In fact he had climbed on to the heap of firewood to be taken to the tower, but she hadn't the heart to tell him.

'Here's Needle with your mum,' said Fingal, lifting him down. Hope set off in the wrong direction, heard Thripple's voice and turned towards her, bumping his paw on something. He stopped to examine it.

'Have I found the Heartstone?' he said hopefully.

Needle dawdled over to look. It was hard to go on being enthusiastic about the Heartstone now.

'No, it's a pink shell, but never mind,' she said. 'It's a nice one to give to your mum. We'll light the bonfire soon. Crackle says they're making hot soup and spice cake.' Crackle, who had been working in the kitchens, came down to join them.

'Urchin's lights will be coming on soon,' said Thripple.

'I sort of don't like it when Urchin's lights come on,' said Crackle. 'They come on every night and he still doesn't come.'

Urchin and Juniper stamped their paws for warmth and watched the mists.

'We're getting closer,' said Juniper. Lugg was gazing into the mists with such intensity that he had forgotten to feel seasick. Cedar leant over the bow as if she wanted to reach out beyond the mists.

'We're moving very slowly,' said Urchin.

'But we're moving,' said Juniper. 'What will happen if we can't get through? Will we just stay here?'

'I've heard about ships from Whitewings that didn't get through,' said Cedar. 'The ship slows down and down, and then stops. It won't go forwards, even if there's a gale blowing and you row with all your might. It'll only turn round and go back.'

'If that happens,' said Urchin, 'we'll lower the ship's boat with you in it, and pray that you get through.'

'Yes,' said Juniper. 'Pray.'

'What in all the island do you think I'm doing?' said Lugg.

'Pray for something wonderful to happen,' said Juniper. 'You never know. We might all just sail through. There must be more in the Heart's way of doing things than we can understand.'

'You sound like Brother Fir,' said Urchin.

They prayed. They watched. They ran up and down the mast to keep warm and to see if the view was any better. They brewed cordials and ate food that still had the metallic taste of Whitewings. Daylight faded. They hung lanterns fore and aft, and in the crow's nest.

'Wouldn't it help if we were up there, too?' said Juniper. 'I still think that if we're not so much on the water, we might get through.'

'If we stop dead and absolutely can't move,' said Lugg, 'then I'll join you up there, to see if it works. But only if I have to. Plague and lice, the things I do for Mistmantle. And speaking of lice, you still smell.'

The ship slowed. Urchin and Juniper climbed the mast and settled in the crow's nest. They looked down on Cedar as she stood like a figurehead with wreaths of mist whirling like veils around her.

'We're still moving,' said Juniper, 'and still forwards.'

The mist made tiny beads on fur and whiskers.

Whiteness folded Cedar and Lugg until Urchin could hardly see them. The lamps glowed softly through layers of white. Urchin pressed his frozen paws to his mouth to warm them. A snowflake landed on his nose.

Were the mists thinner? He might be imagining it, and soon it was hard to tell. The snow grew heavier, falling faster in thick tumbling flakes that twirled to the deck. In the crow's nest, they stretched out their paws to it.

'It's like flying!' whispered Juniper. 'I wanted to fly on a swan, but this is magical!'

Urchin laughed up at the sky. Then he gasped.

'What was that?' he said

'There was something in the snow!' Cedar called up.

Urchin watched. Beyond the mist, he could see deep violet sky where the snowflakes danced and silver swished among them. Awed and wide-eyed, he could barely breathe the word.

'Star,' he whispered.

'Riding stars!' cried Juniper, and the swans rose in the air for joy. 'Urchin, it's riding stars! They're taking us home!'

From Cedar came something like a sob and a cry of joy. Urchin leapt down the mast, ran balancing along the bowsprit, and stood in the light of the ship's lantern, clinging with his hind claws, his face and forepaws lifted to the pouring sky.

Snow over Mistmantle settled steadily on treetops, casting a white hush on Anemone Wood. On Watchtop Hill and on the rocks above the waterfall, animals warmed their paws at bonfires and turned their faces to the sky. On the shore, young animals staying up late to see the stars forgot all about them and were content to watch the snow drift silently down and melt into the sea or vanish in the halo of the bonfire. Padra, his daughter wrapped in a shawl in his arms, watched the small squirrels and hedgehogs hopping across the rocks trying to gather the snow before it melted, tipping their heads back to catch snowflakes on their tongues. Damson stood a little apart from the others, her cloak wrapped about her, Sepia holding her paw.

'Are you cold, Mistress Damson?' asked Padra. 'Won't you come nearer the fire?'

'Thank you, Captain Padra, but the smoke hurts my eyes,' she said. 'Miss Sepia's keeping me company.'

Brother Fir hobbled over the rocks. 'Mistress Damson, will you come to my tower and drink cordial with me?' he offered, holding out his paw. 'Best place on the island for stars, and a great deal more civilised than the sea's edge in a snowstorm. And young Sepia can come if she likes, though I daresay she'd rather be with her friends.'

Sepia looked up at the tower. Urchin had told her that the stars looked wonderful from Brother Fir's turret. They would be breathtakingly close.

'I'll go the quick way, shall I?' she said in a husky whisper. 'I can light the lamps for you.'

She dashed up the wall, having to stop on a window ledge now and again to get her breath back before she scrambled over a snowy window box into Fir's turret. By the time she had set the lamps flaring she could hear his step on the stairs, and knew from the voices behind him that Thripple and Hope had joined him. While Damson warmed herself, Sepia stood at the window holding Hope's paw and watching the stars. They were large and bright as they danced across the night sky and the dark sea, and from Hope's gasps of delight she knew he could see them. Then a shower of stars all hurtled at the tower on a rush like laughing children, so wild and fast that she wanted to duck – but she didn't. If the stars had swept the top from the tower and carried her along with them she could have danced across the sky. But they passed in a rush and all was still.

'That's all for now, sweetheart,' she whispered. Hope said something and pointed, but Thripple was asking her how her throat was and she turned to say that it was much better, thank you, but she had to rest it and she still couldn't sing at all.

'There's a star,' said Hope.

'I don't think so, dear,' said Sepia, looking out.

'But there was one,' said Hope.

'Let's watch, then,' she said, and settled down beside him. 'Oh!'

Something was moving in the mists, a pale, gleaming light. It vanished again as soon as she saw it, but as she watched it came again, glowing with something like muffled firelight. There was another one, lower. Then they vanished, and came back into view again.

Fir was watching, too. And Thripple. And Damson.

On Watchtop Hill, animals turned their heads to follow the light. On the beach, chatter stopped. Animals moved forwards to the shore line. Crispin and Padra stood side by side. Padra passed Swanfeather to Apple. Arran put Tide into Moth's paws, and slipped to join Crispin and Padra.

'A ship,' whispered Padra. 'Lights fore and aft, and on the mast.'

'What have the riding stars brought us?' said Crispin.

'Should we get the young and the old into the

tower?' said Padra, 'in case of danger? But it doesn't feel like danger.'

'No,' said Crispin, 'it doesn't. Stand fast, Padra. Arran, have Docken and Huggen ready in case we do need to get anyone into the tower. Bring Russet and Heath.'

'Star!' cried a young squirrel. One, two, three great stars seared across the sky, and for a second the night was radiantly bright. But nobody could be quite sure what they had seen.

'Something pale, like moonlight?' said Padra.

'Some animal's fur,' said Arran, 'like firelight.'

'There was someone on the mast,' said Crispin. 'And look!'

It was nearer. Dimly lit, barely seen shapes were taking form before their eyes. A ship carried forwards with her lanterns shining through the thinning shroud of mist, stars dancing about her, guarding her, bringing her to shore. She sailed nearer, tall and beautiful, leaving the mists, sailing through snow and stars to Mistmantle. Was that a dark squirrel, in the crow's nest? On the bowsprit, paws outstretched, balanced a figure as pale as moonlight. On the deck something flamed like fire, but it could have been the flame-red fur of a squirrel. They were level now with the small boats that parted to let them through.

All over the island, bright eyes watched. Animals

found their voices.

'Urchin!' said Crispin.

In Fir's tower, Damson rubbed her eyes. 'Juniper!'

'Urchin! Juniper!' cried Sepia, and sprang down from the window.

'Urchin, Urchin, Urchin!' squeaked Hope.

'My dad!' said Moth, hugging Tide.

'Grandad!' yelled two young moles, and pelted towards the shore with yelps of joy.

'It's my Urchin,' said Apple to Swanfeather, and wiped her eyes on a corner of the shawl.

Urchin! Juniper! Lugg! The cries ran through the island. In the tower, with shining eyes, Fir repeated his prophecy and fell on his knees to give thanks. Then he hobbled down the stairs after Thripple, Hope and Damson.

The ship sailed on among the lights of the little boats and her own lights, all shining again in the water. Animals ran to the jetty. Needle hugged her mother, her little brother, Crackle, everyone. Sepia dashed about, gathering her choir, herding them on to the highest rock she could find. And still, snow, stars and swans swirled around the mast head where Juniper stretched out his paws for joy, and round the prow where Lugg waved furiously and wiped his eyes, and Urchin turned somersaults for joy before running back along the bowsprit for the rope, and

Cedar gazed and gazed.

Padra found Arran beside him, caught her look, and grinned.

'Ready for this?' he said.

'It'll be freezing,' she said. They threw down their cloaks and hurled themselves into the water as Urchin threw the rope.

'We'll need more warm cloaks,' said Mother Huggen. 'And one for that tangle-brained Fingal, too, for he's sure to follow them.'

'I'm coming!' yelled Fingal as he splashed into the sea.

Padra's head appeared in the water, his whiskers dripping, his eyes laughing. Bursting with joy, Urchin hugged Cedar, hugged Lugg, and ran up the mast to hug Juniper.

'We can almost touch the stars!' he cried.

'We *are* touching the stars!' said Juniper.

Then the singing reached them, Sepia's choir, their voices high and sweet, blending into the icy air so that Cedar gasped to hear them and lifted her ears. They were near the jetty now, and Urchin sprang down from spar to spar. Crispin flung his cloak to the jetty, leapt on to the taut rope and dashed along it, twisting his tail as it swayed under him, scrambling over the side to seize Urchin in a strong, warm, hug, and finally looking past him at Cedar.

'This is Cedar,' said Urchin, 'and she's wonderful. We owe everything to her. Our lives. Everything.'

Crispin dropped to one knee before Cedar and kissed her paw.

'My lady,' he said, 'you are welcome to Mistmantle and every honour it can offer you.'

'And excuse me, but there's a hedgehog rebellion and a small mole invasion on the way, Your Majesty,' said Lugg. 'I'll get it sorted, soon as I'm off this boat.'

Chapter 23

U rchin started to tell Crispin all he had heard about the Mistmantle hedgehog rebellion, but when he heard that it was all over the surge of relief and thankfulness sent him running down the rope to the jetty. Sepia and Needle reached him first, but it was Apple who hugged him, passing Swanfeather to Sepia to wrap Urchin in a warm and powerful embrace that smelt of soup and spice. The tears in her eyes made Urchin hurt at the thought of her long, worried wait for him, and he tried to apologise for being kidnapped in the first place, but it was no good – Apple was talking so much and so fast that it was no use trying to say anything. With Juniper and Damson, he was dragged to the warmth beside the fire, where the smoke made him rub his eyes and gaze all he wanted at Mistmantle Tower as the bonfire and starlight showed it against the night. Warm dry cloaks were wrapped around them and someone brought beakers of hot, rich soup that tasted of Mistmantle, and not of grey dust. Lugg, hugged by his wife and daughters and with a grandson in each arm, had disappeared amongst a mound of moles. Urchin looked round for Cedar and saw Crispin escorting her, and the crew, from the ship. Needle brought him walnut bread, and Fir hobbled towards them.

Urchin had forgotten the depth and goodness in the old priest's face. Joy and love shone in his eyes.

'I suggest all you valiant travellers come to my tower,' he said. 'Hm. It will be crowded. But the night is passing, and I don't think any of us will sleep.'

When they were crowded into Fir's turret, Urchin finally knew that he was home, and was staying. The apple logs were on the fire and the old saucepan on the hearth. He found himself wedged between Padra on one side and Juniper on the other.

'You smell of Apple's cordial,' whispered Padra. 'She hasn't forced it down you already, has she?'

'No, and I haven't got lice, either, before you ask, sir,' Urchin whispered back.

'Lice wouldn't go near it,' said Padra. Urchin curled up with his arms round his knees. He was back among animals who hugged you and squashed up beside you and didn't mind much what you smelt of.

As the stars faded and the sky paled, Urchin, Juniper, Cedar and Lugg told their story and Needle, Padra and Arran told all that had happened on Mistmantle. The more Urchin heard, the more he realised how long he'd been away and how much he'd missed. No wonder he couldn't keep his eyes open . . . Cedar was talking about her hopes for the future of Whitewings and Crispin was watching her . . . *oh, yes . . . I know who she reminds me of . . . obvious* . . . his eyes were closing again. Was Padra talking about babies? What babies? Oh.

When morning was completely morning and Urchin had dozed enough to be wide awake again, he went back to the shore. Padra, Crispin and Cedar were talking to the ship's crew and discussing the return of the ship with some Mistmantle earth, something to grow in it, and anyone who'd rather live on Whitewings than Mistmantle. Urchin couldn't understand why anyone *would* rather live on Whitewings than Mistmantle.

'You might, if it were the only home you'd ever

344

known,' said Crispin, 'and if all your family and friends lived there.' Cedar didn't say anything.

Various young animals, with a lot of splashing from Fingal, were unloading the ballast from the ship and playing with it. Hope trundled about, choosing pebbles for Thripple. Fir and Needle came down, Fir smiling brightly.

'Your Whitewings friend is an expert healer,' he said. 'She may be able to help poor Sepia.'

'She healed me,' said Juniper. 'I need to talk to you about that, Brother Fir.'

Hope trotted over to Urchin with a pebble. 'That's for you,' he said, and ran away again, making a detour round Arran, bumping into a rock and apologising to it.

'There's one for Captain Lady Arran, and one for Sepia . . .'

'I remember who Cedar reminds me of now,' said Urchin, looking at Cedar. 'I didn't know until I saw her with Crispin, but she's very like Whisper.'

'Oh, is she?' said Arran with sudden interest.

'. . . and one for Brother Fir . . . oops . . .'

Needle gasped. She knelt on the sand by Hope.

'. . . oops, I dropped it again . . .' said Hope.

'Fir!' shouted Needle urgently. 'Brother Fir!'

'It's a nice one,' said Hope.

Fir hobbled over with Juniper beside him. For the

first and only time in his life, Urchin heard Brother Fir shout.

'Your Majesty! Crispin! Here!'

Juniper scooped up the pebble and dropped it into Fir's paw. It lay there as if contented, pale, flecked with pink and peach with a thread of gold. Crispin and Padra stared down at it. Animals, hearing Fir's shout, ran to see what was happening.

'What is it?' asked Cedar.

'It is the Heartstone of Mistmantle,' said Fir gravely. 'Well done, Needle, who never stopped searching. Well done, little Hope.'

'Did I find the Heartstone?' said Hope. 'Where's Mummy, can I tell her?'

'Yes, Hope,' said Needle. 'Does that mean we can have the coronation now?'

'We'll wait for the Whitewings moles to turn up first and sort them out,' said Crispin.

'And then crown him, *please*, Fir, quickly, before he thinks of anything else,' said Padra.

'Can I tell Mummy about that too?' asked Hope.

'Tell everyone!' said Crispin.

'That explains why we had so many ships from Whitewings,' said Fir. 'Hm. I understand it now. Husk must have taken the Heartstone in its box and tipped it into the ballast heap so that it would be taken away from the island. But it was trying to find its way back. From Whitewings it must have been loaded on to a ship coming to Mistmantle, but then, lying in another ballast heap, it would have been taken away again unnoticed. It may have happened many times. It's the Secret, you see. The Secret that brought you home.'

'There are things about Mistmantle that Husk never understood,' said Crispin.

'Dear king, there are things about Mistmantle that none of us understand,' said Fir. 'Where we cannot understand, we can still love. Hm! Dear Mistress Cedar, if you are to stay for the coronation, perhaps you would like something suitable to wear.'

'Mum will make you something,' volunteered Hope gladly, and took her paw. Crispin watched Hope lead her to the tower.

By midday, exhaustion was catching up with Urchin. Most of the young squirrels wanted to go to Watchtop Hill to play in the snow, and were told that they could do what they liked so long as they behaved themselves and were ready for the coronation when the time came. Needle had finally finished some sewing that seemed very important to her. Urchin reported to Padra.

'I've forgotten how to give you orders,' said Padra. 'Go and throw snowballs at Fingal for me.'

Urchin spent a wonderful afternoon with the others, throwing snowballs, making slides, and building snow squirrels with pebble eyes and tails that always dropped off. Even Gleaner joined in, though she couldn't resist telling Needle that whoever Cedar might be she didn't match up to Lady Aspen, and when Needle threw a snowball at her she ran up a tree and sulked. When it was too dark to go on they all realised how wet and cold they were, and slid and tumbled and bounced their way to their homes. After a hasty supper at the tower, Urchin ran through the familiar corridors to the Spring Gate and the little chamber next to Padra's, and to the scene he had dreamed of.

The small, plain bed waited for him. The fire had been lit. Urchin gazed into the flames. There could be nowhere, nowhere in the whole world as beautiful as this, with the sea swishing outside and Padra and Arran in the next room. At last he left the fire and curled up, pulling the blankets into a nest around him and trying to stay awake. He had looked forward to this so much, he mustn't sleep through it now. But as the warmth seeped into him, he could at least close his eyes.

Padra and Arran tiptoed into the chamber.

'What has he been through?' said Padra. 'Will we ever know it all?' He leant closer. 'He's wearing a bracelet. What do you think that's about? A girl?'

Arran looked carefully, and shook her head.

'It's very old. Faded and worn. And the hair in it is his own colour.'

'I wonder if he'll tell us,' said Padra.

In the morning, Urchin met with Crispin, Padra and Fir in the Throne Room, and told them about his parents. They listened quietly, and it seemed to him that they listened as if they were listening to a grown-up animal, not a young page. Then Fir excused himself because, he said, he was expecting visitors at his turret.

Cedar was first to arrive.

'I have seen Sepia,' she said, settling herself on the low stool he offered. 'I may be able to help. But I must ask you to pray, because I don't know if I can do this. Sometimes I don't really heal them. Sometimes, when it's beyond my skill, I think the Heart heals them, if they can receive it. It was like that with Juniper. He's extra-sensitive, isn't he? He's aware of things at levels most of us don't notice. Flame and I talked with him a lot while he was with us. He sensed danger about the Whitewings ship, and about Smokewreath, and I think Smokewreath sensed him, too, and was uneasy, as if something about Juniper threatened him. There's something special about Juniper.'

'Hm,' said Fir. 'I should think that Smokewreath was sensitive, too, but he turned his gift to his own ends instead of offering it to the Heart. Yes, Juniper has great potential. He has loyalty and strength of character, more than he realises himself, I think. Fortunately his heart is turned towards what is good and true. I would be greatly troubled otherwise. But good intentions are not enough, and he needs training. Most important. We must both teach him.'

'Both?' she said, and crossed to the window where she looked down at the woods and the bare trees. The hope in her heart might just be too good to be true. 'Does that mean I'll be allowed to stay?'

'My dear,' said Fir, 'if you think King Crispin will send you away, you're very much mistaken.'

When she had gone, he chuckled quietly to himself at the idea of Crispin wanting her to leave. His next visitor was Juniper, who stood anxiously, curling his claws.

'It's a bit awkward, Brother Fir,' he said, and twisted his weak paw round the good one, wishing he hadn't come. 'You know I nearly died on Whitewings?'

'Yes, I know.'

'Well, I . . . I . . . I think I really did die.'

'Yes,' said Fir without surprise. 'And then what?'

350

'I sort of saw things,' said Juniper, encouraged. 'Things I'd forgotten. I remembered something about my mother, or I think that's who she must have been. I saw a squirrel face. I fell a long way, and there was a scream. I heard a voice. And that's all. That's all I remembered. The next thing I knew I was warm, and everything round me was safe, and Cedar was with me. But in the meantime – it sounds stupid, but I think my heart had stopped. I didn't feel afraid of Smokewreath after that, but I think he was frightened of me.'

'Yes, I see,' said Fir.

'I didn't know what to make of it, sir,' he said. 'But now Urchin's found out about his parents, and . . . and . . .'

'Yes?'

Juniper bit his lip and tried not to fidget. 'Well, he knows about his parents and I still don't know about mine, and . . . well, I couldn't help being jealous, sir, when he found out, then I thought – what's to stop me finding out about mine? So that's what I plan to do.'

'It may not be possible,' said Fir.

'I'm not stupid, sir,' said Juniper. 'I'm not much younger than Urchin. The culling law hadn't been brought in when I was a baby. So I think Damson had another reason for hiding me. She won't tell me, but I thought you might know.'

'Dear Juniper,' said Fir, 'I have no more idea about your beginnings than you have yourself. Has it occurred to you that you may not like the answer?'

'Yes,' he said, 'but I still need to find out.'

'Hm,' said Fir, 'well, well. If you are determined to find out it will be a hard journey to make, and it may be a sad one. But it may be that you need to know your past before you can go forwards to your future, and your future is vital. I see great potential in you, Juniper. I hope you will study with me.'

'But I've never studied anything!' cried Juniper.

'Better start soon, then,' said Fir. 'As Cedar observed, you have great gifts, but they must be trained and disciplined or chaos will result. Your gift of sensitivity is not a good or a bad thing in itself. What matters is what you make of it. You could become a great blessing to the island, or you could destroy yourself and everyone around you. Will you be my pupil? Will you be trained to fulfil your potential?'

'Oh, yes, Brother Fir!' cried Juniper.

'As a priest?' said Brother Fir.

Juniper was quiet for a while. Then he said softly, 'If you think I'm called to it, Brother Fir. I'll do it willingly. But I don't think I'm good enough.'

'Thank the Heart for that,' said Fir.

After Juniper had gone, Fir settled himself by the hearth and contented himself with warmth and firelight. *Firelight and moonlight, anyone could see that meant Cedar and Urchin. The Heartstone was the secret. The true, that was dear old Lugg. So the holy, of course, is the only one left. Yes. And may the Heart let me live to see him ready to take my place.*

Padra ran down the stairs and found a rosemary bush walking in the other direction. But the rosemary bush wore Apple's hat, and had Apple's paws sticking out underneath it, and proved not to be a bush at all, but only a heap of branches.

'For the Gathering Chamber, Captain Padra, sir,' she said. 'The moles are off busy doing them, I don't know what, moley things, and there's squirrels off rehearsing and whatnot and less of us to do the work and I was that pleased to hold your little girl, right little wrigglepot, Heart love her, isn't she gorgeous?'

'Of course she is,' said Padra. He helped her carry her burden to the Gathering Chamber, and they paused in the doorway. Crispin and Cedar were talking at a window. Apple lowered her voice to a confidential whisper.

'Better drop this lot and go back for the rest,' she said. 'He hasn't hardly taken his eyes off her, Heart bless him, and quite right too. We'll no sooner have him crowned than we'll have a big wedding to dress up for.'

'Give them a chance,' Padra whispered back. 'She's only just got here.' They were interrupted by Urchin running up the stairs and bowing.

'Reporting for duty, Captain Padra, sir,' he said.

'Urchin,' said Padra. 'My orders are as follows. Try to stay on the island long enough to finish your training. In the meantime, ask the king for a token to give to the Whitewings crew to invite them all to the coronation, and to Scatter's guards. She should be there, too. But, Urchin,' he glanced at Crispin and Cedar and laid a paw on his shoulder, 'don't go to him yet.'

'You must know the worst of me,' Cedar was saying. 'I pretended to serve the king while I waited to put Larch on the throne. You could say I'm as foul a traitor as your Gorsen.'

'Nobody,' said Crispin, 'could call you traitor. You served your true queen and your island in the best way you could, at great danger to yourself. And as a loyal servant of Whitewings, you can tell me what to do with all these Whitewings moles. As

354

Lugg's troops were ready for their attack, we have a prison full of them. And the ships' crews. And Lord Treeth. And Scatter, of course. I want to give Scatter a chance here.'

'I suppose they should be sent home,' said Cedar thoughtfully. 'The crews and Scatter should be all right. But Lord Treeth and the soldiers might be more trouble than they're worth. Larch has only just established herself as queen, and she has so much on her paws already.'

'Then I'll keep them here under guard for a little longer,' said Crispin. 'When we return her ship with a load of Mistmantle earth, I'll send a message asking Her Majesty's permission to keep her subjects here until they've learned how to behave.'

'Yes, the soldiers will probably obey her when they've got it into their heads that she's the queen,' said Cedar. 'I'm not sure about Lord Treeth. He could be a real threat to her.'

'Then I'll keep him here until she asks for him back,' said Crispin. 'He'll protest, whatever we do, so it makes very little difference to me. And now the tyranny of Whitewings is over, your cause is won, and there are no more battles to fight. I hope you can enjoy your freedom and be happy on Mistmantle.'

Oh, please, thought Cedar. She dared not ask

how long she could stay, but she gazed out over Mistmantle as if she could soak up its freshness. *Please*.

Chapter 24

T he Gathering Chamber was so crammed that Urchin wondered how the smaller creatures could keep breathing. Every ledge, seat and window sill was occupied. Squirrels even sat on lamp brackets, and the new gallery was so crammed that Urchin, wearing a deep red cloak and carrying a sword, couldn't help glancing up at it in case it collapsed altogether. If that happened a band of hedgehogs, the crews of the Whitewings ships, Scatter, Apple, Damson and several small moles would land on the otters. Rosemary and holly, twined with gold ribbons and bright with berries, hung from the walls, and garlands stretched from the ceilings. Cloaks were bright, caps and bonnets were proud with ribbons and greenery, and Apple had trimmed her hat with feathers given by the Whitewings swans. Choirs sang.

357

Everyone sang. And when Padra, as senior captain, and Fir, in a new embroidered tunic, proclaimed Crispin king, the cheering echoed and thundered as if the Chamber could not contain it.

The Heartstone was placed in its box so that Needle could carry it to Fir. Crispin had chosen Needle to do that, as she had looked for it for so long. On Crispin's paw it shone as peacefully as if it had come home, and never wanted to move again. Urchin knew what that felt like.

Scatter was there, looking very tiny, wedged between two large squirrels. Her eyes shone as she watched the ceremony. She wore a small and elegant hat, which Urchin guessed might have been a present from Thripple. Thripple was like that.

Enthroned, Crispin sat upright and alone – but Padra stood to one side and Lugg on the other, with Arran behind them. The otters wore their turquoise blue and silver robes, Lugg wore deepest red, and Crispin was clothed in a mantle of green so worked with golden leaves and spiderwebs and tiny animals that Needle could hardly take her eyes from it.

In old, gnarled paws, Fir lifted the crown high. Animals craned their necks to see it, whispering to each other of the craftsmanship. Oak leaves and acorns were woven into a wreath and, small but clear in the workmanship, worked in white shell, were stars and a swan. A shiver ran through Urchin. *Stars and a swan.* He had been there.

Prayers were said. Crispin made his promises to the islanders, and heads were bowed as the animals made their promises to him. And Urchin, joining in, with his paw on his sword, remembered that this was the young squirrel who had picked him up from the shore on the morning of his birth. He glanced over his shoulder at the Threading of another flame-red squirrel.

It's all right now, Lady Whisper, thought Urchin. *He'll be all right.*

As Fir pressed the crown over Crispin's ears it was as if a sigh of joy and relief ran through the Gathering Chamber. With a billowing of cloaks, every animal knelt. And a sweet, clear voice sang from the gallery like an enchantment.

Here we bring Crispin,
Swanrider Crispin,
Sing for the king to the mist and the tide . . .

It was Sepia. Urchin looked for Cedar and caught her eye.

'Thank you!' he whispered, and she smiled back.

When the procession had left the Chamber, Urchin followed Padra and Crispin to the ante-room. Tables were set up in the Gathering Chamber for the feast. Even in the depth of winter the Chamber had become misted and hot, and Urchin went to open a window, welcoming the cold fresh air. It was snowing again, and it would lie till tomorrow.

There was one thing still to do. Urchin, helping Padra and Crispin with their robes, told them what it was.

'The sword the ambassadors offered you?' said Crispin. 'It's still in the Throne Room. Do you want it?'

'No,' said Urchin earnestly. 'No, I don't want it. It was meant to trick me, and it was used against you. But I don't want it lying around, either, and as it's mine I think I should do something about it. All that's happened, Whitewings and everything, it isn't properly finished until this is done. And I'd like a witness, please.'

Later that evening while Sepia and Needle danced at the party, a small boat rocked its way across the dark waves towards the mists. When it was as far out as it needed to be, Padra shipped the oars.

Urchin held up the sword in the moonlight. Its exquisite workmanship was as beautiful as ever, but its pattern of twists and knots seemed to tell him of deceit and imprisonment and the trickery of silver. Pushing back his cloak, balancing himself carefully so he could throw hard, he flung the sword forwards towards the mists. For a moment it twisted and flashed, and there was a gentle splash as it hit the water.

An overwhelming sense of peace fell on Urchin. It filled him, and made him warm, like being loved. Softly, as he had said it in his prison cell on Whitewings, he whispered, 'Goodnight.'

Then he took his place beside Padra, and side by side they rowed back to Mistmantle.

M. I. McAllister

Margi McAllister's first novel, *A Friend For Rachel* (now called *The Secret Mice*), was published in 1997. Several more titles followed, and Margi then began to write full-time. For a long time she had wanted to write a book about a secret island, but couldn't find the way to make it work – then somebody suggested that she should try writing about animals instead of humans, and *The Mistmantle Chronicles* began to come alive.

Margi has spent most of her life in the north-east of England. When her first novel was published, she lived in Corbridge, Northumberland, in a house with a big garden shared with hedgehogs, rabbits and a red squirrel called Yo-yo. As a good Northumbrian, she is very fond of red squirrels.

Margi is married to Tony, has three grown-up children, and now lives in Yorkshire.

Urchin and the Heartstone is the second book in *The Mistmantle Chronicles*.

www.mistmantle.co.uk